VOLUME 1

Passions of the Gods

LEAH NIGHTINGALE

Cover Design By: Miblart

Copyright © 2024 by Leah Nightingale

Excerpts from Calling of the Gods and Forbidden Loves

Copyright © 2018 by Leah Nightingale

All rights reserved.

No part of this book may be reproduced in any form or by any electronic or mechanical means, including information storage and retrieval systems, without written permission from the author, except for the use of brief quotations in a book review.

Dedicated to everyone who longed for a story solely centred on the Gods and Goddesses of Greek Mythology.

CONTENTS

1. Blood + Water — 1
   Ares & Aphrodite
2. The Curse — 14
   Hephaestus & Hebe
3. The Perfect Trick — 22
   Hermes & Artemis
4. Affairs Of The Heart — 32
   Zeus & Demeter
5. Naked Dance — 37
   Athena & Apollo
6. All Tied Up — 44
   Zeus & Prometheus
7. To: Err Is Human — 49
   Xander The Mortal
8. Apollo 13 — 53
   Apollo & Hebe
9. FWB — 60
   Hermes & Artemis
10. Kill(H)er — 70
    Persephone (Kore)
11. The Bodyguard — 75
    Xander & Hebe
12. Death's Wish — 78
    Hades & Zeus
13. Queen B — 84
    Hera & Hebe
14. Loose Lips — 92
    Aphrodite & Hermes
15. Battle Of Wits — 100
    Ares & Athena
16. Do You Know Who I Am?! — 109
    Hermes & Hallirhothios
17. The Prisoner Prince — 114
    Hephaestus & Hebe

18. **Inquiring Minds** — 120
Hermes & Athena

19. **Philadelphia** — 128
Ares & Hebe

20. **The Full-Borns** — 140
Athena & Aphrodite

21. **The Wing(less) Man** — 143
Apollo & Hermes

22. **(Hermes) Has It** — 148
Artemis & Athena

23. **Big Brother** — 155
Ares & Hephaestus

24. **When Jealousy Rears...** — 162
Apollo & Athena

25. **Watch The Throne** — 166
Ares & Aphrodite

26. **Distant Lovers** — 171
Zeus & Hera

27. **Kissing, Cousins** — 180
Ares & Hallirhothios

28. **The Wine'd Up** — 188
Ares & Hermes

29. **Sister, Sister** — 193
Aphrodite & Hebe

30. **Lot In Life** — 200
Hermes & Zeus

31. **Thrill Of The Hunter** — 208
Artemis & Ares

32. **A Gift And A Curse** — 214
The Royal Family

33. **Indecent Proposal** — 226
Ares & Hera

34. **Blackout** — 236
Zeus & Hephaestus

35. **S.M.I.L.F** — 241
Hermes & Hera

36. **Daughter Dearest** — 248
Athena & Zeus

37. **Off With Her Head** — 256
Hera & Aphrodite

38. **Dressed Down** 260
Ares & Hebe

39. **Stranger Danger!** 267
Persephone & Demeter

40. **Touch Me, Tease Me** 271
Hebe & Hermes

41. **Between The Sheets** 284
Aphrodite & Ares

42. **Herbs And Spice** 294
Minthe & Hades

43. **Undercovers** 305
Zeus & Hera

44. **The Monster** 309
Xander

Epilogue: A Gigantic Problem 312

Desires of Olympus 315
Where to find Leah Nightingale 317

1

BLOOD + WATER
ARES & APHRODITE

HE STOOD BEFORE HER, SOAKED IN BLOOD.

Aphrodite's gasp resonated throughout her newly crafted home as the rising smell of burnt flesh hung in the air. The room seemed to hold its breath as an unexpected intruder, Ares, Prince of the Gods, stood at its center in full warrior attire.

"My prince," she murmured, her voice trembling.

His response came not in words but through the subtle clench of his jaw, a silent protest to being addressed as *Prince*.

"You are bleeding."

The gods seldom bore the marks of violence, yet dark stains marred Ares' once-immaculate form.

Aphrodite's instincts urged her to reach toward his breastplate, but she hesitated to follow through. *I do not want my white nightgown to be covered in blood.*

Ares tore his helmet from his head, revealing the unruly,

thick black hair that lay underneath. The heavy metal crashed against the marble floor in a resounding thud.

His cheeks up to his brow remained untouched by the aftermath of the bloodshed, allowing the natural olive hue of his skin to stand in stark contrast. He then shed his long cape, marked by the royal crest woven into its fabric.

The open wounds along his biceps had since healed, and the bruising on his calves would soon disappear entirely.

Through narrowed dark brown eyes, Ares examined Aphrodite with careful scrutiny, tracing a path that began at her crystal blue eyes, moved along her delicate features, and —inevitably—settled at her alluring cleavage.

"Your blood is dripping all over my floor."

His voice cut through the air like the tempered edge of a warrior's dull sword. "It is not my blood."

Ichor, the blood of the gods, was a gold liquid. The red color splattered all over his body could only belong to the mortal men of the earth.

The warmonger glanced around the surrounding area. *Why does Hebe's room look so different?*

The rectangular table that should have been in the center of the room was replaced with a long sofa; the doorway that was supposed to be to the right was instead to the left, and most of all, Aphrodite, who was standing by the balcony doors, was not supposed to be on the premises.

"Where is Hebe?" His eyes darted back to the goddess with a raised brow dipped in a lake of suspicion. "What are *you* doing here?"

Aphrodite threw her head back as she laughed and traced

her delicate fingers down the line of her cheekbone. "You asked me the wrong question." After reconsidering her earlier decision, she no longer cared about staining her negligee, and searched for the latches on his breastplate. "Instead, you should ask me to draw you a bath."

The Prince knew better than to deny a beauty her offer, so he relented as she unclasped his armor and let the hardware drop to his dusty sandals. The mortal blood on his shoulders followed the path down the creases of his sculpted chest.

Not wanting a pool of blood collecting on her floor, Aphrodite stared directly into his dark eyes and batting her full lashes. "Shall I...draw

All the warring thoughts that had once churned within his mind fell by the wayside. As if yielding to an invisible current, Ares surrendered to her guidance, hoping he would not regret his actions by morning.

With her form illuminated by the soft play of torchlight, she beckoned him to follow with a curl of her finger and they headed down the hall toward another unfamiliar room. With each step, he pulled off another article of clothing until there was nothing more to remove.

The chamber that awaited them bore a scented air of sweetness, a haven nestled within the clouds of the highest mountain. The centerpiece was a large, empty tub, promising the embrace of healing waters. Like a pool carved from the hands of giants, it held the potential to wash away not just the battle's grime but the weight of the world itself.

"It is your luck. I was preparing a bath for myself." Pointing to the large vessels behind her filled with hot water, she added, "Little did I know, The Fates meant for me to be preparing a bath for you instead." She led him over to the tub, and he stepped inside.

While Ares sat down, she went over to the row of vessels and brought one back to him. Then, gradually, she poured the mineral water mixed with scented oils all over his body, starting with his broad shoulders.

"Ahhh!" His eyes rolled to the back of his head as a wave of relief washed over him. His muscles relaxed while water tainted with foreign blood trickled down to his legs. Settling further into the hot tub, he let out another deep sigh. "This is everything I needed."

"Ares, Ares, Ares. You speak much too soon." Slowly, she rubbed a wet cloth over his muscular body toward the center of his being and circled his thick manhood.

His eyes shot open in response to her boldness.

"Are you sure a bath is *only* what you need?" Her hands continued to move innocently down his muscular thigh toward his leg and ended at the heel of his foot.

She is toying with me. He suppressed a smile but could not hide the gleam in his eye. *I shall let her toy.*

Ares leaned back and rested his head on the edge of the tub. He reminisced on the Bathing Ritual that regularly awaited him once he returned home from a long journey.

"Whenever I come home from a battle, Hebe would always have my bath drawn. She ensures the water's temperature is to my liking and she fills the tub as close to the brim without a drop spilling over."

The blonde goddess listened intently, noticing the change

in his tone as he spoke about the Princess of the Gods. His once-heavy voice had suddenly switched to a lighter cadence—his hardened face, turned soft.

She poured more water over him to wash off the remaining suds and placed the near-empty jar on the ledge between them.

"Hebe says to be of service to others is her calling, and I do believe servitude is her gift to the gods...more so, it is her gift to me. When she bathes me, she does so with such care and affection."

With his lips sealed and eyes again closed, Aphrodite thought it was the best time to safely roll her eyes. *Far be it for me to encourage adoration of another goddess in my presence.*

Hebe, Ares' younger sister, was on her first solo mission into the Land of Men. A journey into the world was a tradition all gods followed once they reached their Day of Understanding, which arrived at differing stages unique to each god.

"I purposely planned to war with men during her first venture into the world to distract me from worrying about her." However, try as he might, Hebe was never too far away from his thoughts.

The Princess is hardly little. Aphrodite tried her best to contain her annoyance. *Unless he means she is little in stature...and intelligence.* Circling the wet cloth around his nipple, she pouted her plump lips, "I am sorry that tonight, instead of your little sister, you have to settle for little ol' me."

Ares opened one eye, catching her aloof demeanor in the torchlight. She was a full-born after all, a type of goddess he always found unsettling. And on top of being a full-born, she was exceptionally gorgeous—a dangerous combination.

Faintly, he traced a finger along her arm to her neck. "Aphrodite." He latched into the roots of her wavy locks and firmly yanked her face closer to his menacing stare.

She fought desperately to maintain her balance, keenly aware it would not take much force for her to be pulled head-first into the tub.

In a low, stern voice, Ares asked, "Where...am...I?"

The goddess struggled fruitlessly against his brute strength. She clung to the edge of the tub, but with each passing moment, his grip grew stronger, drawing her closer. *Will he dunk my head underwater?*

A vase that rested precariously between them teetered and then toppled, spilling the remaining water onto her clothing. She caught his playfully dark expression. *He does not wish to overpower me. It is more fun for him to watch me struggle.*

Unable to endure the mounting pressure any longer, she relented, "You are in my home!"

In an instant, Ares released her, the tension between them dissolving as abruptly as it had arisen.

Aphrodite took a couple of breaths, enough to settle her pounding heart. Forcing a strained smile, she warned, "Do note in the future, the next time you pull my hair, it should be followed by an impassioned kiss." She rubbed the back of her neck. "Lest I think you a tease."

"So, you like it rough?" It took everything within him to withhold a chuckle. "I will be sure to remember that."

Taking another glance around the unfamiliar room, he furrowed his brows.

I see the poor god is still confused. The beauty adjusted her posture and smoothed out her disheveled nightie. She decided to forego her mysterious approach and instead let him in on the cause of his disorientation.

"Zeus, God of the Sky, finally agreed I could build a home on Mount Olympus. But, unfortunately, it is lower than the main home," she mumbled, then scrunched her face as if she had tasted something bitter. "Alas, you just happened to stumble into the wrong palace."

My father allowed Aphrodite to build on the mount reserved for the Council of the High Gods and home to the Royal Family?

The High Gods consisted of the offspring of Uranus: Zeus, Hera, Demeter, Poseidon and Hestia. They formed a council that ruled over all the creatures of the earth. The Royal Family consisted of King Zeus, Queen Hera, Prince Ares, and Princess Hebe. Their duties entailed ruling over the gods.

I wonder what the Queen thinks of this? Even with all the added details, nothing was making any sense to Ares. "How were you able to *convince* Zeus to build a house on the hill?"

Aphrodite lifted and dropped her shoulders, as clueless as could be for an answer. The rise and fall of her breasts were accentuated because of her wet see-through attire, displaying her noticeably pointy nipples.

He stared at her pronounced bosom, fuelling a rush of Ichor through his veins. *Is her damp nightie making her cold, or did yanking her hair make her...hot?* The Prince did not intend to wait too long for the answer.

Easing up in her direction, his distrust of her dissipated at the same rate his body ached for her to touch him without the rag. "Is it possible for you to be more beautiful than when I last saw you?"

She noticed his growing arousal through her peripheral vision but ignored his desire. Blushing, the goddess twirled the ends of her golden hair. "Why, anything is possible."

Before he could pounce on her, she emptied the last of the steaming water over him, leaving behind a freshly washed, tanned body.

"There you are, nice and clean." She inhaled and exhaled deeply. "Smelling as flowery as the Garden of the Gods."

When Ares rose from the bath, Aphrodite could no longer feign indifference to his imposing physique. Not only was his impeccably sculpted form fully revealed, but one part, in particular, was at eye level, begging for her undivided attention.

Hmmm. Thick, long and hard. Just the way I like it.

She raised her gaze to meet his as he loomed above her and instead of offering him a helping hand, she gave him a taunting smile.

"First born to the King. I am sure you know many goddesses and nymphs who would have already been on their knees willing to please you."

This is undoubtedly true. However, I know better than to confirm it.

"But I promise you this. Whatever they can do," standing up, she made sure to lightly caress his balls, "I can do better."

Before he could relish the sensation of her tender grip, she spun around and made her way to the door, fully aware that he would be in close pursuit.

Does she not know never to tempt a beast? I guess I will have to teach her.

The Prince hurriedly stepped out from the deep tub, his robust frame glistening with water droplets. She was like a magnet, drawing him ever near and if he drew any closer, he would impale her...again and again.

Ares was so entranced by the hypnotic bounce of her shapely bottom he almost bypassed his armor on the floor.

Almost.

He stopped.

The goddess vanished into another room yet her departure barely registering in his mind. Acting on impulse, he bent down to retrieve his bloody breastplate.

"Leave your armor be." Aphrodite popped back out from another room with an offering of fresh clothing wrapped over her arms. "You will only dirty yourself again."

Leave it be? He hoovered over all the pieces that made up his armor: Golden helmet, steel sword and metal breastplate. *If only it were so simple.*

His helmet shielded his features from prying eyes. Without it, he felt as though his innermost thoughts were open for all to judge. And his sword, an extension of his very will, could no longer fend off an uninvited touch. Even his breastplate, the emblem of his invincibility, could no longer protect the heart that lay beneath.

Each piece of armor that had once been a barrier against the world's cruelties, remained scattered on the floor—revealing a newfound emotion…vulnerability.

Ares did not expect Aphrodite to understand the feeling of nothingness, nor did he feel the need to explain it to her. It was the first time they had ever had such a lengthy conversation in their entire existence. Indeed, what would a Bloodied Warrior and a Beauty Queen have in common?

"Your armor can stay on the floor for one night." She held out her clothes for him to take. "Do not worry. I will protect you."

One thing was sure. Ares admired Aphrodite's persistence. Taking the robe from her hands, he quickly realized it was an outfit made for her. However, it was oversized enough to fit his large frame. "Pink?"

She shrugged her shoulders and pressed her lips together to stop from giggling. *I better not laugh, or he will never wear my robe.* "The pale color brings out your rugged features."

Reluctantly, Ares put an arm through one sleeve as she helped him get the other arm in.

The goddess then stood before him and tied a knot at the center of the robe, noting that his erection had since been tamed.

Although Ares would not admit it, the snug material felt like paradise against his damp skin. The droplets of water quickly absorbed into the robe, leaving the only moisture on his feet and hair.

Ares followed his guide to a stretched white sofa. She sat down first and let him stretch out and rest his head on her lap, while stroking his wet hair. The goddess ceased all conversation for a moment so he could be still. Only the soft crackling from the burning torches could be heard.

"How were your battles with the men of the land?"

"Invigorating!" A distant rumble rolled through the clouds from a far away land.

Easy does it. Aphrodite could feel the burst of energy surge within him, but she gently soothed him back into a calming state. "I am so glad you could have fun with men. Now you can have a *different* type of fun."

Even though he knew she was teasing him, he found her flirtatious demeanor alluring. "Is that so?"

The beauty continued to pet him, again lulling him into a relaxing frame of mind. She wanted him to be short of sedated so he could lower his defences and she could freely speak her mind.

"Ares. Why do you run away from your royal responsibilities?"

He did not respond, and so she carried on.

"Why do you disappear for eons at a time? Son of the King and Queen of the Gods. First in line to the throne and yet you are out gallivanting the earth."

He scoffed.

"You are not Dionysus, a wanderer with only himself to live for."

Did she not appear to us not too long ago? And yet she speaks as if she has known me a lifetime?

"*You* are the next king."

"What good is being an heir to an immortal god?"

"It does a lot of good. The Titans are immortal and were defeated. Being an heir means everything if another enemy arises to overthrow our King."

"My dear goddess, any god who would be courageous enough to overthrow my father as the rightful heir, *I* would be next on the murderer's list." Yes, he was condescending, but at that moment, he felt like he was talking to a mortal.

"By the gods! You are not taking me seriously." It surprised her that she was the first to lose control of her temper. Then, pausing momentarily, she loosened her muscles to release the tension stored in her body and tried again. "You are a prince."

"And you also come from the same loins of a king. Therefore, you are a princess."

If it were only so simple. "You know I am not a *real* princess."

"And you know my home is not on the Mount of the Gods but on the battlefields of men. Therefore, I too, am not a *real* prince."

"The gods may dismiss your abilities, but they are not lost on me. It takes a great deal of skill and forethought for warfare." She stopped massaging his scalp. "I see you. You are more than you know."

More? The day that Ares first discovered what a swift motion from a sword could do to a mortal body was the day he did not look back from warfare. *What more could there be when I am everything I want to be right now?*

"You are more than you know." She answered him as if she heard his thoughts. "I see you on the throne ruling over the gods. I see you on your chariot commanding troops to battle. I see you at your wife's side while tending to your future children. I see all of this for you. I *see* you. You are more than you know."

As her last words brushed against his ears like the gentlest of caresses, his body surrendered to a deep slumber nestled in the comfort of her breast.

"Ares? Are you sleeping?"

He snored in response.

"That is good."

How much of her words had penetrated the armor of his heart and mind? Aphrodite could only wonder. The inner workings of a god, especially one as formidable as Ares, were a mountain of complexities too vast to decipher.

"One thing is for sure. In order for you to be on the throne. I will have to be there as well."

Although, there was one small problem—the thrones she craved were already occupied.

Aphrodite smiled so brightly; she was saddened that no one was around to bask in her beauty. She curled a finger tightly around a lock of his hair, only pausing when his body jerked in response.

I will have my throne.

2

THE CURSE
HEPHAESTUS & HEBE

"May the gods be with me..."

Princess Hebe boldly entered the dark cave with her torch held high. The flames were strong enough to brighten a couple of steps ahead of her. However, there was still enough darkness in the corners for anyone or *anything* to catch her by surprise.

The expedition marked her first foray into the Land of Men, a right of passage to signify the transition of youngling into godhood. Rather than treading the well-worn routes of safety, Hebe had deliberately chosen to journey into the dangerous Unknown Territories, a realm her father forbade her to explore alone.

With each cautious step, she could not help but cast a regretful glance over her shoulder. Her thoughts wandered to Pegasus, the majestic winged unicorn she left behind by the forest's edge. She had commanded the loyal creature to stand guard, but a nagging uncertainty lingered in the night.

Peg is as stubborn as the day Uncle Poseidon created him for me. Oh! This is the first time I wish he had disobeyed my orders to 'stay put' and instead trailed behind me.

A heavy sigh escaped her lips once she accepted her beloved pet was nowhere to be found. No Pegasus, Father, Mother, or Brother will rescue her. For the first time, she was indeed on her own.

My brother, Ares, says the Unknown Territories is the home of the Cursed Monster. But everyone tells me lies to keep me from discovering the truth. And so, tonight, on the eve of my Day of Understanding, I will no longer be kept from the—

Whoosh!

The Princess heard a rumbling pass her shoulder and spun around with her flame to identify what was there. "Hello?" Her voice was soft, and she mentally berated herself for how weak she sounded.

Great! I just upped my chances of being eaten by whatever lurks here.

Whoosh!

Another shape darted to the other side of her as she spun around again in the other direction. "Who is there?" she asked with more gusto.

Out of nowhere, a swift, strong wind swopped by and blew out the torch's fire. Instantaneously, she was surrounded by complete darkness.

Until...

Four pairs of glowing red eyes appeared from high above.

Great Zeus!

Without much thought, Hebe dropped the fireless stick from her grip, letting it tumble to the ground. Panic surged through her veins like wildfire, and she spun around, retracing her steps back from where she came.

The cavern walls seemed to blur into a chaotic frenzy as she sprinted. Screaming, giving voice to her fear, felt as impossible as it was futile. Each pounding footstep only intensified the thunderous drumming in her ears, drowning out the sound of her own breath.

There's the opening! She could taste the cool kiss of outside air as it brushed against her cheeks. *I am so close.*

Yet, as her escape neared, so did the threat that pursued her. A guttural growl echoed, and the fabric of her clothing tore as unseen jaws snapped at her gown.

I made it!

Finally, she burst forth from the confines of the cave's mouth, and her once-dark world changed into a blur of sand and sky. The rocky beach beckoned, its jagged terrain offering little refuge.

Oh no!

Hebe's world seemed to shatter as her footing betrayed her, sending her crashing onto the ground. She landed heavily onto her stomach, the sharp edges of the rocky beach sending a jolt of pain through her body.

The snapping jaws behind her, hungrily nipping at her sandals, was a haunting reminder of her father's warnings. She had disobeyed her father's orders and ventured into the forbidden Unknown Territories, and now, the consequences bore down upon her with merciless ferocity.

If I cannot survive here in the Land of Men, how can I rule over the gods in the sky above?

Summoning every ounce of courage, Hebe lifted her head in a last-ditch effort to power through. What met her eyes was a figure hovering above her, cloaked in a whirlwind of darkness.

Could it be? The Cursed Monster!

Her voice caught in her throat, a petrifying scream that dared not escape her lips. What would it matter? There was no one around the desolate place to hear her.

The cloaked figure's gaze shifted, drawing his attention to the advancing onslaught of the wild beasts. With effortless movement, he cultivated fire from his fingertips. The flames swirled around and surged forth, over Hebe's head, hitting its intended target.

The wild beasts cried out in agony as their forms were consumed by the fiery ball of wrath. Their lifeless husks crumbled to charred skeletons, shrouded by a billowing cloud of dark smoke. A chilling silence was all that remained, followed closely by the horrid stench of burnt flesh.

I made it out in one piece!

Her adrenaline still flowing, Hebe's heart continued to race in her chest. She sprang to her feet, her eyes wide as they took in the pile of bones and ashes that lay mere inches from where she had fallen.

Once the smoke cleared, the remnants of vicious jaw

bones was enough evidence for her to admit that the flames had saved her from a gruesome fate.

Hebe wanted to be proud of herself for overcoming danger. However, she did *not* defeat her attackers—she was rescued.

Or was she?

The young one snapped her head back in the other direction and examined the dark, intimidating figure who stood tall on the rocky shore. His shadowy expression made it difficult to distinguish his features beneath the hood.

Even though she could not make out his face, his clothing was instantly recognizable. He wore a cloak with a crest patched over the heart, depicting Mount Olympus, a crown, and two winged creatures.

Hebe squinted before opening her eyes as wide as her mouth. *We are wearing the same Royal Crest! Members of the Royal Family have the right to wear the sacred symbol. Besides my father and mother, only Ares and I wear the crest as the children of the King and Queen of the Gods. Which means...*

"Hephaestus?" Her voice sounded like the squeak of a mouse.

"Who dares speak my name?" The god answered in a husky voice. "It is a curse."

By the gods! I was right! The quiet, shy goddess stood tall, placing her hands on her hips. *Let me just forget I was attacked by creatures and running scared for my life.*

She tried her best to mimic the boldness of her father. Dusting the mud off her knees, she declared, "I dare to speak your name. I am Princess Hebe, daughter of the King and Queen of the Gods."

As if she channeled the essence of the Sky God, a low rumble, followed by a bolt of lightning, flashed in Nyx's sky.

His eyes widened in utter shock. *Why would a royal risk harm in such an unforgiving place?* Not knowing what else to do, he collapsed to his knees and cast his gaze on the muddy ground. But it was not enough. He longed to bury himself in the sloppy dirt to hide from the goddess.

"What are you doing in this wasteland?"

"Hunting for food." He lifted his large satchel as evidence. "You should not be here. This is no place for a princess."

"Neither a prince."

He glanced up from his bowed position, only fleetingly looking into her big brown eyes. "I am no such thing."

"You are the son of Zeus and Hera, and yet you live in the caves overlooking the deep ocean?"

Is this a joke? The son of Zeus has laid in squalor for many of Selene's moons. What is so different now? Why should anyone care now?

"I do my work in the caves where I forge, hidden away from all. There is enough light from the sun and, at night, the stars. The redfish are my company, and the purple critters of the beach are my food. Besides the wild beasts, there is not much else here in the Unknown Territories."

Hebe squatted down to his level, trying to look into his hidden eyes. "I would hear through whispers about a son of the great Zeus living amongst the sea creatures. I thought it was all a tale of make-believe." Raising her voice, she continued, "Now I see you are not a story to scare mortal men. You are my brother."

Brother? There, he kneeled, covered in mud and misery, yet she was covered in the riches bestowed upon all the gods by the very nature of being gods. "I am nothing."

The pretty Princess stood up, not willing to take no for an answer. "You are Prince Hephaestus, son of the King and Queen of the Gods. Come with me and take your proper place. It is your birthright."

Out from his lips came a long, steady breath as if he had been holding it in for all eternity. Reluctantly, he stood up in the fullness of the moonlight and pulled off his hood. Only then did Hebe see his scarred appearance.

One side of his face was perfectly normal, handsome even, but the left side had scratches running down his cheek.

Hephaestus was a god in name only.

She gasped despite herself but could not cover her mouth fast enough to mask her disgust.

Her vocal outrage was nothing more than a slap to his horrid face. The outcasted god stepped back in response.

His hair was unkempt, and his teeth were stained. However, instead of recoiling further, she swallowed hard and stretched out her delicate pale white hand.

What is she doing? He had a million questions but not enough time to seek any answers. Not wanting her to suddenly come to her senses, he quickly grabbed hold of her, before she could withdraw her hand.

Hephaestus was struck by the contrast as her soft, delicate skin brushed against his rough and scaly palm. Never before in his long existence had he experienced such a juxtaposition—a sensation that was both foreign and oddly enticing.

Only then did Hephaestus dare look directly upon the Princess, allowing his eyes to roam over every facet of her petite form. Her jet-black hair framed a perfectly round face. The charm of her cute button nose and the fullness of her inviting lips captivated his senses. Her thick robe, though concealing her curves, only served to fuel his imagination, which eagerly filled in the hidden details with fervent creativity.

Hephaestus felt an insatiable need to explore every part of her. Here, in the secluded land, there were no prying eyes, no restraints to hinder his desires. It took everything he could muster to hold his feral instincts at bay.

He closed his eyes and took a deep breath before releasing it again into the air. Anything to bury his dark thoughts deep into the recess of his mind.

After years of abandonment, he was content to live the rest of his immortal life in the caves with the creatures of the sea for companionship. A disfigured god, he believed, did not deserve a traditional happy ending. Yet, as he willingly took Hebe's hand, he felt a glimmer of hope, a belief that perhaps there was more to his story than he had once believed.

They walked along an invisible path that would eventually lead to their home on Mount Olympus.

Still, Hephaestus could not help but wonder if he was merely leaving behind the savage world he knew only to enter another savage world he knew nothing about.

3

THE PERFECT TRICK
HERMES & ARTEMIS

Ready...

Artemis concealed herself amid the towering grass, her stare unwavering as she tracked her prey with the keen precision of her razor-sharp, brown eyes. Her curly hair was artfully secured in a high bun, ensuring no errant strand would dare obstruct her line of sight. One of her breasts was left exposed, allowing her to extend her arm fluidly across her chest. Every aspect of her being was attuned to the hunt—the goddess and the wilderness merging into a single entity.

Just beyond her vantage point stretched a narrow shoreline, cupped by a secluded beach filled with dark waters. While Artemis knew she was secure in her present location, the border between safety and danger lay but a few strides away.

Aim...

Her fingers wrapped around the polished grip of her well-crafted bow. The taut string quivered with potential energy, and the arrow perched upon it waited, suspended in breathless anticipation. Artemis slowly pulled her bow, ready for its release as seconds ticked away in silence...

Fir—

"Even though I cannot see you, I know you are there!" A clearly amused voice rang out into the night.

By the gods! Grumbling, she dropped her hands to her sides. *I have been spotted.*

After adjusting her grab to again cover her breast, Artemis stepped into the shallow light of Selene's moon, revealing her tall, athletic form from the hidden forest surrounding her. Against the light breeze of the night, she followed the path out of the bushes onto the rich yellow sand.

Finally, my stalker shows herself. The god Hermes sat neck-deep in the waters of the warm sea. His eyes were fixed upon the shore at the sight of Artemis emerging from the sandy beach.

With every step she took, the sand clung to her feet, leaving a trail of footprints in her wake.

Hermes stood up, the water catching him at his waist. He quickly ran his hands through the sea and splashed his face and curly, brown hair.

He narrowed his eyes with a cheeky grin. "Why were you spying on me?"

"I was not..." her voice trailed off as she found herself engrossed by the scene unfolding before her. As Hermes stepped out of the water, his nakedness was revealed more fully.

"...spying on..." her words faltered and fell away, eclipsed by the sheer visual impact of his form.

He stood unapologetically naked, droplets rolling down his slender, well-toned physique. A masterpiece carved by the gods themselves, his body exuded an air of perfection that would inspire artists for millennia.

Hermes was many things—confident, audacious, and daring—but bashfulness was not among his traits. With a playful flicker in his eyes, he wiggled his brows, casting the goddess a knowing stare.

Artemis struggled to rein in her thoughts, to resist the magnetic pull of curiosity that urged her eyes to sneak a peek between his thighs. Swiftly, she averted her gaze, pretending indifference as she glanced over her shoulder at the forest line behind her.

"You should not be out here in the waters leading to the Underworld," she managed to say, her voice betraying only a smidgeon of its usual steadiness. "It is not a safe place for a god."

"Nor a goddess."

She met his gaze. "Zeus would be very angry if he saw us here."

"Well then, it is good he cannot see us," he countered with a wink.

The moonlight cast its silvery glow upon them, revealing a telltale golden flush that graced her high cheekbones. Her lips, full and inviting, unleashed a subtle smile. *Since we are hidden from the world, what harm can come if I explore everything before me?* Her eyes flickered downward as they traced the contours of Hermes' rock-solid abdomen and beyond— *Great Zeus!*

"Shall I stare into your forehead since I cannot stare into your eyes?"

She looked back at him in a flash, utterly embarrassed by her wandering stare. The huntress had never laid with a god before and could not deny the unusual stirrings within her, begging to be coached up to the surface.

His hand reached out, fingers encircling hers with a gentle touch. "Come with me into the sea."

"I will."

"But first," he smirked, "you must undress."

Before she could say yay or nay, he moved with deft precision, his finger tracing a delicate path around the gold rope that hugged her waist. With a gentle tug, the release of its grip on her dress allowed the fabric to fall and pool at her feet.

Once loose from the constraints of her clothing, Artemis responded with a shimmy of her shoulders, embracing her newfound freedom. With her long-toned legs, she stepped over her discarded outfit, never breaking her grip on his hand.

Hermes led her into the warm waters that got hotter with each step. A mist hovered just above its surface.

"See? Not so dangerous after all." Turning to view the shore, he spun her around, resting her back against his front, and settled his hands on the curve of her hips.

In the distance, pillars of smoke rose above the dense

forest, signaling impending doom for the mortals trapped within. The flames relentlessly engulfed everything in their reach, leaving a trail of destruction. It was a sight to behold.

Although brilliant, the distant swirling of fire faded away from her mind while the god, whose fingers rubbed against her skin, raced to the forefront.

What is Hermes doing out here? He is a clever one—a god to always keep an eye on. Now that she was no longer distracted by his naked body, her ever-present guard shot back up. "We are not allowed to venture so far into the deep waters, yet you float here without a care. I do not know how you get away with such things. You can do no wrong in Zeus' eyes."

Although she could not see him, she felt the shrug of his shoulders.

"I cannot help my natural charm." Hermes was barely listening, enthralled by the contrast of her dark skin against his own. He was far too busy trying to prevent his growing staff from penetrating her ample cheeks.

Charm! What charm? In a flash, Artemis forcibly removed herself from his grasp and turned to face him. She swayed her arms back and forth, adding ripples into the sea. "Tell me. Is that also what *the Banshee* sees in you?"

He dared not chuckle at Artemis' unaffectionate name. "You mean the Queen the of the Gods?"

"Yes. Queen Banshee."

Bending his knees, he submerged himself in the water until it reached his mouth, concealing any signs of deception that might have given away his genuine emotions.

"She cannot stand any of Zeus' bastards, yet she dolts all over you?" The swaying of her arms stopped. "Why is that?"

His hands clenched, but she did not notice because they were hidden beneath the dark waters.

"Apollo, Aphrodite, Athena, Dionysus, and I are all Low Gods, destined to serve our elders, the High Gods. But not you. Yes, you are also a Low God, but you have managed to finesse your way into becoming the King's personal messenger and the Queen's confidant."

Hermes purposely chose to remain silent, forcing her to draw her own conclusions.

"You treat the High Gods as if they are for *your* pleasure and not the other way around. You get your way because you trick them. You trick them into doing whatever you want."

Unable to bite his tongue any longer, he raised his head high. "*That* is where you are wrong. The High Gods do whatever they please—the trick is, they do not know their desires pleases me as well." Pinching his thumb and index finger together, he added, "It is ever so slight, but there *is* a difference."

"So that is how you get your way?" She furrowed her thin brows. "That is the secret to your charm over them?"

"Ta-dah!" he said with a simple wave of his magical hand.

An owl flew overhead, momentarily attracting their attention. Talk of the High Gods no longer interested her. Instead, Hermes undressed, so close to her, again ignited her curiosity.

The only naked god she had ever seen was her twin brother Apollo, and she never thought of him with hidden desires. And yet, Hermes could ignite sensations throughout her body without so much as a word.

Never has a god enflamed my passions, such as Hermes. Could it be? Maybe he does have charm.

The tallest of the Low Gods, his light brown eyes had a permanent twinkle so that even if a harsh word escaped his lips, one never knew whether to be angry or to laugh. His smooth skin was always freshly shaven, giving the mask of youthful innocence to an audacious thief. And if such advantages were not enough, he had effortless charisma, a mischievous grin—the *bad* god with a *good* reputation.

How is that possible?

It just was. Hermes was a conundrum wrapped in a riddle.

A rumble and a quick bolt of light temporarily lighted the black sky. He took a glance above. *The sound of thunder with no rain clouds? Wherever Zeus may be—he is angry.*

Artemis was too far gone to take notice of the King's mood. Suddenly overtaken by lust, the huntress floated through the waves over to him and latched onto his shoulders, wrapping her firm legs tightly around his narrow waist.

Her sharp nipples brushed against his bare chest, a touch that sent an onslaught of tremors between them, setting a fire that smoldered beneath the surface.

As her body melded against him, she felt the unmistakable rise of his erection grazing against the curve of her buttocks. *There is it.* The realization that she could evoke such an immediate response from him filled her with a sense of victory.

He moved his hands down her back and took her bouncy

cheeks into his tight grip, slowly spreading them apart for greater access to what hid in between.

For the first time, Artemis' active brain, went on mute, and her heart, overflowing with untamed emotions, roared throughout her body. A low moan escaped her lips. Her eyes locked onto his, the space between them dwindling as she leaned closer, desperate for more—their lips to touch.

Surprisingly, Hermes swiftly turned his head to the side, abruptly halting her advances. "We should stop. There is no need for us to go further."

Huh? She clamped her legs together, tightening her hold over him. "Why not?"

He continued to fondle her buttocks, but he did not respond. Like before, his silence only forced her to answer her own question.

"Because your heart belongs to another?" She found no reason to wait for his verbal confirmation. "Perfect. It is not your heart I am after." With a sheepish grin, she reached for the delightfully long member between his legs and teased him with her playful fingertips.

His body responded immediately to her touch with a jolt.

Again, Artemis lowered her head for a kiss, and he hungrily returned it, not giving her time for a breath. She held onto the back of his neck as their tongues wrestled together, neither wanting to admit defeat. He pulled her roughly against his length, brushing her never opened slit with a taste of what was to come.

By the gods! She broke away from his kiss, shocked by how far she was willing to experiment with Hermes. "Are you now glad you decided to not stop and instead go further?" she asked, breathing heavily.

Slowly, he nodded his head in response, thrilled to learn that Artemis foolishly believed *she* was the one in control.

Ta-dah!

As they were about to go in for another kiss, the sounds of approaching flames were getting closer to the beach. Over the burning foliage, cries from the men of the land pleaded for the gods to have mercy on them.

Panic started to creep into her limbs once she remembered they were not meant to be anywhere near the dark waters. "What is it?" Her voice trembled with a breathlessness that did *not* stem from their interrupted kiss.

"The fire is getting close. If we stay any longer, we may feel obliged to help mankind, and in doing so, we will disobey the High Gods." Reluctantly, he pried her arms from around his neck. "Run. Go into the woods and find your way back to Olympus, the Region of the Gods."

"And what will you do?"

"I will stay a moment longer. I want to witness what death brings."

Artemis swam back to shore and quickly picked up her clothing and weapons before darting into the forest, away from the haunting screams of mankind.

Hermes remained steady in the current and looked on until she disappeared from his sight, seemingly safe from harm.

What harm exactly? After all, they were gods. Harm did

not find them easily. And as such, Hermes was not in any hurry to leave.

Death's door was left open for the men of the land, and he had every intention of watching them as they entered, one by one.

The oblivious god was so enthralled by the dancing flames and the putrid smell of burning flesh, he did not notice that he was, once again, being hunted.

4

AFFAIRS OF THE HEART
ZEUS & DEMETER

"I love you."

Even as her back remained turned to her lover, Demeter could not shake the instinctive impulse to shield herself. Her fingers clutched the folds of her robe with a tension that mirrored the storm of emotions rolling within her. A lone, black braided hair fell over her shoulder, almost as if it could replicate a veil to obscure the turmoil in her weary eyes.

Staring out of the window, she yearned for the ability to count every star in the sky—anything so an eternity could pass before her inevitable response to the one who stood mere steps behind her.

Demeter clenched her jaws and swallowed hard to brace herself. "We must not ever do this again."

Zeus, The God of the Sky, closed the distance between them, enveloping her in his embrace as his hands gently settled around the nape of her slender neck. He was muscular with a large frame. Being able to throw lightning bolts would give anyone such immense stature. Yet in the presence of the quiet beauty of Demeter, his overbearing presence seemed to shrink, revealing a sensitive side of his character.

Gently kissing her bare shoulder, he repeated, "I said, I love you."

She shrugged his hands off of her and spun around in a huff. "Why do you not listen to me?"

He could not help but smile in the face of her anger. The god's fingers lightly traced over his curly, dark hair and continued down to his well-groomed beard. "I do not listen because you always say the same thing to me after we make love."

"Well, this time, I mean it." If she were a mortal child, she would have stomped her foot.

Zeus narrowed his sharp eyes. Yes, her words were the same as always, but her stance was a bit troubling to him. "What makes this time so different from all the others?"

"I am a hypocrite every time I lay with you." Fiddling with the material of her covering, she sighed. "I am supposed to be a virgin goddess. I made a vow of chastity to honor the earth and everything on it."

He would have rolled his steely blue eyes if he knew it would not provoke her further. "I lift you of those vows." Zeus carelessly swirled his hand in the air. "See, there? No more vows."

The goddess pounded her fist against his hairy chest, only

to find that it felt like striking a solid wall. "You make fun when I am serious."

Suddenly, the memories of her youth engulfed her chaotic mind like a whirlwind. Memories she had spent a lifetime trying to forget to no avail. *Long ago, I was surrounded by endless darkness and I would have gone mad if not for... my dearest one.*

A long breath escaped her as she lowered her rounded brown eyes. "Not to mention my sister...your *wife*," she whispered.

It was now *his* turn to have his anger stir from within. "Then make no mention of her."

"I cannot betray Hera any longer."

"What is one more time after countless others?"

"It is wrong."

"It is right!"

A bellow of thunder and lightning lit up the night sky through the window.

Zeus' electricity prickled through the pours of his skin. He grabbed her arms and pressed her against his chest. "We were meant to be together. We were *supposed* to be together."

He reached for her clothes and tore open her robe, exposing her nakedness. Roughly, he pulled her waist against his ready body.

With no space between them, she could feel how hard he ached for her because he would not have it any other way.

"I said no more!" The goddess swiftly slapped him across the cheek.

He did not flinch. Instead, his eyes drifted slowly to the rise and fall of her swollen breasts—her sharp nipples peeking through her open robe.

I know that look all too well. "Or will you take me against my will?"

Her question was met with a deafening silence that left a loud mental impact.

Only then did the Sky God recapture her gaze, but he did not release her. No, Zeus remained still—as if he were weighing his options.

And finally, he let her go. "I will not."

Zeus moved away from her, leaving a clear path to the door. His warm skin grew cold, his golden blood all but drained from his face. He sat on the edge of his bed, watching silently as she retied her robe and retrieved her crumbled dress from the corner of the room.

"I know you still love me. But I do not know why you are pushing me away."

When her hand reached for the doorknob, she hesitated, caught in a moment of contemplation. The late-night trysts with Zeus would be sporadic during their many years together—a constant reminder of how she betrayed her sister. *There is nowhere for me to hide from my guilt.* It was a painful burden that Zeus could never truly comprehend, and she had taken great lengths to ensure he would remain ignorant.

"I will be here, right where you left me. Always."

She dared not look behind her, for she knew one glance

could become another lifetime entanglement. Finding the strength to open the door, she was finally able to leave him alone.

Still she could not escape a nagging thought.

But for how long?

5

NAKED DANCE
ATHENA & APOLLO

"My mind is spinning," Athena said, hopping out of her dress.

Apollo swayed to the music of his lyre as he played a melodic tune. The instrument rested on his lap while his fingers glided along the strings. Before him danced Athena, her long fiery red hair, her only source of covering, resting just below her small breasts.

His rhythm became faster as she picked up her pace, arms swaying and legs stepping to the music. Her movements were hypnotizing. Each note he played was inspired by every move of her body.

It was night, and the stars twinkled in the sky, illuminating the dense forest. As Apollo played the last note, he stood up from the large stone he had been sitting on as Athena ended her dance with a playful curtsy.

"I declare, every love song composed from now until the end of time to be inspired by your beauty this very night."

She was taken aback by his words. "Beauty? Me?" Yes, the gods and goddesses were all beautiful by their very nature, but she still was not used to hearing that kind of compliment regarding herself. "All my life, I was praised for my wisdom, not my appearance."

"Can you not be praised for both?" he asked but did not pause long enough for her to respond. "Yes, you are wise, born from the mind of the great God Zeus. And yet, you are more than just your intellect." Standing before her, he grazed a finger along her lower waist. "Much more."

Only then did Athena realize she had so lost herself in the dance that all her clothing had been removed. Yet no shame had overcome her. Instead, she stood taller and relished his touch guiding her closer to him.

She loved the feel of his fingers on her bare waist. Not only was it pleasing, but it also helped to steady her and stopped the world from spinning around. "Your songs, they make me forget everything."

"Is that a compliment?"

"Yes, it is!" Her laugh was loud enough to carry along the winds. "I overthink everything. It is so nice to be in the moment and not continuously think about every possible outcome—all different types of scenarios."

"Great! I *want* you to be in the moment."

The way she moved, with an effortless and commanding presence, left Apollo in awe. His infatuation with Athena only grew as he observed every inch of her body. Every glance, every smile, and every word from her lips fueled the flames of his desire, leaving him helplessly and hopelessly enamored with the goddess. Never mind that she also stood before him as bare as the day she was born in full-form.

It took all the strength he could muster not to throw her onto the grass that very moment and ride the wave into ecstasy.

What god could have this much self-control in front of a naked goddess? Although he was proud of his restraint, he did not know how much longer he could last.

"I know of the yellow nectar of the gods, but I have never seen red nectar until tonight." Athena picked up the silver chalice that lay at her feet. Her cup was half-filled, while Apollo's was empty. "What is this funny-tasting drink called?"

"The drink is called wine. Supposedly, Dionysus took an eternity to perfect the substance. He created it to make the gods merry. It is said, 'A little is good. Too much is trouble.'" Laughing, he added, "What kind of trouble? I do not know."

Her slow mind started to race. A question unanswered—a problem unsolved, was all it took to get rev up her thoughts. "Do you think this concoction is what is causing mortal men to behave like brutes?"

"Mortal men need no excuse to behave like brutes." Apollo thought little of her theory, not caring one way or the other about the plight of the earthly creatures. "Forget about them for tonight and think only about us. This is why I invited you here tonight. After all my invitations, I am happy you finally accepted one."

"I do not know why I never did before." Upon further

reflection, she added, "Actually, I do know why. It was because..."

He stopped her before she would retreat back to her over-calculating ways. She was like a rabbit that would hop away when one went to grab it. He could tell she was about to hop away if he did not redirect her attention. "The past does not matter now. What matters is that you are here and how much I want you."

Instantly, he embraced her and kissed her lips with the passion that rumbled within him. She opened her mouth to his surprise and returned his kiss with the same intensity. A slight tug at his tunic was all she needed to do for him to be naked before her.

Athena had always found Apollo mesmerizing since the first day she laid eyes on him and his twin, Artemis, in the Royal Court of Mount Olympus. Back then, his full face bore the innocence of a young god. However, now his features were chiseled from perfect marble. Golden locks framed his face, reminiscent of the rays of Helios' sun, and his eyes were as vivid as the blue sky.

My, has he grown so much in stature!

Turned on by the sight of his massive biceps, Athena grabbed onto his bulging muscles. "If Atlas can hold up the world with his hands, you can brace the universe on the strength of your shoulders."

"I would much rather use my strength to spread your legs than to brace the universe." He could no longer restrain the lust of his heart, and with a swift motion, he scooped her into his arms and placed her onto a knitted blanket covering the grass.

A wave of distant thunder rang out as Athena lay on her back. The surrounding trees blocked the following bright flash of light from her view.

Again, Apollo kissed her, inching his fingers melodically up her inner thigh with the same fervent he would strum a chord.

She widened her legs subconsciously, urging him to explore deeper into her warmth. Caught in the intensity of his knowing touch, she tightened her arms around his neck.

His finger slipped into her hot, sticky core, causing a low moan in his ears. Her sounds of pleasure drove him wild as he pressed down on top of her, pushing her flat onto the blanket.

His hardness throbbing against her stomach was enough to snap her back into reality.

No. This is going too fast! With both hands, she pushed against his hairless chest. "Wait. Stop."

He did not stop. "Remember. Do not think."

He kissed her lightly down the crawl of her neck, drawing her back in before finding her breast and sucking her nipple until it sharpened between his lips.

Athena thrashed her head from side to side, her body responding to his fingers so much that she thought she had suddenly turned into a lyre. *By the Gods!* Already, she could feel herself carelessly falling into carnal desires. Yet she knew how to break free from the power of lust.

"I said, stop!" Not waiting for him to take the initiative,

with all her might, she shoved Apollo completely off her and sat up, breathing heavily.

After calming her nerves, Athena turned her back to him, pulled her knees against her breasts, and hugged her legs.

Damn, The Fates! Apollo could not believe how fast everything that felt so right, flipped into something so wrong. *I scared her off.*

Cautiously, he reached out to touch her back but thought better of it and lowered his hand. Even though it was probably best to leave her alone, he did not want to. Instead, he asked, "Why are you shutting down? I know you feel this...*thing* between us."

Athena already had a million answers to his simple question but did not speak. She observed the trees that surrounded her and how they swayed in the breeze with not a care in the world and wished she had a life so simple. But no, she was the wise one, a goddess as complicated as they come. A life of love was not at the forefront of her mind. She was far too ambitious to settle for something so...simple.

"I do feel it...this *thing* between us," she whispered as light as the breeze. "Which is why we must stop." Reaching for her dress by her feet, she stood up, still too weak to challenge the god any further. "Have a good night, Apollo."

And with all *his* might, he controled his passion long enough to let her leave without trying to convince her to stay. It would take an eternity to convince her to change her mind and his obsession with Athena was such that he had put off a mission commanded by the King.

As the crickets chirped through the night, he watched Athena go back to her natural essence, like a rabbit hopping away.

Yes, she may have gotten away this time. But next time will not be so easy.

6

ALL TIED UP
ZEUS & PROMETHEUS

The King of the Gods contemplated his next move as the sun hesitated to grace the sky. The aftermath of his affair and subsequent breakup with Demeter would have to be dealt with at another time; as it stood, there were far more pressing matters to settle.

For now, Zeus was a lone god in the Land of Men, heading toward a land of *no* men. By foot, along the darkened path, Zeus traveled with no servants nor harem. He had dreaded this treacherous journey and avoided the inevitable for as long as he could—but no longer.

The suspicious thoughts he forever tried to bury in his mind would not stay hidden. Instead, his thoughts replayed on a never-ending loop. If he were a weaker god, the constant barrage of mental attacks would have been enough to drive him mad.

After trekking over hills and valleys as the black starry

night changed to shades of dark blue, the King finally stopped at the clearing ahead.

And there he is.

Zeus stood behind a huge boulder—where the incredible Son of Iapetos, chained naked, unable to see him, lay. With long steps, he emerged from the rock and made his presence known.

"It is I, Prometheus." His long shadow fell over Prometheus, casting a looming silhouette that the prisoner could not yet see but could certainly feel.

Carefully, the Titan's son turned his head to face the unwanted visitor.

The two gods stared at each other for a long moment, their expressions guarded and wary. The silence stretched between them, broken only by the occasional clink of the chains as Prometheus struggled against them.

"Well, well, well," The chained god's voice was as thunderous as a storm-filled night. He tried shifting his body but could not move much because of his restraints. "My long-lost cousin. Zeus, how good of you to visit."

The King was momentarily caught off guard by the mischievous glint that danced within the depths of the trickster's eye. "Yes, it has been a while since I last saw you."

"Welcome to my rock. I would offer you a drink, but my hands are tied at the moment."

The dried blood on Prometheus' abdomen briefly caught Zeus' attention. "A god in your predicament making jokes?"

"I laugh to keep from crying." His joyful face instantly changed to one of curiosity. "Why are you here?"

"The last time I saw you, you prophesied my future." *Prometheus was always a schemer. Although, he is now confined in the middle of nowhere, I am sure he still schemes all the more.* "You warned, 'from your declared offspring, will come one who will defeat you and take all that is yours'. Your foreboding words have weighed heavily on my mind ever since."

As much as it were possible, the Titan's son leaned forward in an attempt to whisper in the ear of the King. "Good."

His nails dug harshly into his palms. *Prometheus, the one who stole fire from my Mount to give to men. The one who then tricked me into accepting bones and fat as a sacrifice from men instead of flesh...* Zeus' anger festered, aching to be released. *He has robbed me of my rightful sacrifice, stole my fire, and now tries to steal the love I have for all my younglings by igniting my paranoia.*

"I still do not know why you were so shocked to hear my premonition." He would have shrugged if his shoulders were able to move. "After all, it is a family tradition for the youngling to usurp the father."

It is lies he tells! All lies! Yet, I cannot help but believe his lies. Taking another step toward the elder, Zeus said, "You told me what lies in my future...but you did not tell me *who* the perpetrator will be."

Looking toward the semi-dark sky, Prometheus remained quiet.

"So, tell me now! Which of my sons will dare strike me down?"

"After all this time, you do not have an inkling?"

"All my young ones love me. And I love all of them, each more than the last." Zeus became louder the more desperate his plea.

"Release me and I will tell you all you need to know."

His eyes darted frantically from side to side. Again reminding himself that he was conversing with a known Trickster. "Maybe all this is a ploy...a lie for you to escape divine punishment."

"So you know my words are true, I will tell you what will come to pass before your betrayal."

Before Zeus could protest, Prometheus relaxed his head back, his eyes glowed a strange color and a voice as piercing as a windstorm bellowed:

> *Now minus 1*
> *Will soon be undone*
> *An addition to 5*
> *Can subtract and divide*
> *When it comes to 3*
> *The end will it be*
> *Lastly, multiply by 2*
> *But the result, you cannot undo*
> *Woe, woe, woe is you!*

Zeus waited for more to be said but the shackled one turned his face from him and back to the sky, the vast darkness disappearing with each second that past.

"Instead of clarity you give me more riddles? Relieve me of this madness and tell me who will take all that I have!" The

God of the Sky would have fell upon his knees beside the rock, if he were not a king. "I cannot bear the thought of my own blood wishing me ill."

So says the one who stole all that he now has from his blood. Prometheus laughed softly at first...but then his laughter became louder with every passing moment. And just when it could not get any louder, his laughter stopped.

"Oh, but you *will* bear it. If you are driven insane from the unknown, all the better." Staring the god deep into his eyes, Prometheus taunted, "You torture me your way, and I will torture you my way."

For one brief second, Zeus looked at the prisoner with pity. An elder once of immense strength and vigor, pinned to a rock for all eternity. "So be it."

Once that brief second was over, Zeus' pity was also over. "Oh, look," he mused, taking note of the multi-colored sky as an eagle passed overhead. "It is now dawn."

Without another word, Zeus turned and began his journey down the unseen path. When he took his last step out of the desolate terrain, a blood-curdling scream echoed throughout the early morning.

7

TO: ERR IS HUMAN
XANDER THE MORTAL

Dearest Father,

The very first time I opened my eyes, your face was what I saw. Swirly dark hair, prominent nose with flared nostrils. Your cheeks were gaunt, hidden behind a thick, long beard. I would later learn that your olive skin had a red tinge, born from countless hours over sacrificial fires.

Soon thereafter, I found out I had an older brother, who eventually taught me all I could ever know about the world around me. Although there was much to digest, he preferred that I focus my studies on the earth's soil and how best to grow food from the fields.

While I spent many years toiling the ground and reaping the harvest for the family, my brother defended our village while you spent those same years at the Temple serving the High Gods.

You taught me to pray to the goddess Demeter for the health of my crops and to keep the locus at bay. Each week, I was to set aside a portion of grain to leave at her Temple in her honor and I made sure sure to light her favorite fragrance on the specified holy days. I did all that you commanded in body...but never in spirit.

What a wonderful life I could have had if all my worries were centered around which seeds were best planted at what time. Imagine if my biggest trouble was that the basket I carried to reap my harvest needed to be larger to contain the overabundance of produce.

But alas, that was never all of my worries. Instead, warring villages surrounded us, filled with ~~neighbors~~ enemies on every border who did not want to rest in peace. And so, I was a farmer and a soldier, standing as a last line of defense if worse came to worse and our army was overrun from the battlefield.

~~Unfortunately~~, or Fortunately, I was a better soldier than a farmer, considering I had more practice in one than the other.

As my brother and I fought for peace, you prayed for peace. I argued that our life would be ~~perfect~~ better if you fought beside us since prayer did no good. What an outlandish thing for me to say to my father, the High Priest of the King of the Gods.

Every morning, you dressed in ~~imacu~~ immaculate purple robes, smelling of minted incense, and humming old hymns. You would return home stained with blood from a goat, bull, or whatever else sacrificed to the gods that day. You asserted the gods filled our household with blessings because of your worship when I contended that only a metallic-tangy stench filled our four walls.

Inwardly, I knew we were blessed because my brother and our soldiers were skilled with the sword, and our village settled on fertile land.

What you call blessed, I call good-old fashion 'luck.'

I write to you sitting on the log where you left me, mere steps from the path toward Mount

Olympus, the so-called 'Dwelling of the Gods.' All this time, I have stayed here in obedience to your orders, having never disobeyed you before.

You said I was destined for greatness if I remained at this spot and waited for a visit from the gods. When I cried out to you, 'I will die waiting!,' you promised to return in a fortnight and take me home if what you prophesied did not come to pass.

Father, when you return tomorrow, you will not find me sitting on this log. I am leaving you, Nikolas, and our village behind in search of a world unknown. I have held my tongue for far too long, but no more! Finally, I will say my peace.

When Helios graces the morning sky within the hour, 13 days will have passed since we parted ways—enough time to confidently tell you what I had suspected long ago:

1) Our life is meaningless.
2) Your worship is in vain.
3) The gods are not real.

~ Xander,
Son of Zir

8

APOLLO 13
APOLLO & HEBE

"I am late!"

Apollo swung his yellow cloth, one of many colors that adorned his body, over his shoulder as he rushed through the forest.

'Late' and 'early' were relative terms to the gods compared to mankind. The creatures of the earth were bound to the wanderings of Helios' sun and Selene's moon. However, the objects of the sky did not rule the divine—*unless* the King of the Gods commanded it to be so.

The twin of Artemis, whom Zeus gave a timely task, dashed along, determined to avoid getting sidetracked by a beautiful red-haired goddess or an undiscovered melody until his mission was completed.

"Today, nothing will stop me from my errand—"

Arrrrrfff!

A small creature with ferocious teeth and pitch-black eyes

ran rapidly toward the god without a hint of slowing down. With no apparent cause for panic or need to hurry, Apollo lazily reached for the quiver strapped to his back and slowly pulled out one of many arrows. Bringing his bow out, he aimed his arrow steady.

"...Not even you," he finished readying the release of his weapon.

"No, Apollo! Stop!"

He looked up just in time to see the terrified face of the Princess of the Gods. Her unexpected interruption was enough for the four-legged beast to jump and bite into the god's skin with razor-sharp teeth.

"Bloody Hades!" he cursed, taking the animal by the neck and tearing it away from his flesh. Golden ichor flowed from its snapping teeth, foaming savagely at the mouth. "Ugly brute!" Apollo threw the mini monster onto the ground, pointing the arrow at its face.

"Please do not hurt her!" Hebe, once reaching the two, fell to her knees and wrapped her arms around the feral beast. "She is my new pet."

Great Zeus! As if he could kill the wretched creature now, knowing it belonged to Hebe. Gritting his teeth, he placed the arrow back in its quiver.

"There, there, Wolfie. You cannot eat Apollo." Wiping Apollo's ichor from the great wolf's mouth, she added, "He is the twin that I *actually* like."

"My dear Princess." He ripped a length of one of his linen. "If my dear sister were here, *Wolfie* would already be shot, skinned, made into a satchel, and gifted to you at your celebration."

Hebe combed her fingers through the pup's whitish-gray fur and scratched behind her ears. "I am so sorry she bit you." Wolfie lapped the Princess's cheeks happily. "I have not fed her yet."

What a wild beast—able to pierce the skin of a god! No doubt she was specially made to protect the goddess. Apollo was too busy wrapping his wound to grumble any further.

After settling the young Wolfie, Hebe stood up with an outstretched pale hand. "I know you can heal wounds, but at least let me help you with your pain."

"No!" Apollo sharply backed away from her touch as though it would burn and not soothe his skin. "And risk *further* pain if Helios spins a tale of me fondling you in the forest to your brother?"

She withdrew her hand, but the tremble of her lips was impossible for him to ignore. His words were harsh, much too severe for a goddess so sensitive.

She is only trying to help me. He forced a small smile, more so for her benefit. "My pain will soon go away."

Hebe nodded, hating that she could take away the sting if only he would allow her.

As long as she existed, Apollo and his twin Artemis rarely frequented the palace compared to Athena and Hermes. It was a shame since she did grow to appreciate Apollo's rather unusual disposition.

Sometimes, he was calm with slicked-back locks, wearing a simple white tunic and humming sweet melodies. Then, there were other times when he was erratic. His hair would be perfectly messy. He would layer his tunic with clothes of many colors and never put down his inked pen.

Examining him as he stood before her with slicked-backed hair and colorful clothing, Hebe reasoned Apollo was in an in-between stage.

"Promise me you will not tell my father what Wolfie did to you?" Her big brown eyes peeked through her dark tresses. "He hates all my unruly pets, and I do not want her punished."

Apollo looked down only to be met with the pet's sneer. *If I did not know any better, I would think Wolfie was threatening me to keep quiet.*

"It is your good fortune I do not attend to meet with the King before the festivities. Therefore, he cannot ask me about my day." His slight smile became genuine and grew more prominent when she stood on the balls of her feet in delight. The young Princess was no longer young, per the ways of the Gods. "Congratulations on your entry into godhood."

"Thank you." She gave a sheepish grin. "Did you, by any chance, get me a gift?"

"I did." His clear blue eyes twinkled as he wiggled his brows. "For you, I composed a Hymn that your worshipers will sing for all time."

Hebe clapped her hands together, filled with explosive energy. It was any wonder how she could restrain herself from leaping into Apollo's arms. "I cannot wait to hear my song!"

"All in due time."

She laughed, and he found the bubbly sound infectious. Actually, he found her very essence infectious.

No wonder Ares did his damnedest to keep her under wraps, hidden from unwanted gazes. "My, have you grown after all this time."

Hebe stood beaming, her white face blushed with a golden hue along her cheeks. She wore a green and white flock, the flowing hemline stopping below her knees. Except for a few locks framing her face, her braided raven-colored hair hung in two long pigtails below her petite breasts.

Soon, the length of her hemline will grow, and her braided hair will loosen. And sooner still, her white face will lose its plump innocence. "After today, you will have many suitors vying for your affection."

"Not if Ares has any say." Her sigh was long and sorrowful. "One scow from him, and all my suitors will scatter."

"My Princess, it was easy for Ares to keep the gods at bay because you were a youngling." He crossed his bulky arms as she twirled the end of her braid. "Now that you are of age, not only will he have to fight to keep the gods away, but he will also have to fight to keep *you* from running to those very gods."

"I do not wish to have *gods*." Her eyes traveled over his layers of multicolored clothing. "Only one will suffice."

If she were any other goddess, Apollo would have mistaken her behavior for flirting. However, he knew better thinking such things about one as naive as Hebe.

She is grown yet still so young of mind. How easily I could take her away from Ares as he took away my sister so long ago. It would only be fitting—and Ares could not fault me...even though he would try. Alas, I am so madly in love with Athena that I cannot scheme as cleverly as the Hermes' of this world.

Securing his weapon to his back, he drifted away from his thoughts. "You must excuse me, my Princess. The King sent me word to perform a task, and come tomorrow, a fortnight will have passed since I have delayed my duty."

"Then I shall not keep you any longer."

The god bent forward with a perfect bow, allowing her the perfect opportunity to do what she wanted after all.

"And please forgive my carelessness." Hebe touched his cheek.

Instantly, his eyes glowed with a strange light, and he snatched ahold of her wrist.

She gasped but was unable to twist her arm free from his grasp. Wolfie sat by her feet, also caught in the hypnotic brightness of Apollo's eyes.

His voice was monotonous, and his face lacked all expression:

> Your gift is not wonderful
> It is poison
> Woe to the one who tastes
> your poison.

Her limbs tightened as though an unseen aura held her in place. Blinking profusely, she stammered, "What?"

Before he could speak further, his eyes clamped shut, and when they reopened, the haunting light had disappeared.

Not again! After gathering his bearings, he saw two water-filled doe eyes staring back at him. *Great Zeus!* His grip still held her hostage, and at once, he flung her hand from his as if her skin was coated in boiling lava.

"I am so sorry, my Princess." Quickly, he looked overhead, his trembling body only ceasing because Helios' watchful eyes hid behind the clouded sky. "Please forgive me."

"What did you mean?" Her search for answers outweighed her panic. "I did not bring my father poison."

"Forget everything I said." Apollo rubbed his temples to combat the sharp pain clawing inside his skull. He took off without another glance at her, not wanting to face any more distractions. "I must go!"

9

FWB

HERMES & ARTEMIS

"So, how was I?" Artemis asked, wiping the edge of her mouth.

"You were..." Hermes searched the clouds for the perfect words to describe the toe-curling experience. "Amazing!"

"Amazing?" Even though she did not need the verbal confirmation, she smiled triumphantly at a job well done. After rearranging her dark tunic, she eased onto the soft blades of grass. "Why, thank you for the compli—Ow!" Her words were abruptly interrupted by a sharp hiss of pain, followed by a swift slap to her forearm for added pressure to the sore spot.

Hermes swiftly intervened, gently prying her hand away to inspect the source of pain. To his surprise, all he saw was her unblemished skin. "Are you alright?"

A fleeting grimace flitted across Artemis' face before she

composed herself. "Yes, I am fine." She sighed, shaking her head. "My brother, unfortunately, is not."

"Huh?"

"Apollo must have been injured somehow..." Artemis trailed off, her voice tinged with worry.

"You can feel each other's pain?"

"Sometimes."

A flicker of realization danced across Hermes' features as he tilted his head to the side. "What other sensations can you two feel?"

The goddess rolled her eyes, refusing to indulge Hermes' probing questions further.

The sky was still dark, but Helios would soon be gearing up to pull the sun overhead in his usual fashion. And when Helios was in the heavens, it was always best not to draw his attention.

"I trust that you will keep our little *excursion* between us?"

Hermes turned to face Artemis, thrilled they had finished where they had left off hours before. *Her plea for silence can only mean one thing.* "You do not want me to tell your brother."

"I want you to keep a secret for *once* in your life."

There were many situations when Hermes found it necessary to reveal secrets. Because of his previous exposé, the Low Gods declared him untrustworthy, never realizing there was always a method to his madness.

It does not benefit me to tell anyone about our... arrangement. Focusing back on Artemis, he explained, "Apollo and I had a rocky start to our relationship. However, we have become far better acquainted once we overcame the indiscretions of our youth."

She zeroed in on him through her dark brown eyes. "Indiscretions of *our* youth? You mean…*your* youth."

"No need to be weighed down with pesky details," he said, brushing away her judgmental response with a flick of his hand. "In order *not* to draw your brother's wrath, I will not tell Apollo how much of me you can fit down your—"

The twitch of her brow was enough for Hermes to stop talking—and let the calming sounds of nature fill in the gap. Eventually, Artemis' muscles relaxed, and he could safely ogle her in peace as naked as the day he was born.

He marveled at the darkness of her body. Her umber-brown skin was unique in appearance, her tone physique was intimidating, and her attitude was *never* to be tested.

Out of all the goddesses, she was the one Hermes knew would be a formidable foe in hand-to-hand combat—not that he would ever want to try his luck. Artemis was so disciplined in her training, and with anything, she was the perfect specimen of a goddess.

"May I ask, where did you learn your…technique? It is not every day I run into someone who can handle my length."

The huntress smacked a red spider crawling up her leg. "Your crush, Aphrodite, is a well of knowledge," she said slyly and continued on before he could interject. "However, there is only so much theory one can learn without application. So, you happen to be my first—the one I want to practice everything I have been taught." Artemis beamed with pride. She always wanted to be the best at anything she participated in, and leading a god to climax was no exception. "For research purposes, I was curious to know what it takes to please a god."

The birds, perched on their branches, whistled throughout the forest. He leaned his head onto his hand with an ever-present smirk. "Then let me know how it is to please a goddess." Not one to leave anything to chance, he licked around his top and bottom lip so she knew exactly what he meant.

This cheeky one. "I am sure you already know all the ways to please a goddess, Hermes."

If she does not want me to stick my head between her legs, there is only one more thing I can stick in there. "Then let me show you how we can please each other…at the same time." His entire body reignited at the thought of being the first to take Artemis to the heights of pleasure. Hermes traced his fingers along her well-defined thigh, and she promptly stopped his wandering by covering his hand with her own.

"A god's seed is extremely potent. The last thing we need is a little Hermes running around."

He wiggled his brows. "What about a little Artemis?"

She laughed wholeheartedly, impressed at his persistence, and lifted her hand, leaving him to roam free over her leg.

"I promise I will be careful. I will spill my seed on the ground and create a new race of rock gods."

Artemis giggled. *The Fates are a curious lot. Always finding new, unconventional ways to make creations for their will to be done. Aphrodite says The Fates can and will make new rules as they see fit. However, one tried and tested rule is that a god's seed spilling on nature will produce a living being—what kind of being is up in the air.*

Hermes continued to slide his fingers along her leg until he reached the warmth between the lips of her body. "I want to do more with you."

Her hips raised involuntarily to greet his two fingers at her entrance, tittering on the edge of no return.

I have already kissed his balls, licked his head, taken his entire shaft into my mouth, and swallowed his load with one gulp... "This is not about what you want. This is about what *I* want." Abruptly, she scooted away on her bum, breaking contact with him. "Right now, pleasing you is all I want to do."

Liar. As if I cannot hear her heavy panting, see her swollen nipples, or feel her juices dripping along my fingers. However, if Artemis wants to lie to herself while I hold onto the truth, so be it.

He sighed in disappointment. "As you say."

She smiled, ignoring the slow shrinking of his erection. "I say."

Again, he laid on his back with his arms tucked under his head, not caring enough to get dressed.

On the other hand, Artemis grabbed the yellow fabric beside her and began wrapping it around her limps. "It seems like forever since I was last here."

Here? "The forest of Mount Olympus?"

Nodding her confirmation, she tied a golden rope along her waist.

This is true. While I am a constant fixture in the palace, even though I am a bastard, Artemis would be around the outskirts of the Mount but not much further inland.

Because of my close association with my father's kingdom duties, I am extended special privileges the other bastards cannot access. However, the limited luxuries I attained were due to my persistence—nothing was ever handed to me.

Artemis sat crosslegged next to him. "I am only here today to honor my father and no more."

"A word to the wise. The King loves you dearly as he loves us all, but this ongoing war you have waged against the Queen keeps you at a disadvantage. Since I worked tirelessly to gain the Queen's favor, she does not begrudge that I have some sway over the King."

"What good is it to bend over for Hippo Hera?"

He surpassed a grin.

"Athena has the King's ear as much as you do…maybe even more so, and she did not have to kiss the Queen's enormous *ass* for the privilege."

Her burst of anger revived his settled passions enough for him not to interrupt her rant.

"What happens when you both give the King an opposing council? Athena was born the oldest from the very mind of Zeus. Will he not take her advice over yours?"

He blurted before he could control his tongue, "Athena may have the King's ear, but I have the Queen's lips. I can make her speak my words, and the King often relents to her desires if only to prevent a quarrel."

"Hermes, if you truly believe you have *any* part of Hera,"

she said, crossing her arms, "you are the dumbest fool on the face of this earth."

"Shall I instead employ your tactic and antagonize the Queen? It does not behoove you to war with Hera. You are playing this game all wrong."

"Everything is a game to you, Hermes." Artemis eyed him with great suspicion. "But tell me, what is the prize you hope to win at the end?"

The answer was simple. *I want Aphrodite and to be the next in line to the throne.* Instead of giving away his entire game plan, he replied, "I want love and power."

"Hermes, do you not know?" Artemis shook her head adamantly. "It is impossible for you to have both."

Impossible? Nothing is impossible as far as I am concerned. Even though he spoke more words than he intended, he knew enough not to talk anymore.

Her superior attitude was such that he wanted to wipe the smug smile off her face. "And if you one day wake up and decide to play the game of gods, what prize would *you* fight for?"

Artemis pretended to think long and hard when the answer was already waiting to jump out. The answer was the one thing she wanted more than anything in the world. With a voice so faint, she whispered, "Freedom."

Hermes let her words hang in the air before he burst out in a loud, obnoxious laugh.

"What is so funny?"

His lips curled into half a smile. "What is funny is you believe freedom exists." Hermes changed the subject to avoid an arrow jammed into whatever bodily orifice Artemis saw fit. "Today is a day of celebration. Our Princess will be officially presented to the court and her subjects."

"Who cares?"

"I take it you are not impressed."

"Hebe is afraid of her own shadow. There is *no* way she will be able to navigate through the Land of Men, never mind bringing back a gift worthy of the King."

"Yes. Y*our* gift to the King on your Day of Understanding will never be outdone." *No one can take away the bold gift Artemis presented to the King and the tale she told to go along with it. It was a gift for the ages, no doubt!* "But today is Hebe's day, and she is our Princess. For that, we must honor her by attending the ceremony."

"Earlier, I saw Poseidon from afar presenting a new four-legged creation to the young one…Wolfie."

Hermes' eyes perked up. *Hebe has already returned to the palace? I must make sure to see her before the ceremony.*

Artemis sighed, then muttered, "It must be nice to be gifted such nice things just for being born to the King in wedlock."

Hermes refocused on the clouds moving along the sky. Because they were bastards of the King, their station in life was already predestined. The path The Fates determined for all those born was set in stone. A life already planned out was maddening to most…but not for Hermes.

He did not believe in The Fates.

"Have you seen Apollo? I feel he has been avoiding me as of late."

His boredom was setting in. "Not since last night."

"You saw him last night?" She thought a moment, slightly confused. "He told me he had plans."

Hermes picked up on her curiosity. *This conversation got a lot more interesting.* "Oh yes, did he ever have plans!"

Artemis sat up in an instant and slapped his bare chest. "*Spill* it!"

"Where?" He could not resist. "On your breasts this time?"

She pressed hard onto his chest. "You *know* what I mean."

I better answer before she pokes her finger straight through my heart. "Apollo and Athena are spending a *lot* of time together."

"What?" *This is so unlike my brother.* "He never told me this."

"It is true." He sat up to get a better view of the outline of her nipples. The fact that her breasts were now covered intrigued him more than when they were free. Subconsciously, his hand drew back toward his groin. "I helped him plan the night. Even giving him a bottle of a special drink courtesy of Dionysus. If all goes well, there may be a wedding in the future."

"My twin...married...to Athena." *Who would have thought?*

"Might I add that a love-sick Apollo is such a pleasure to be around? It is the only time he is *not* obnoxiously cocky."

"So says the cockiest one of them all." Usually, she would defend her brother's reputation, but Hermes was too ridiculous for her to be offended. "And even if Apollo married Athena, it would not mean he was in love with her. Zeus and Hera prove that love is not needed in marriage."

His thoughts were no longer on Apollo and Athena but on

the growing hardness protruding from his grip. *If only I could fondle her tits with my free hand.*

Artemis noticed the remains of his crooked smile. Seeing him so confident in his domain of spreading rumors caused a stir within her—as did the view of him butt naked, jerking his erection while penetrating her with his eyes. "What are you doing?"

"Since I cannot touch you, I will just have to touch myself."

She bit her bottom lip, watching his solid abs flex as he gradually increased the speed of his pumping.

Although I have set boundaries with Hermes, it does not mean we cannot play within them.

"Alright, time for round four." She pushed him flat on the ground and straddled his stomach, preventing him from moving...not that he would have gone anywhere else. "Quickly, before Helios makes his way closer."

"Again?" he asked playfully.

She winked. "Practice makes perfect."

10

KILL(H)ER
PERSEPHONE (KORE)

"What lie will we tell the elders when we return to the village?" Nikolaos scratched his growing beard.

He and Andreas were sheltered beneath the gnarled branches of an ancient tree. The soft light of dawn could not penetrate the thick morning haze that seemed to follow them like a bad omen.

Andreas, the weathered soldier, bore the marks of countless battles carved into his features. He was clad in sturdy leather armor, tarnished from the trials of never ending combat.

A faint smile formed on his lips. "My father would say: A lying tongue is cut for a truthful mouth." The smile soon turned to a frown as the image of his dying father left on the battlefield bombarded his thoughts. He shook his head adamantly. "No lie will suffice. The elders will call us cowards for running away."

Nikolaos, his comrade, possessed a more refined demeanor, with sharp, calculating eyes that betrayed a keen intellect. His attire was similarly practical but well-maintained. "I would rather be called a coward than to be called dead." A well-worn sword was belted at his side, stained from his last kill.

Andreas lowered his head in shame of what lay ahead. "We will face decimation."

"From who?" The harshness of his voice was echoed by the furrow of his brows. "We will tell a false tale when we return home, and no one will be able to counter us with the truth. Dead men tell no tales. All the other soldiers were burned alive as fire rained down from heaven." Nikolaos cleared his throat and spat thick yellow phlegm onto the soil. "Ares be damned."

The birds stopped chirping, the winds stopped blowing, and Andreas stopped breathing.

By the Gods! Frantically, he pressed his palm over his chest to ensure his heart was still beating. "You dare curse the name of the Prince of the Gods?" he hissed.

"I fear no other gods than the High Gods."

"If you fear the High Gods, you should fear their son."

As they bickered, a distant, sweet melody filled the silence of the air, prompting both men to rise from beneath the tree and peer deeply into the fog.

Soon, a figure came into view, stepping toward them draped in a flowing blood-red cloak and a glowing torch.

Nikolaos elbowed his mate, curiosity piqued, "What is that over there?"

The mysterious one before them stood in place and removed her hood, allowing her scattered braided and twisted brown hair to fall past her waist. Her eyes were the color of murky waters, and her cheeks were as plump and rosy as a new baby.

The warriors were in awe of her beauty, having rarely, if ever, seen femininity in motion.

What is she? Andreas wondered aloud, his voice tinged with disbelief, "Is it a mermaid?"

"She has no tail, you moron."

Mortal men were created and destroyed in various ages and now lived in the Bronze Age. Prometheus fashioned all men, some as babies, some as children, and the rest as adults all at once, although they awoke into existence at different times. He only created a fixed amount in the masculine form to reflect the image of the mighty gods. Per his decree, male and female duality would only be represented in the animals and the divine.

Andreas did not take his eyes off her. "Then what creature is this?"

"I am no creature." Her perfectly sculpted lips parted, "My name is Kore."

Andreas marveled, "It talks!"

"Of course, I talk."

Unlike Andreas, Nikolaos was far from enamored with the beauty and closer to suspicious. He made it a point to grab the hilt of his sword, though it remained in its sheath. "What are you?"

"I am a goddess."

"There are only two choices to explain this mystery. Either this one is mad or she is a fool!"

"She can also be both!"

Nikolaos exchanged a glance with his partner and burst into laughter, one clutching his stomach while the other doubled over.

After regaining his composure, Andreas pointed to her in disgust. "A goddess appears dressed in the silk of clouds, not in the tattered clothing of men. What creature are you really?"

"I am no creature. I am a goddess," she insisted.

Again, the memory of Andreas' father entered his mind. However, instead of sadness, a haunting smile crawled along his face. He signaled to his friend with a nod. "This one uses the tongue to lie."

"Then we...will cut it out." Nikolaos wasted no time removing his sword and pointing it at the goddess, and the two began a forward march in her direction.

As the men approached, her feet remained planted on the ground. "I shall warn you to step no further."

The former cowards only hesitated enough to laugh once more before continuing their offense.

Oh, stubborn, stubborn men. The goddess shrugged with indifference and raised her torch high. "You were warned."

...

And after the goddess finished disposing of her victims'

bodies, she continued on her merry way with only her haunting melody lingering in the air as she vanished into the distance.

11

THE BODYGUARD
XANDER & HEBE

"It is poison?" Hebe's voice echoed softly in the secluded Garden of the Gods, her words meant for her ears alone, save for the attentive presence of her faithful companion, Wolfie. "What was Apollo trying to tell me?"

As if sensing her distress, Wolfie nudged against her leg, coaxing her to move. Hebe sighed, reluctantly allowing herself to be led out of the peaceful park, her steps guided more by instinct than intention. "No, Wolfie," she murmured, her grip tightening on the leash as she steered the curious creature away from its chosen path. "We are going this way."

Apollo's cryptic words lingered in her mind, refusing to be dismissed despite his insistence to forget them.

I serve the High Gods at my pleasure. I pour drinks for my father often. Why would my drinks be poison? What sense does that make? None at all—

Arrrfff!

Hebe's mind raced with questions as she came to an abrupt stop, her eyes narrowing at the sight before her. A red-capped soldier, spear in hand, stood sentry at the entrance to her quarters. *Who could this be?*

With cautious steps, Hebe approached the figure, her curiosity piqued by the unexpected visitor. *Another puzzle to unravel.*

Wrapping the leash securely around her wrist to ensure Wolfie stayed close, Hebe marched forward. Planting her hands firmly on her hips, she fixed her gaze on the soldier. "Who are you, and why are you standing at my door?"

The soldier, tall and dark-haired, stood at attention, his eyes flickering as he avoided direct contact with her gaze. Instead, he cast his eyes downward, his voice barely above a whisper. "Zeus, King of the Gods, commands that I stand guard at your door."

Hebe huffed at the mysterious figure. "What for?"

"Pro—protection."

Grrrrr... Wolfie nipped inches away from his toes.

The soldier gripped the spear directly at his side but dared not point it in either of their direction.

Hebe raised a bemuse brow for once, happy with her pet's actions. "As you can see, I already have protection." With a swing of her wrist, she ordered. "Down, Wolfie."

The cub settled at once, not because of her command, more so because she found a new game—playfully pulling on her leash.

"What shall I call you?" Hebe asked as Wolfie tugged at her tethered arm.

"Xa—Xander," he answered, still without eye contact.

Xander. His olive skin stretched over his large muscles, yet his face gave hints of reddish coloring. *Is not the blood of men red?*

Choosing not to contemplate further, Hebe spoke on, "Xander, I will be preparing for my upcoming celebration. I do not want any visitors. Understand?"

He gave a firm nod and stepped aside as she breezed past him. "As you wish, my Princess."

As Hebe headed up the spiral staircase, there was only one question remaining on her mind.

How can a mortal protect the immortal?

12

DEATH'S WISH
HADES & ZEUS

Dark. Death. Hades.

The Underworld: A land of mystical creatures, the souls of men, and the God, Hades.

Zeus never liked the treacherous journey into his brother's kingdom, but once he settled at the Dark Palace, it was worth the trip.

Guided through the shadowed corridors, he was led to a room with nothing but a solitary imposing table, with Hades seated at the helm, dressed in an exquisite silk robe in various shades of black.

In the shaded corner, the formidable dark Cerberus lay at rest, its three heads displaying the satisfaction of a recent meal.

Zeus took the seat opposite his brother. His dark, unruly curls hung above his piercing eyes. He quickly surmised that

Hades was fairing well, although his skin appeared pale next to the otherworldly blue and green torch flame.

"I am sorry I took so long to get here."

Hades waved Zeus off with little care. "No need for an apology," he said, though he was curious. "How many *detours* did you have to make on your journey?"

Thinking it best to ignore Hades' innuendos, Zeus continued as if he did not hear him, "It is good to see you, brother."

"Brother." Hades sat tall in his chair. Although he had a smaller frame than Zeus, he still had the same intimidating stature. His hair, so blonde it was almost white, was cut low, and he had steel gray eyes that only seemed to light up whenever a new soul entered his territory.

The Sky God loosened his V-neck blouse, exposing more of his chest. "It is hot in here."

"May I offer you some water to drink? Food?"

The fruits on the table seemed sweet by their vibrant color, the meat smelled divine, and the drinks would very well satisfy his thirst, but Zeus knew better. Indeed, if he indulged his appetite, the land of the dead would become his permanent home.

"I know not to eat or drink in the Underworld."

"I had to try." He had a twinkle in his eye. "Maybe one day you will accept my offer."

"Not today."

Hades snapped his fingers, and at once, the servers appeared, took up all the plates on the table, and left them alone.

"I know I do not visit a lot. This place takes a while to get used to. When I leave, it takes a while to prepare myself to come back."

"Well, it is your luck and good fortune that picking Lots worked out in your favor. Poseidon gained the sea, you the sky, and me the Underworld."

He wiggled uneasily in his seat. "Yes, my good fortune."

Hades rubbed the arm of his extravagant walnut chair. Anytime the topic of Lots would come up, he could never hold his tongue. "As the oldest reborn son, I should have sat in the sky."

"In theory, some would say yes. Although others would argue I became the oldest once..."

Hades gripped the forearm of his seat. However, Zeus knew better than to finish the rest of his sentence.

Even without mentioning how the others spent decades in our father's stomachs while I grew in stature, I still deserve rights to the sky. "Since *I* was the one who freed you and the others from our father's stomach, it was only right we settled on a fair way to divide his territory amongst his sons."

"Speaking of sons. One of yours likes to flirt with the boundaries we have set between our two worlds."

Zeus' mood changed at the thought of his younglings being on Hades' mind. *He better tread lightly.*

"The young god wades in the dark waters, leading to the underworld, tempting fate."

Only one of my brood would dare test the boundaries so brazenly. "I will have a talk with Hermes."

"Or...you can let him—"

"I will *not* let him," he stated sternly, cutting off all conversation.

Hades chuckled at Zeus' ability to forget where he was now sitting. *Very soon, I will have to remind him.* "Let us then discuss the matters you have come all this way to settle."

"We have lived peacefully for a millennium, and now you want to disrupt the balance of peace?" Folding his hands together, he asked, "What do you want?"

"More."

"More?"

"More souls."

What is this nonsense? "You have more souls than I can count."

"And I want more still."

How can I argue when he is so unreasonable? He already has creatures only native to the Underworld on top of the souls of men who have died. "If things continue as they are now on the earth with the uncontrollable fires, mankind will soon no longer exist."

Zeus folded his hands on the table. "And then you will make more." He flippantly waved his hand in the air. "It has already been done three times before."

"Mankind was living peacefully in a primitive state until Prometheus thought it best to defy my orders and steal fire from Mount Olympus to gift mankind. At first, men used fire to keep warm, and then they used fire to hunt and cook food. Not much later, they used fire to melt steel and make weapons to kill and war with one another. Prometheus' gift suddenly became their curse."

Hades listened intently without interrupting.

"They are killing each other at an alarming rate. Time goes much faster for them than for us, so no more men will be left before long, but I will not expedite the process. You will wait your turn for your souls. They will come to you in due time...naturally."

They were at a stalemate.

Hades waited until the tension left the room, and once it was gone, he summoned it back with only three words.

"How is...Hera?"

Slowly, Zeus leaned into the table with a snare on his face and a pointed finger. "You do *not* speak my wife's name."

"She was supposed to be *my* wife. *I* was supposed to marry the Queen of the Gods." Sitting back in his chair, as calm as possible, he repeated the forbidden name, "Hera."

A bang of thunder echoed throughout the room as Zeus catapulted from his chair with such force that it toppled over.

Instantaneously, Cerberus, the fearsome guardian of the Underworld, leaped into action. With all three of its heads baring razor-sharp teeth, the monstrous hound charged toward Zeus.

Zeus instinctively raised his hands in a defensive posture as Cerberus lunged at him. The beast's assault was halted only by the taut leash that encircled each of its three menacing heads. The beast barked and snarled in Zeus' face but could move no further.

Only when Hades calmly raised a single, commanding finger did Cerberus abruptly cease its aggressive assault. The hound settled back down, its thirst for blood and bones quelled for now.

Still seated in the same position, Hades sneered, "I will speak any name I want. Remember, God of the Sky, you are now in *my* kingdom."

Without another word, Zeus picked up the chair from the ground and sat back down. It was not time to dredge up the past but to secure the future. Prometheus' looming prophecy made it so he had no other option but to maintain the bridge between their two Kingdoms. *I cannot risk war with my son and my brother at the same time.*

"You will have your souls. I will have mankind wiped out to quench your never-ending thirst. The High Gods will then create a new mankind once this generation has passed." *Indeed, this was now the third generation of men. If he wants them so badly, he can have them all.*

Hades nodded, yet Zeus could sense that everything was not settled.

"Is there anything else you want?"

"Yes, one more thing. In the name of peace."

He rubbed his dark-trimmed beard while contemplating. "Name it, and you shall have it. In the name of peace."

Clasping his hands together, Hades stated plainly, "A wife."

13

QUEEN B
HERA & HEBE

Where is he?

The Queen of the Gods released a heavy sigh, her melancholic gaze lingering on the sight of her neatly made but empty bed. It stood as a stark reminder of Zeus' absence and grew cold the longer he was away.

Slowly, she pivoted in her carved chair to confront her reflection in the vanity mirror. Her sharp hazel eyes held a hidden vulnerability within the reflection—eyes that had witnessed eons of darkness, trials, and triumphs. Her rich brown hair was elegantly secured in a tidy low bun.

Am I still as breathtaking as the day we met?

Although she asked the question, she need not dignify herself with the obvious answer. Her husband's gasp in awe whenever they reunited would always settle her wayward thoughts.

What is taking him so long?

Whenever her husband's journeys took him far from Olympus, he would let it be known the day he would return but never the hour. This deliberate mystery was his way of ensuring Hera's unwavering anticipation. It was a pattern she had grown accustomed to, a dance of expectation and impatience that only deepened the mania she had yet to crawl out of.

I can wait for him no longer. I have a Queendom to rule.

Hera rose from her seat, mentally preparing for the long day ahead. She wore a colorful silk gown flowing around her, the edges finding rest at her ankles. Upon her brow, she bore a golden crown with diamonds that sparkled with a brilliance rivaling Helios' sun itself. It symbolized her queenly authority over all the gods, an honor bestowed on her the day of her rebirth.

Every step Queen Hera took through the palace halls commanded attention even though she did not utter a word. Along the way, servants in her line of vision halted their tasks to lower themselves in deference. Hera acknowledged their reverence with a graceful tilt of her head but no more as time did not allow her to patronize all those who would seek her presence.

Anticipation heightened her every step as she moved closer to the entryway leading to her daughter's recently occupied quarters. *I cannot wait to hear how she fared on her journey.*

Suddenly, Hera came to an abrupt halt.

What...is...this?

An unfamiliar figure in the realm of the gods stood at the entrance to her daughter's door in the common foyer.

Intriguingly, the stranger bore the physical stature of the divine, with forearms the size of the gods. However, there was no denying he was only a mortal.

"Greetings, Your Highness. Queen Hera." The bare-chested man said with his head down, a spare in his right hand, and a sword at his side.

With an arch of her brow, Hera observed the man, suspicion flickering in her eyes. She was no stranger to the machinations of gods and mortals alike, and this particular figure was no exception.

She spent a moment sizing him up. Scars of varying sizes decorated his bare, tanned upper body. Faint etchings of past conflicts bore witness to his many battles.

This mortal man is obviously battled tested, yet he grips his spare so forcefully his hand shakes.

His attire and weapons were imposing, but his demeanor told another tale. *What a timid fellow to be given such a great responsibility.*

"And who are you?" Her voice was as smooth as her skin... and as icy as her heart.

"Xa-Xa-Xander," he finally managed to spit out.

When Hera refused to speak further, he got the clue and continued on.

"I was a—appointed by King Zeus, God of the Sky, to stand by Pr—Princess Hebe's door now that she no longer dwells next to Your Grace's chambers."

What foolishness is my husband up to now?

There was not much time left to ponder her question. Hera shifted her gaze up to her daughter's balcony. "Xander, has the Princess returned from her journey into the Land of Men?"

"Yes, Your Majesty." Without thinking, he rambled, "However, the Princess has instructed me that she does not wish to have any visitors."

Would he dare assume I take orders? Luckily for him, he amused her. "Well then. It is a good thing I am no visitor. I am her mother."

"Yes of course, Your Majesty." Before finishing his sentence, he readily stepped aside, not wanting to embarrass himself further.

Hera headed into the Princess' Quarters and did not flinch at the loud sound of Xander whacking his forehead with his rod.

The rooms she passed displayed the grandeur of Olympus. Gilded accents graced the walls, catching and reflecting the golden light that streamed through tall windows. Lavish drapes, dyed in hues as rich as the gods' realm, captivated the gaze like precious stones.

Once through the maze of the palace, the Queen turned a corner and was met with the youngest one at the other end of the hall.

"Mommy!" Princess Hebe dashed ahead, only stopping once she was face-to-face with the one she so longed to see.

"Oh! My dearest one." Hera placed her hands over her daughter's plump cheeks and beamed as if they had been reunited after a millennium. Her eyes scanned over every inch of Hebe's body to ensure no harm was done to her. "You have returned to me in one piece."

Oh no! Hebe's brows raised suddenly as she took a slight step back. "I thought I was not to see you until the ceremony."

"Nothing will ever keep me from you—or any of my children. Besides, I wanted to see for myself how well you settled into your new quarters—"

From an open room door behind Hera, a furry four-legged creature ran circles around her sandals before excitedly jumping at Hebe. "What is this beast?"

"Her name is Wolfie." Hebe scooped the young pup and giggled as it buried its nose against her neck. She stretched out her arms and held Wolfie close enough to happily lick her mother's lips. "She's Uncle Poseidon's present for my special day."

Hera turned up her sensitive nose when she caught a whiff of the stench. *Poseidon is determined to turn my beautiful home into a stable!* "Make sure she has a proper place to sleep outside. You already know your father does not allow your pets in the palace."

She motioned toward the balcony and mumbled, "Then why does father allow me to have Xander?"

"My daughter." Shaking her head, Hera gently cupped Hebe's chin. "What am I to do with you?"

"Love me to pieces."

She brushed aside her raven hair and kissed her forehead. "Always."

Hera waited until Hebe released Wolfie before she

continued on. "And how was your first journey into the Land of Men?"

"More than I ever could have expected." She squealed with excitement. However, her stomach ached at the thought of what was to come. "But..."

"Yes?"

"Ares once told me it did not take long for him to be permitted to take his first journey to the Land of Men. Neither did Artemis, Apollo, or Hermes take long to reach their Age of Understanding. I fear that I cannot measure up next to them."

"Growing up, what have I taught you to believe? The King's bastards were *never* beside you. They will always be beneath you."

Reluctantly, she nodded her head. The Queen had raised Ares and Hebe in the knowledge that they were special because they were born into wedlock of the Ruler of the Gods. As such, the Royal Golden Blood that pumped through their veins set them apart from Zeus' other offspring in stature and in family relations.

"You are the Princess of the Gods and your brother Ares is the Prince of the Gods. Never compare yourself to the King's bastards." Hera clenched her teeth hard enough for visible bulges to appear on her jawline. "Besides, all of the gods reach our true potential at varying points. No need to pout now that your time has arrived. Today is a day of celebration."

Hebe forced a smile and eventually, her smile became genuine. "Will my dear Aunt Hestia be well enough to attend my ceremony?"

Her daughter's innocent question was enough to rattle Hera's senses. She held her tongue in anguish, her emotions too much to bear, and shook her head in response.

My poor darling sister. The Fates know how I hoped my sister would be well enough to attend. However, Hestia's up-and-down days did not pan out in our favor.

As the seconds ticked by, the rawness of her emotions began to subside, allowing her to regain her composure. "Today is a day of joy, and Hestia would want us to honor her by being of good cheer."

"Will mummy-Demeter be here to witness my ascension into godhood?"

"Darling, how could you ask such a thing? Demeter loves you and Ares as if you were her very own. Nothing will stop her from sitting in the front row." Focusing back on her youngling, she asked, "Now, did you follow all the rules of your first official outing and bring back a gift for your King?"

Hebe brimmed with youthful confidence. "My gift to the King will rival everything he has ever received, past and future."

"Really?" The Queen pressed further, her curiosity piqued, "What is this gift?"

"I cannot say." She twisted her finger around the ends of one of her pigtails. "It is a present for you as well."

"I love surprises." Grabbing hold of her daughter's hands, Hera squeezed in delight. "You will do well, my love." As a gentle sigh escaped her lips, Hera's gaze turned inward as though peering into the wellspring of her heart. "I still recall the first moments when you graced my arms as a fragile babe, your laughter bringing a sparkle forever brightening our once-dark palace. And even as you grew, you would always be wrapped all around me. But little by little, you moved further and further away until I could no longer cradle you in my arms."

"Because, I am no longer a youngling. I am a goddess."

"That you are!" Soon Hera's smile turned into a frown while taking hold of one of her daughter's braided hair. "But tell me this, should a goddess be wearing pigtails?"

Hebe hesitated. A question she did not know the answer to, and so, she looked to her mother in search of the answer.

Hera slid her fingers along her daughter's clothing. "Please tell me you did not intend to wear this outfit for the ceremony."

Her dress was pale green and white with little detail to captivate the eyes. *How can I be a Goddess if I still rely on my mother's wisdom?* She swallowed hard, her confidence leaving as quickly as it had arrived. "Then what shall I wear, mom?"

"A dress of silk clouds..."

Hebe's eyes sparkled. "...wrapped in the stars."

14

LOOSE LIPS
APHRODITE & HERMES

Ah-ha! Perfection!

After an intense selection process, Hermes finally plucked a flower from the many that overwhelmed the scenery where he stood. The rest of his plan would be easier to execute because Aphrodite was precisely where he knew she would be, taking her usual early morning stroll through the Garden of the Gods.

The garden, bathed in Helios' sunlight, was a blend of vibrant colors and intoxicating fragrances. Blossoming flowers of every hue lined the path, their delicate petals swaying gently in the morning breeze. Towering ancient trees provided shade, with birds perched on the branches chirping away.

Aphrodite wore a flowing gown of shimmering golden silk with patterns of pearls. Her lustrous hair topped with a fresh makeshift laurel wreath.

The quick-footed god stood a moment to watch as she sat by the crystal fountain, dipping her fingers in and out of the shallow pool of water. She was humming a tune only she knew and he could have stared at her in a trance for all eternity.

Happy was I the day Zeus introduced the goddess Aphrodite to the Royal Court.

His hesitation was all it took for the beauty to ease up from her spot and again glide softly down the marble path.

Wake up, Hermes! Snapping out of his temporary hypnoses, he quickly caught up to her from behind. "My dear, love."

As she turned to see him, he had a flower already in front of her.

"The prettiest flower for the prettiest goddess."

"Oh, Hermes!" She lowered her head a tad so he could place the flower in her hair. "You spoil me so."

He gave a carefree shrug. "It comes naturally for me whenever I see you."

She giggled and, with a spin, continued ahead of him, knowing he would follow suit. "My day just keeps on getting better and bet..."

"Watch your..." Hermes reached out to stop her, but it was too late.

"Oh!" Her right foot had plunged into a soft pile of... "Ugh!"

"...step."

"Yuck!" Aphrodite raised her leg and wiggled her filthy-covered toes in disgust. "Cannot Hebe clean up after Pegasus?"

"By the look of it. I would wager that disgusting pile did not come from Pegasus." Hermes spoke on as Aphrodite made her way toward the trickling stream ahead. "That mess looks like it came from Princess Hebe's *new* pet. Wolfie."

"Wolfie?" With both feet, she stepped into the cold water and splashed about until no trace of waste was left on her otherwise perfect skin.

"Yes. I heard that Poseidon gifted her the new creation to honor her entry into Godhood."

Hermes offered his hand, and Aphrodite held on as she made her way out of the stream. "Hebe is unbelievably spoiled!"

"Jealous?"

"Me? Jealous?"

"Hmmm. I wonder where the Princess might be?" His sandals glimmered as he effortlessly glided along the path. "She is back from her journey, and I have yet to see her."

First Ares and now Hermes? I will be damned if a god is preoccupied with another goddess when in my presence. "Why do you bother me with talk of Hebe when there are far more interesting things to discuss? You were gone for a long time. Where were you?"

"I had some things to take care of. All is accomplished."

The normally chatty god was much too vague for her liking. She narrowed her warm blue eyes suspiciously. "You always go on some top-secret mission for the High Gods and never tell me why."

Aphrodite is curious about my whereabouts? He had every right to be suspicious of *her* newfound curiosity when she usually cared very little about things that did not concern her. "You have never asked me before."

"Silly me." Thinking more deeply into the matter, she knew it to be true. "I guess I never ask because I do not care," she said, combing her luscious curls with her fingertips.

They found a nice spot to sit as sunlight filtered through the lush foliage, casting dappled patterns on the ground. "And what have you been up to in your free time? On my returns from my travels, I could not help but notice that monstrosity carved into Mount Olympus."

With her lips perched, she slapped her hands against her cheeks. "How dare you call it a monstrosity?" She looked up at her house in the sky from where they sat. It was positioned underneath the palace atop the mountain and looked like a quick build. "That is my new home, and you know it!"

"How did you get Zeus to agree to construct a home on the mount of the King and Queen of the Gods?" Her unabashed ambition amused him like no other. "Hera must be livid."

"Not my problem." She had an air of defiance about her. "I may not be a princess, but by the gods, I *will* be treated like one."

He suppressed a chuckle. "It is any wonder why Hera does not love you," his words were drenched in sarcasm.

"Toad-face Hera. The old hag!" Staring out towards the morning sky, she sighed. "I have the cruelest stepmother in the world. My life is simply unbearable."

"Says the non-princess with a castle protruding out of Mount Olympus."

His mockery was lost on her. *My new home is only a step-*

ping stone for me, and it has already paid off its worth. A wry smile covered her face. "You laugh now, but imagine my luck when I had a special visitor last night who mistook my home for the royal palace."

"Who would be so stupid?"

"Ares!"

"Of course." He snapped his fingers. "I would have guessed the answer had I more time. Anyway, why would that be your luck?"

She became excited, thinking back to the previous night. Ares standing before her, armed and ready for a fight. "It is my luck because he had just come straight from the battlefield when I saw him. Blood still pumping through his veins, his body ready for another conquest."

The gods! Yes, he always liked being first to hear new information, but *this* new information greatly troubled him. "Aphrodite, what did you do?"

"I did what I always do." She rolled her tongue subconsciously over her pink upper lip. "I seduced him."

The professional gossiper was too shocked to respond. He felt as though his heart exploded in his chest.

Aphrodite was, of course, oblivious to the pain she inflicted on him. "Tell me, Hermes. How does one become a queen?"

"...Marry a king."

"And how does one become a princess?"

"Marry a—no..."

She grabbed his hands before he had the chance to protest. "You must promise to keep my secret."

"Of course I will." *I see where she is going with this, but she is in way over her head.* "But you will never get Prince Ares to marry you. He is *the* most sought-after bachelor by goddesses and nymphs alike..."

"As if anyone compares to me..."

"The fact that Ares has yet to produce a litter of bastards proves he is at the very least making sure his conquests *swallow*. Which means you cannot marry him or trick him into marriage—but pushing all of that to the side, Ares is *not* marriage-minded. His heart belongs to the charred remains of war."

A challenge? Her eyes sparkled in delight. "Ares thinks a life of war is what he wants because he has never known my love." *And still, he does not know my love as we both fell asleep until the early morn.* "I did not get a chance to complete my seduction. But I will."

Hermes took a slow breath, not caring that he did not hide his relief. He realized Aphrodite was so overcome by her plotting that she did not notice his reaction.

"By mere...*chance*," she winked, "Ares left his helmet and breastplate at my home. Surely he will have to return to retrieve his armor and I will be better prepared to lure him into my—"

"Vagina?"

Aphrodite winced her beautiful face. "Can we not leave some things to the imagination?"

One night with Aphrodite would be a gift, followed by a curse if the night could never be repeated. "There is no doubt Ares has a stable of Nymphs and Goddesses to warm his bed at night. The competition for his love is fierce."

"As if anyone can compare to me. Please believe I will do whatever it takes to secure Ares' heart."

"And for what? Royal status? If your plan works—you marry Ares and become princess. We will then have Princess Aphrodite and Princess Hebe. But Hebe will always outrank you by right of birth."

"Silly, Hermes." *Why must everyone think so small when we know how big the universe is?* "Marriage to Ares is only the first step. The end goal is to become queen."

"You cannot become queen. Hera is the Queen of the Gods, and she married Zeus, thus solidifying his Kingship."

"Yes. For now."

Hermes quickly glanced around the garden, making sure they were truly alone. His eyes quickly shot up above. *Thank the gods that even though Helios can see us from the sky, he cannot hear us.* With a hushed voice, he warned, "Aphrodite. The words you are speaking now are treasonous."

His concern for her, radiated from within him, and so, she relented. "Alright, fine. I will stop speaking. But one day, one day soon, you *will* greet me as Aphrodite, Queen of the Gods." She was over the moon with herself, almost forgetting she spilled her secret to the god who was as unscrupulous as he was handsome.

What have I done! Even though she was in no position to make any demands of him, she could not resist. "Do not tell anyone of my end goal."

"Of your *treason*?" He raised a mischievous brow. "Why,

that is a crime against the High Gods *and* the Royal Family. I would not want to be charged as an accomplice. Therefore my lips are *not* sealed."

She glared at him sharply.

With a shrug, he added, "You will just have to seal my lips for me."

Oh, Hermes! Giggling, she inched closer and placed a hand underneath his clean-shaven chin. Closing her eyes, she gave him a sweet, playful kiss on the lips.

His godly urges stirred up, ready to flow out of him. Hermes opened his eyes to witness love sitting before him in the body of a vivacious goddess.

Oh, the irony! It is a shame the very kiss she gave me to seal her secrets has only made me more determined to spill all I know, so I can have her for myself.

15

BATTLE OF WITS
ARES & ATHENA

Ares droned on to deaf ears.

"...defeated the army. And when they chanted victory, I commanded fire to rain down over them, destroying..."

Athena did not listen to anything Ares had to say. Even though she invited herself to join him on his usual outing, she was far more intrigued with something else.

The goddess followed a step behind the soldier, her grayish-blue eyes observing every detail of his gold-plated armor. His yellow shield resembled a halo strapped to his back, and she examined every weapon hanging off his leather belt. The goddess yearned to experience the feeling of leather intermingling with precious metal against her tender skin. As he gleefully rambled about the carnage of war, Athena pondered the weight his weapons bore and how they responded to movement versus stillness. In silence, she admired the long red cape he wore, fixed with the Royal Seal, and how it swung at an angle off his shoulder, revealing his bulging chest.

The Warrior God finally stopped speaking mid-sentence after not hearing any objections from her for some time, which was unheard of. He caught her staring at him, exploring every inch of his muscled body with intense focus.

Along with my helmet, I left my breastplate at Aphrodite's home, so there is much more of me for Athena to feast on. Ares mimicked her by letting his glance dip slowly down the emerald dress, which loosely draped over her. Visualizing her naked did not take much effort since her bare breasts were already etched in his mind's eye.

She has round perky tits, a slight curve of the hips, and a trimmed red patch to match her curly locks. He lowered his voice, his words so deep she could barely hear them. "Is there something I have that you want?"

Huh? Athena's furrowed brows soon relaxed once she realized what he was implying. She rolled her eyes. Ares was many things, but subtle was not one of them. "You have nothing I want." Choosing instead to ignore his innuendoes, she added, "Your armor. Is it easy to maneuver in?"

He matched her step as they continued. "It is relatively heavy, but I am used to the weight. It is like a glove on a hand. I do not even notice it is there."

"The design is so intricate. It is obviously very well made."

"When you find a good craftsman, you keep him." His thoughts wandered onto something else. It was unusual for Athena to ask him for anything. She made no secret of thinking him to be a waste of intellect, yet there she was, demanding something that only he could provide. *The tables have indeed turned.*

"I must admit I was surprised when you asked me to teach you my ways of war. It is good of you to put away your huge ego and admit you could learn a lot from me. After all, I am the firstborn of King Zeus."

"True, you are the firstborn. However, I was born *older*."

"This I know." Every time he looked at Athena, he would remember the day she was born. "Was it not I who brought you into this world?" Although he faced her, his eyes seemed to travel elsewhere, to another place and time of his memory. "You arrived straight from the skull of Zeus, naked and unashamed." He raised his thick brows, showing a hint of amusement. "You were the first fully nude goddess I had ever seen."

"Is that why you wasted no time tending to me instead of our wounded King, whose head you cut open with an axe?"

Ares brushed away her question with a wave of his hand. "He survived, did he not?"

Athena's birth had been nothing short of a spectacle, and from that moment onward, along with Hermes, Athena was a constant presence at the side of Zeus.

"I would notice you around the palace, though you have been absent lately." The little mystery distracted his thoughts from battle plans and armor. "Where have you been when not in the mind of Zeus? You are his wisdom, yet you have not been around him."

He is one to speak. "And how would you know? You are rarely at his side."

"I hear things. That is how I know."

Against her better judgment, she decided to divulge the mystery of her whereabouts. "I have been reading and learning about the tales that happened before I came to be. Before we all were here."

Her words were like the babbling of a baby to his ears. "And what use is learning such inconsequential matters?"

"The past is surely doomed to repeat itself. It is better to learn what happened before us to avoid repeating the same mistakes in the future."

"Such nonsense you speak." He unleashed his long sword and pointed straight ahead as if it were his index finger. "The path ahead is clear and will be whatever it is."

She paused a moment, reflecting on his choice of words. After all, it was an interesting theory. "Based on what?"

"Huh?"

"To what, are you basing your opinion on?"

Her question seemed simple enough, but he stumbled, trying to come up with a reasonable answer. "Whatever I think."

This dumb response is my reward for trying to have a thoughtful discussion with a fool. "Please remember always to wear your helmet in battle. You must not lose what precious few smarts you have left." She picked up her pace. "It is a wonder you can walk and speak at the same time."

Now he remembered why Athena was his least favorite god to be around—next to Hermes. "Please go ahead of me. At least that way, I have an incentive to continue walking behind you."

Oh! She covered her ample buttocks with her hands to hinder the view he craved. *I am not like the nymphs he uses for his pleasure!*

Spinning around to lecture him further, she continued to walk backward. "If my intelligence is too much for you to handle, I shall surely…"

"Stop!" Not having much time to react, he thrust both hands in front of him.

Athena froze as if she were a statue.

"We are here." He gently touched her elbow and spun her around.

She caught her breath at the sight before her. She was standing at the edge of a cliff. Another step, and she would have fallen to the rocky ground below.

"You said you wanted to observe me at my essence."

At the bottom of the cliff, for miles and miles, laid the scorched remnants of war.

"And here it is. The aftermath of my last battle." Pointing to a clearing on the field, he added, "We will land right there."

Together, they disappeared from the top of the ledge and reappeared at the landing. Without a word spoken, they both knew to make themselves invisible as a scattering of men made their way through the dead. It was a rule imposed by the High Gods:

Mankind must not see the Low Gods,
Lest he fall on his knees and worship them.

Athena pinched her nose as the stench of the dead traveled around them with the wind—sounds of crying as loved ones cradled the dead bodies scattered throughout the valley. The sight was one of devastation she had not witnessed before.

Her mouth opened and closed several times as she searched for the proper words to convey her emotions. "And what was the purpose of all this destruction?"

Ares surveyed the landscape in awe. "Purpose?"

"Yes, purpose." The corpse at her feet died with his eyes open—his face twisted at a moment of excoriating pain. "What was the reason?"

"Reason?" Lowering to the ground, he scooped a pile of ashes and let it slip through his fingers as he stood up. "There need not be a reason."

"Are you mad or just stupid? Sometimes I cannot decide."

"You know not of what you speak. The only *reason* you sympathize with mankind is because you only *learn* about them through worn-out pages instead of through real-life interactions. You sit and read and gain your knowledge. But if knowledge is not practiced and tested, what good is it?" Ares dusted his hands together as the remaining debris scattered in the wind. "These men are my playthings of which I can do what I want...as long as I adhere to the High Gods."

"The High Gods," she repeated scornfully.

Athena made herself visible so she could touch the dead man and feel his cold skin against her warm flesh.

Ares followed suit, noting she seemed entirely out of her element as she toured the area. Her steps were quick and disjointed, not wanting to dirty her sandals in the mud. She sometimes pinched her nose as the smell was too much to bear. Her eyes were squinted, and her face contorted because of the mangled body parts she accidentally stepped on. He did his best to suppress a chuckle.

"Athena, just admit it. Your curiosity got the better of you, so you had to see what I was doing on the earth. And now that you know, it is clear that *you* belong at the right-hand side of Zeus. I belong here, surrounded by destruction, for the glory of the High Gods."

"Still a fool, I see." She shook her head hopelessly. "Do you not want more for yourself than to be a foil for the gods to bless men?"

The war god stared blankly, not knowing what to make of her assessment of his role for the High Council.

How can I spell it out for the moron? "Your *purpose* is only a means to an end for the High Gods."

If she thought she was manipulating him into questioning the High Gods' Decrees, she was sadly mistaken. Ares cared nothing of the politics in the council.

His voice grew loud. "I need no purpose to incite violence. A rush of excitement runs through me, something that cannot be replicated in your dusty old books." Turning away from her, he mumbled, though loud enough for her to hear, "You full-born gods."

She clenched her fist, knowing Ares was purposely trying to upset her by mentioning the state of her birth. "And what about us?"

"Always so calculating...something is missing."

How dare he? "Just because I was not born a babe does not mean—"

Suddenly, balls of fire cascaded from the heavens, launched from a distant source of men not killed in the previous battle. Athena found herself taken aback, unable to react swiftly enough.

In the nick of time, Ares swooped her into one arm, unceremoniously leading her to safety while blocking the raining inferno with his sturdy shield.

Her heart pounded as flaming embers fell around them like deadly rain. Ares' powerful biceps enveloped her, offering refuge from the impending peril. As she cautiously reopened her eyes, she found herself gazing into his intense, smoldering pupils, and she realized how tightly she held onto his waist. An electrifying sensation coursed through her entire body, faintly reminding her of the night before with Apollo.

Their heavy breathing crescendo until it was louder than the ensuing chaos. With each breath she took, her breasts grazed against his bare chest, and the heat from the fire circled them like an inferno.

Ares spoke hauntingly, "Do you feel that? The pounding of your heart. The bead of sweat building on your forehead. The excitement of not knowing what will come next. No time to think, only time to act. You can experience all of this here on this battlefield. Or...you can experience this same *sensation* somewhere else."

He held her firmly in his arms, allowing her little room to escape. "Again, I ask, are you still sure I have *nothing* you want?"

The balls of fire had long ceased, and the flames lowered instantly once the War God took control of the element.

Her mind started spinning. She was in Ares' clutches for a few seconds too long. No longer in danger, she broke away from his grasp and whispered, "I have learned all I need to know."

A slow smile appeared as he watched her storm away. "You are welcome!"

16

DO YOU KNOW WHO I AM?!
HERMES & HALLIRHOTHIOS

PERCHED ATOP A COMMANDING HILL, HERMES STRATEGICALLY positioned himself to overlook the various paths leading to the King's Palace. He observed the parade of horses and banners representing prominent families across distant lands. If one did not know any better, it would be easy to misconstrue the intimidating convoys for a renegade army. However, Hermes knew better, having personally been entrusted by Zeus to deliver all invitations for Princess Hebe's upcoming ceremony.

Becoming the unofficial messenger of Zeus was a duty that Hermes secretly vied for. Before Hermes took up the mantle, the King would entrust his letters to a select few depending on who was available. When Hermes noticed the Royal Delivery Method lacked efficiency, he made it a point always to be available and he used his vast speed to deliver letters quickly. And in time, Zeus had no choice but to rely solely on his youngest son. Once the quick-footed god had acquired the great responsibility, he wisely used the opportunity as a way for him to form and maintain relationships with the elite of all the lands.

Well, what do we have here...

An enclave of dark horses from the East caught his immediate attention. Without another thought, he zipped down the hill and floated over to the god, riding the lone sapphire-coated horse in a sea of midnight black.

The rider wore a robe of rich fabric mixed with deep shades of emerald and gold, decorated with a broach depicting a shimmery octopus pinned to his chest.

"Hallirhothios," Hermes greeted as he landed on the dirt road, forcing the beautifully blue creature with a burgundy mane to halt.

The young god, roughly the same age as Hermes, examined him with sharp green eyes before tossing his head of orange curls in the air. He strained every muscle in his face as if it pained him to speak. "And who are you again?" He strained every muscle in his face as if it pained him to speak.

As if we have not met countless times before. I see his newfound godhood has made his big head all the more bigger. He blew a breath of air to brush the bangs away from his bright face. "I am Hermes. The son of the King."

Hallirhothios snapped then wagged his pointed finger. "Oh, right, Hermes. The glorified servant of the King." His soft, dark curls blew lightly with the wind as his voice grew louder. "You are one of Zeus' brood of bastards."

Hermes leaned in closer with a wink. "Takes one to know one."

Faint chuckles rumbled between the lesser gods and militants on the surrounding horses. However, Hallirhothios went on as if he did not hear their laughter. "Yes, like you, I am also a bastard. But I was not born amidst a brood."

Enough with the back and forth. "Son of Poseidon—"

"The *one* and *only*," he said with the dip of his head.

"The God of the Sea was invited to the soiree, but his bastard son did not get an invitation."

"I come with my father."

Hermes looked around in vain. "Did you lose him at sea?"

"Poseidon is ahead of me," he said, gesturing toward the mountains. "He wanted to see Princess Hebe before her ceremony."

Hermes nodded profusely. "Which is his right as a High God." Locking eyes with the other bastard, he added, "A right that *you* do not have."

"A right that neither of us have." Hallirhothios bent down from his high horse to meet Hermes beneath him. "And here is where *my* father looked out for my best interest as his only son. Instead of raising me to be a servant of the gods, when Poseidon came to Olympus for High Council meetings, he made sure to bring me along so that I could spend time as Princess Hebe's playmate in our youth."

Hermes averted his eyes, not wanting Hallirhothios to see his crossed expression. Even though Hermes had spent more time in the King's dwelling compared to Posidon's son, he was never afforded the freedom to act as though the Palace were truly his home. The Queen made sure Zeus' bastards knew they would forever be visitors.

"Back then, I was far too innocent to see my father's intentions. However, today, everything is crystal clear. The more time I spent with the Princess, the more I could ingratiate myself into the Royal Family." Shifting his immaculate clothing, he mused, "Who would have thought that I, the son of a Nymph, had the potential to become a—"

"Fool?" his quip let loose another round of laughter from the surrounding mighty creatures.

Hallirhothios forced a yawn. "I expected a wittier insult from the god everyone says is so clever."

"Now, why would I, a clever god, waste my wit on a fool?" The cheeky one gave a slanted smile, egged on by the snickers throughout the crowd.

Poseidon's son waited for the noise to cease before he continued, "Hermes, we may both be bastards of High Gods, but we are *not* the same. As my father's *only* son, I am the sole heir to his Kingdom. All that he has is mine."

His servants and soldiers let out a low moan in agreement with all he had said.

"You will do well to step aside and not insult me further." He gripped the reins, and his face turned as hard as stone. "Lest I inform my father of my poor treatment in his brother's Kingdom."

For once, Hermes' mouth remained shut, not because he did not have a stinging response, but because he thought better than to antagonize the god any further. And so, he did what was asked and stepped aside.

Hallirhothios' hard face then cracked with a soft smile. "I knew you would make the right decision."

Holding up the reins, with a quick whipping motion, he directed the horse to proceed. After taking a couple of steps forward, the horse again came to a sudden stop. "And Hermes?"

The brilliantly blue creature raised his long orange tail and without further warning emptied its bowels with a big, wet...

Plop!

A pile of manure landed all over Hermes and the dirt road.

First Aphrodite and now me. He raised his foot, covered in mess, in disgust. *If The Fates are real, surely they have a sense of humor.*

Looking over his shoulder, he said smugly, "Make sure that gets cleaned up."

And for that alone, Hermes refused to hold his tongue any longer. "Hallirhothios?"

"Yes?"

After kicking off his sandals, the smile returned to his face. "Only a fool would believe his immortal father will never marry and one day have a *legitimate* son."

17

THE PRISONER PRINCE
HEPHAESTUS & HEBE

Did I make a mistake?

Grrr!

Hebe could not answer her question with her new pet nipping at her heels, and she stood in front of a rising doorway.

"Stay, Wolfie!" she commanded the cub with a pointed finger.

To her amazement, the animal decided to listen and sat on her hind legs.

"Good girl."

With a heavy heart, Hebe entered through the opening and made her way into the dreary-lit dungeons of the palace. The burden of her vow to her newfound brother pressed heavily upon her shoulders. She had pledged to restore his royal status, only to find herself imprisoning him within the confines of Mount Olympus' cruel iron bars.

When I went in search of a monster, I never thought I would find my brother. Everything I did after rescuing him was unplanned.

She braced herself before turning the last corner and making her presence known, determined not to let Hephaestus sense her uncertainty. *Ares always tells me to be brave.*

As a young goddess, she constantly strived to prove herself and match the knowledge of the more experienced gods. *I want to be who I am, not who everyone else wants me to be!* The relentless battle was wearing her down, and she longed for rest.

Without more thought, she turned the dark corner and approached her deformed brother, who sat alone in a cell with nothing but a satchel strapped around his shoulder.

The newfound Prince's heart gladdened to see her friendly expression, and he stood up as fast as he could to rush to the steel separating them.

Hephaestus no longer wore the hood of his cloak, but his long hair framed his face so that his scars remained concealed.

"I brought you some blankets just in case it gets cold and you need some comfort." She slipped the folded blanket between the bars, and he grabbed them from her. "How are you doing?"

He wrapped the brown knitted sheet around his shoulders. He was not at all cold but much appreciated the sweet gesture. "I am doing well, my Princess. It is much warmer here in this palace than in my cave. The only thing is, these bars restrict my movements."

Hebe almost laughed. *Does he believe this will be his new home?* "This is not the actual palace, but a section beneath the Mount where evil-doers await punishment. It is not your home. It is only temporary."

"Oh." Her strange response took him aback. *What could be better than this room?*

"This prison is special. It can hold even the strongest gods, so we cannot blink in and out."

His one visible eye was wide in shock. "I would never dream of escaping. I am warm and content and have your company most of all."

Oh my! He is easily pleased. "Here, I got you something to eat."

"I do not want to be a burden to you." He patted his satchel and the contents moved from within. "I have food to eat."

"The Earthly food you have is needed for men to live. But for gods, the food of the land is neither here not there." She reached into her pouch and pulled out a dark purple fruit. "What I have for you is ambrosia. The Food of the Gods. It is good for you. One bite and you will feel better than you have ever felt in your entire life."

He reached for the food and bit into it. It was juicy and sweet, filled with seeds that did not taste bitter. "Never has something so delicious touched my tongue."

How is it possible he has never enjoyed the taste of ambrosia? "I can hardly imagine what you endured alone in a forbidden land."

Hephaestus shrugged his uneven shoulders, having lived a life with nothing else to compare it to. "Not everything was horrible. I had help along the way. Food was plentiful. There was shelter and clothing at my deposal."

Her eyes scanned his robe. Although it was old, it was clothing only a Prince was entitled to wear. *Even after all this time, he wears the Royal Seal, which means someone of note did look after him.* Hebe scrunched her buttoned noes. "Then why were you banished from the palace?"

Hephaestus looked away from her onto the dirt floor for the first time since she entered. "I...I do not know."

My poor brother. "Never mind all that. Forgiveness is greater than any offense you may have committed. Cheer up!" Hebe wanted nothing more than to have a smile return to his face. "Soon, everything will be good. I promise." She placed her hands on the bars, and he covered his hand over hers.

The touch of her soft skin sent a pleasant shiver down his crooked spine. "I will never be able to repay your kindness."

"You do not have to. We are family." His smile was not beautiful, yet it radiated an outpouring of love. "Once Father is present at my ceremony, I will finally let the Royal Hall know I brought you here."

He froze, not quite registering what she had just said. "You did not seek me out on their orders?"

"No, I found you all by myself." She beamed proudly with her chest puffed out.

By the Gods! Hephaestus felt the metal bars were bending, twisting around him, and the approaching darkness would consume whatever was left. Still covering her hands, he pleaded, "Hebe, you must let me out."

"What? Why?"

He squeezed her hand tighter. "Open these gates!"

"I cannot—"

"Did you bring me to my death?"

She struggled to free herself, but he would not let her go.

"Let me out!" he roared in a panic.

"Let go of me, or I will scream so loud my father's bolt will reach you before he does," she warned.

The blurred image of the angry King was enough for Hephaestus to snatch his hands away. His jagged nails sliced her skin, and she stumbled backward as golden ichor trickled from her wounded flesh.

"Hebe, you must let me out!" He panicked as she backed up toward the exit with a horrid expression.

Slowly, she shook her head, too stunned to speak.

He shook the bars, trying in vain to break free. "Hebe! Hebe!"

The louder his voice, the more her fear intensified. At that moment, he seemed to transform into the nightmarish creature of her youth.

The Cursed Monster! Without uttering another thought, she fled from the looming creature through the tunnels, evading any possibility of becoming his prey.

Once outside the trappings of the dungeon, she collapsed

onto the ground in despair. Wolfie nestled beside her, licking her open wound, and the Princess hugged her with all her might.

I made a huge mistake!

18

INQUIRING MINDS
HERMES & ATHENA

"All men are destined for Hades."

Athena positioned herself within the heart of a small gathering of mortals, their senses oblivious to her divine presence. The chaos around them unfolded as panicked individuals scurried in all directions, attempting in vain to rescue others from a blazing structure.

Although it lay within her power to douse the flames and ensure the survival of those who remained, Athena maintained her passive stance as the unfolding tragedy played out before her eyes. Among the many mandates issued by the High Gods to the Low Gods, one rule stood prominent:

Never show favor towards mankind.

If I help these men, without question, I will have a temple dedicated in my honor. Priests will do rituals around my name and offer sacrifices for my blessings. In doing so, I would be taking worship away from the High Gods, and they alone are to be worshipped by men.

She shook her head at the ridiculousness of all involved.

Ares can get away with warring because his antics cause mortals to curse him rather than worship him. The High Gods allow his destruction so that, from time to time, they can appear as if they are the bearer of the good fortune of men.

Hermes strolled up to Athena, also concealed from mortal sight, and observed her deep in thought. He noted that strategizing was common for her. She perpetually seemed to be pondering one thing or another. "What are you doing all the way out here?"

She answered without acknowledging him. "I was personally escorted by Ares to a village or two away when I saw the flames over here."

Ares? They never speak to one another.

Her gaze locked in on the burning structure. "This is horrible. Dionysus' wine, mixed with Prometheus' fire, is destroying everything."

Hermes took in the thick smoke that covered the surrounding area. The cries of men, once alarming, had become little more than background noise to him over the decades.

The longer he analyzed Athena, the more evident it became that the men were not her concern but the blazing building they were fleeing.

"I watched mankind get the gift of fire and build many great buildings. This pile of rubble was once their library. The pinnacle of all they constructed. They had thousands of ancient books, passing knowledge to anyone traveling to learn." The glow of the blaze added an orange hue to her subtle skin. "And in an instant, it is all gone. The loss of knowledge is the beginning of the end for them."

Hermes soaked in her every word. "Knowledge." *I see now why she is so concerned. We also have a library on Olympus, though Athena is the only god I notice who makes good use of it.* "Is that why you spend your time cooped up in a room, reading our great books of yesteryear?"

"Yes." Finally, she turned her full attention to him. "Our library is filled with so many great revelations begging to be discovered."

"We have lived for so long and *seen* so many great discoveries. Why do we need to read about what was before us?"

She suppressed a grin though her face was beaming with pride. *Hermes' instinct to question everything sets him far ahead of Ares. One seeks out knowledge, while the other seeks to destroy it.* "It is good to read about what happened in the past to learn what may happen in the future."

"So the future can be predicted...can be known?" *That seems a little farfetched.* "How so?"

"By seeing patterns. By noticing repetitions."

"Have you noticed any patterns?"

"Good question." The energy from the flames blew heat in their direction, warming the surrounding area. "Something stuck out as I read the stories about how history unfolded so long ago. Zeus was born of Cronus, our grandfather. After our father came of age, he defeated Cronus and eventually won his crown."

That is nothing new. "Yes, us Low Gods were born after the Titanomachy. However, the greats wrote songs of the battles, and we recite the vivid poems as if we were there. It is known that Zeus rebelled against his barbaric father."

She pointed an index finger in the air. "Ah, but did you know Cronus was born of Uranus, our great-grandfather? Uranus was also defeated for his crown by *his* son...Cronus."

"I did not know of this." *One learns something new every day.* "We seem to have a history of sons taking the crowns of their fathers."

"So much can be learned by reading about what has happened in the past." *Which is why the destruction of the library of men is so horrid.* "Their memories are being burned before our eyes. We still have our memories, our libraries, but if no one reads our books, they might as well be consumed by fire."

And such was the reason why Hermes respected Athena. *Her wisdom knows no bounds.* "Do you think another uprising is in our destiny?"

"History shows that it is a possibility. More so, it is inevitable."

"Then why has it not yet happened?"

"That is an excellent question." *Hermes is as bright as he is clever. He can figure it out.* "You tell me why."

He thought back to the aftermath of the last battle of the Great War. The High Gods defeated the Titans, yet all was not over. "After that final battle, the gods threw Lots. The brothers

Zeus, Hades, and Poseidon divided the world into three parts."

"A fair way to give powers over to the winners."

Fair. Hermes felt a pang at her choice of words but did his best to overlook it. Again, he wondered why another rebellion had yet to take place.

The brothers shared power, and the sisters received titles to govern...

It finally hit him.

Yes, the older gods divided the world between them, but we Low Gods have nothing to show for our contributions to keeping the peace. Cautiously, he glanced her way. "Not *all* of us gods share in the power of the winners. At least, not us bastards."

Athena furrowed her brows and cleared her throat respectively.

"Present company excluded, obviously."

"Obviously." *I may be many things, but a bastard is not among the many.* "As you were saying, we do not hold any power in governance, which means..."

"Given time, a rebellion *will* happen. Not from the High Gods, but from the rest...*us?*"

"Peace is only maintained when the powers that be are satisfied with their lot in life. Let us just hope the sons and daughters of Zeus remain satisfied."

"And if we are not?"

Instead of answering, Athena remained silent, leaving him to ponder the thought alone.

Never would I presume the Low Gods would go to war for increased power. But my rage after my encounter with Hallirhoth-

ios...Oh, how I would have given anything to sit on my father's throne and have that smug bastard bow to me. And to think, there is a possibility that Hallirhothios could one day become my prince!

Hermes shook the thought from his mind, lest it consume him into a whirlwind of fire that would devour even the flames before him.

Athena had an unmatched quality about her that stirred more in him than he could ever stir on his own. *If Apollo has his muses for bursts of inspiration, then Athena would be my muse for all eternity.*

Zeus spread his seed enough to have a multitude of younglings whom he loved beyond measure. However, the Low God's ties to each other were fractured at best. Ares and Hebe, having Zeus and Hera as parents, had a profound and unbreakable connection. The same could be said for the twins Artemis and Apollo, sharing Zeus and Leto.

Unfortunately, Athena and Hermes did not have the same mother, so they were deprived of a solid sibling attachment like the others. Since Zeus held both so dear to him, his love allowed them to forge a path toward a semblance of trust resembling a brother and sisterly bond.

Athena and I try our best to carve a spot within a family structure that does not exist. As such, we have an unspoken pact to mimic sibling behavior even though we fail at every aspect. Hermes laughed to himself. *And with each failure, we pick up the pieces and try, try again.*

Athena refused to witness any more of the destruction and she lifted her dress and turned away to take her steps over the mud.

Feeling the urge to act *like* an annoying little brother, Hermes decided to tease her. "If the Low Gods are destined for a rebelling if not content, maybe the addition to Mount Olympus will satisfy Aphrodite for another millennium." His choice of words had his desired reaction as Athena halted in her tracks.

"What are you talking about?"

"You are telling me you have not seen that monstrosity?" He gave a wry smile. "Count yourself lucky!"

"Hermes, unlike you, I cannot keep up with all the latest gossip." Continuing on her journey, she left him behind. "I am actually using *my* free time wisely."

"Your free time?" He could no longer resist saying what he really wanted to talk to her about. "And how did *you* spend your free time last night?"

She stopped but did not turn around. "To what are you referring?"

"I am referring...to your night with Apollo." He caught up to her and stood in front of her so she could not leave again so easily.

"How do you know about that?"

"I helped plan it with him." Sticking his chest out proudly, he asked, "Who do you think supplied the red nectar?"

"I should have known *you* would be involved."

"Did the wine at least set the mood?"

"I will not discuss my relationships with you."

"Ah-ha! So you and Apollo *are* in a relationship." He loved the fact that his assumptions were driving her mad. Something about her fiery hair and hot-gold cheeks did it for him. "Do not worry. Your secret is safe with me."

She clasped her hand over his big mouth, though she really wanted to pull out his always moving tongue. "I am wise enough to know my secrets will *never* be safe with you." Maneuvering around him, she stomped away in a huff. "And just when we were having such a pleasant conversation, you have to go and ruin it!"

Hermes could not stop the laughter from coming forth. He yelled after her, "I guess I will just have to get the rundown from Apollo!"

19

PHILADELPHIA
ARES & HEBE

Woe to the King who drinks your poison...You brought me here to my death.

Hebe shook her head, forcing Apollo's bad omen and Hephaestus' pleas out of her mind . She rubbed the scar on her hand, hoping to find a way to hide the blemish before the ceremony. Although she was able to take away pain with a touch, it was Apollo who possessed the power to heal fresh wounds.

There is no way I can tell Apollo what happened to me. He will tell my father without question that Hephaestus did me harm.

All she could do was hug the many stuffed dolls that covered half of her bed for comfort and hope that within time, healing would come naturally before her ceremony.

It was still early in the afternoon, with the mighty sun working its way across the bright sky.

The Prince had finally made it to the new dwelling of his

sister located on the other side of the mountain, away from the quarters of the King and Queen. After a *very* brief interaction with her bodyguard, he skipped up her winding staircase and paced down the halls leading to her bedroom.

Quietly, Ares pushed opened Hebe's door and entered her chambers. He beheld the Princess, seated upon her bed, lost in deep contemplation. A slow breath of air escaped his lips. Seeing her filled him with an overwhelming sense of joy and an even greater sense of relief.

Following each of his journeys around the earth, when he returned home, he never failed to marvel at the subtle changes in Hebe's growing figure. Long ago, all it took was one hand to effortlessly toss her playfully into the air. Those days were long gone. Not the tossing in the air, but now using two hands instead of one.

Watching her from across the room, he could tell she was a little taller than before, and her form was increasingly shaped with gentle curves. Yet she retained an undeniable innocence that had remained since he first held her in a tiny blanket and never wanted to let her go.

Softly as not to make a sound, he peeled off his satchel and placed it on the floor and leaned his sheath and sword against the wall. Then, Ares stood proudly at military attention. "Little sister."

His voice did nothing to lighten her mood. She pouted and cross her arms, turning her head to the wall. "I am no longer little."

"Really? Then I shall find another little sister to give my gift to."

She looked back to see her older brother at the door. Her aggravation was short-lived once she noticed the satchel by his sandals. "Brother!" Hebe jumped up and leaped into Ares' waiting arms.

The god easily hoisted her as she wrapped her arms around his neck and her legs around his waist. He squeezed her tight and he planted multiple kisses along her cheeks. "Welcome to godhood!"

"It is about time, is it not?" She pulled out of their hug long enough to make sure he was in one piece. "I am so glad you are home safe."

"Likewise." His words were an understatement. Feeling her steady heartbeat against his chest and seeing her unharmed after a lone trek into the lands, lifted an unprecedented weight off his shoulders.

He set her down and stood with his hands on his hips, scanning every inch of the room. "I see your new furniture has arrived. Would you like me to check under your bed for monsters."

Although his teasing remark came with a wink, Hebe pressed her lips firmly together. *Of course my big brother has to remind me of how much of a scaredy-cat I was growing up.* "There are no such things as monsters." She puffed hard enough to disturb her bangs.

Wait a minute... "How did you get past Xander?"

"Xander?" *Was he the bug masquerading as a guard that I crushed on my way inside?* "Has anyone on land, sea, or sky ever prevented me from seeing you?"

Hebe giggled, knowing he asked a question that needed

no answer. And as if to belabor the point, Wolfie bolted out from another room, headed toward them, her razor sharp fangs growing with each step.

Before Hebe could speak, Ares swiftly set her down behind him and crouched down enough to have the ferrel beast leap into his arms.

The princess wanted to scream but instead covered her eyes knowing that when she again opened them, her precious, albeit rebellious, pet would be ripped to pieces on the floor.

To her surprise, she heard lapping, instead of yelping. *Huh?* Slowly, the young one uncovered her eyes to see her brother cradling the pup against his chest as her tail wagged excitedly. *I cannot believe it!* Her eyes were as big as two full moons. "Wolfie has growled at every god she has seen get too close to me except you."

Standing back up, he turned to her while the creature licked his delectable neck. "Her instincts tell her I mean you no harm. She knows I am your brother."

Hebe giggled. "Wolfie tore a chunk out of Apollo earlier."

"Good work!" Holding the pup up in the air, Ares gently shook her, rubbing their noses together. "Next, you can attack Hermes." He placed her back on the ground and shooed her into another room before locking her away.

They ignored her clawing at the door trying to get let back in.

"If Wolfie knows my brother means me no harm, why did she attack Apollo?"

His face stiffened when he turned back to Hebe. "Apollo is

not your brother. Neither is Hermes the weasel. None of Zeus' bastards are our siblings."

She nodded firmly, having heard the same rhetoric her entire life. As a royal, all the other gods were beneath her and as a sibling, she only had her brother, Ares.

But not anymore. Her heart quickened with the new realization that she now had *two* brothers.

"Be sure to put Wolfie outside before Zeus finds her."

She sighed heavily in response.

Ares moved passed her and picked up his satchel and placed it on her bed. "Come and see what I brought back for you from the Land of Men."

Anticipation bubbled up within her as it did every time he returned with a gift from far away lands. It was a cherished ritual that Ares had initiated since she had taken her first steps.

Reaching into his bag, he pulled out a simple chain tied around a short blade with a curve at its helm. Beaming pridefully, he placed the present in her opened palms.

"It is wonderful." Hebe inspected the sharp metal between her fingers before bringing it close to her dark brown eyes. "What is it?"

He chuckled. "Men call it a gut hook. They use it to pull out the intestines of animals," as he spoke, he jabbed forward, twisted his arm and sliced across the empty space, "sometimes other men."

This looks nothing like Apollo's arrows. "Why can men not bring forth lightning like father or call down fire like you?"

She rubbed her finger over the pointed tip in dismay. "They are so primitive."

"Yes, they are." Ares noticed something as she twirled the object between her fingers, which caused a slow burn in the pit of his stomach. "What are those jagged scratches on your hands?"

Great gods! "Nothing." Turning her back toward him, she placed the arrowhead on her dresser as she desperately searched for an excuse. "I came back from my first journey of the lands alone. You know how clumsy I can be. I must have tripped here and there."

He stepped behind her, closing the distance she so desperately wanted. Ares knew what defensive wounds were, and her injuries did not come from a slip and fall over the terrain, as she implied. *Four long claw marks on each hand only means one thing.* "Where did you get those scrapes?"

Hebe could feel the warmth of his breath against her ear. He already towered over her but he made it a point to lean closer to invade the tiny personal space she had left. Intimidation tactics were second nature to him, and what better way than to use them to force his younger sister into submission—for her own good, of course.

"Answer me, Hebe."

"I do not remember." Facing him, she clasped her hands behind her back. "Anyway, they shall soon disappear."

Which means her wounds are recent. Hebe is lying to me. But why? To play the part of an uncaring brother, he relaxed his tense shoulders. *I will let it go for now until she is again at ease.* "I did not see you last night as I came home from battle. You were not around to draw my bath."

As he stood before her bare chest without his breastplate, there was no denying that someone else had cleansed his body from the grime and filth of warfare. *But who?* "Looks like you survived without me."

"Barely." He squeezed her shoulder taking care not to crush her in the same manner as the hundreds of soldiers he led into battle. A soft smile, reserved only for her, appeared. "I missed seeing you."

Hebe was happy Ares had missed her Bathing Ritual—a duty she prided herself on being the best at providing. *I was much too busy with Hephaestus to fulfil my obligation to my brother. But I am glad the person who replaced me this one time could not outdo me.* She settled herself in the center of her bed, legs neatly crossed, and Ares took his place beside her.

The Princess looked over her Prince dressed in common black trousers, and a red Royal cape draped around his shoulders with a golden clasp. She whipped her pig-tails behind her shoulders and scrunched here face. "I hope you are planning to change your outfit for my celebration."

Looking down at his tanned pecs and dusty pants, he shrugged before raising his brows. "What is wrong with what I am wearing?" he teased.

"Trousers are informal attire."

"But they grant me flexibility in combat. A long tunic is much too constricting."

"I can assure you there will be no fighting at my party."

"For shame," he said with a crooked smile.

Hebe tugged on his massive arm but he did not budge. "Will you dress nicely for my ceremony to please me?"

"You are asking a lot of me."

Resting her head on his shoulder, she wined, "Please."

Ares exaggerated a heavy sigh. "Have you picked your gown?"

"Yes. Mother helped me."

Of course she did.

"I have an idea! We can wear matching outfits."

The Prince painfully rubbed his temple in a slow circular motion. "What color?"

"White!"

He likened her enthusiastic response to a drawn-out death march. His nails dug into his palms. *My most hated color!* Although his every limb cringed at the thought, her adorable round face and infectious giggle nudged him over the edge—as always. "I will think about it."

His answer was as close enough to a yes as she could drag out of him. Excitedly, she squealed and kissed his stubbly cheek before twisting her lips in response. "And a nice shave will also do you well."

Give an inch, she will take a mile. "Do not push your luck." *Hebe knows there is nothing I would refuse her.* "I am proud to see you have completed your first outing as a goddess. So? How was your first journey into the lands?"

"It was wonderful!"

Paying close attention to her every movement, he asked, "And where did you go?"

I know him all too well. My brother is already suspicious of me, so why hide any longer? "Remember when I was young and you would tell me the story about the monster hiding in the Unknown Territories?"

"Ah, yes." He chuckled reminiscing on how he would scare her as a babe. "And if you say his name three times, he will appear and eat you!" Unexpectedly, he grabbed around her ribcage and tickled her relentlessly.

Hebe tumbled and turned amidst her disheveled covers while Wolfie sulked in the other room as if she was missing out on all the fun. Although her laughter resonated wildly from within, Hebe could not help but harbor resentment—resentment directed at Ares for still having the power to provoke her to youthful antics.

"Ares! I am no longer a youngling." In a tizzy, she swatted him away and rose to her feet while he remained seated, allowing her to gain a height advantage over him, albeit a slight one. Having calm down some, the rush of gold soon faded from her puffy cheeks. "The story you used to tell me is not a tale. It is real."

"Of course, it is real." He wagged his finger as though she was an unruly toddler. "And the monster loves little ones who stray too far from home."

"I said I am not a youngling! As of today, I am a goddess." She stepped closer to him and added, "I am your equal."

"My equal?" he roared. Ares accepted her challenge as his nostrils flared, and a familiar fire ignited within him. It was akin to the fiery emotions that would engulf him when faced with an armored foe on the battlefield. "Do you know what it means to be *my* equal?"

Startled by the intensity of his response, she retreated. Hebe was well aware that she stood no chance against the might of her brother, so why pretend otherwise? "No," she sighed.

Although he would never admit it. A part of him was proud she had the audacity—the strength to stand up to him...even if it were only for mere seconds.

"Ares, I *know* about Hephaestus."

His eyes widened in complete shock. *That name had not been spoken aloud in ages.*

"He is a prince. He is our brother, and he should be here with us."

"Hebe." The warmonger was cautious about the next question. "What did you do?"

She tried her best to remain strong. "I found him...and I brought him home."

The match was lit, and he sprang to his feet. It took everything in him to refrain from shaking some sense into her. How else would she comprehend the gravity of the situation?

"Did you not think there was a reason Hephaestus was banished to the outer regions?" he demanded, running his fingers through his hair. "Why his name was told in tales as a curse? And yet you still went and sought him out and brought him back here? Not to mention you were in the Unknown Territories where you should *never* have been alone!"

Even though Ares was a ball of clashing emotions, he was soon able to steady himself. *But she is here safe with me now, so there is no need to lecture her further. I should not be surprised. Even as a child Hebe was sensitive and followed her heart. Still, she left alone and returned with a god raised amongst creatures. Such a naïve soul. Not even aware of the unknown danger she put herself in.*

"Where is he now?"

Her nerves started to get the best of her. The little princess fiddled with the hem of her short garment. "I did not know what to do with Hephaestus, so I hid him in our dungeon."

"You threw our *prince*, our *brother* as you so eloquently put it, in prison?"

His sarcasm stung her ears.

"I would think he was better off with the red fishes." *Given that he was raised in solitary by creatures unknown, without realizing it, she did do the right thing.* "At least you *did* put him in the proper place. Prison."

"I did not have enough time to think."

"No, that is the *one* thing you did right. Still, our father will have your head for this. Figuratively speaking."

Father? She could feel the tears begin to well in her eyes. *How will I explain to the king that I was in a danger zone?* She wrung her hands together, unsure of how to escape the situation she created. "I need your help, older brother." Her wide eyes became even wider. "Tell me, what shall I do next?"

So now, I am her older brother. "You are a goddess, my equal," he said mockingly. "Help is only for youngling." Crossing his arms, he again asked, "I will ask you one more time. Hebe, where did you get those marks on your hands?"

Once more, Hebe looked at her hands and a small smile appeared. She held her wrists up to show off her perfectly healed godly skin. Her stance was defiant, and her tone haughty, "What marks?"

Slowly, he nodded his head. *If this is the game she wants to play, she can play it alone.* "Since you insist on lying to me, you are now on your own. Good luck, little sister. When it comes to the King, you *will* need it."

The Prince headed toward the door, leaving her right where she stood.

Alone.

20

THE FULL-BORNS
ATHENA & APHRODITE

"How did you do it?" Athena's eyes flashed with rage as she stood over Aphrodite.

The beautiful goddess was knelt before a headless statue and at any other time, Athena would have respected such a sacred act, however her temper would not allow her to extend any form of grace.

They found themselves within the confines of an ancient temple, a relic dating back to the second generation of men. Although the structure had aged and weathered, it still stood resilient. Nature had claimed it as its own, with creeping vines and overgrown shrubs masking the entrance. Abandoned for centuries, the shrine had lost its connection to the worshippers of old.

It is about time the wisest one of all showed up. Aphrodite's head was lowered, and her hands were folded together, suppressing a triumphant grin. "Be mindful to pay your respects to the High Gods."

In a huff, Athena knelt down with Aphrodite before the headless statue with her hands raised and hurried a prayer. "May the High Gods have mercy on us all." And with that, she stood back up.

Aphrodite opened her eyes. "Lovely to see you too, Athena."

"Quit all the nonsense." Athena placed her hands on her hips, not liking Aphrodite's smug tone of voice. "Our father saw it fit to hide your existence and only recently revealed you to us all. In such a short amount of time, how did you get our father to allow you to build on Mount Olympus?"

Aphrodite effortlessly shrugged her shoulders. "I simply asked him." She spoke as if the answer to the question was so easy to understand. "There is much to be gained by just putting your wishes out into the ether. A closed mouth does not get fed."

Interesting choice of words. Athena was willing to admit when something was right. "This saying is true."

The beauty twirled a finger around a lock of hair. "You need not be angry. So I may have our father's heart, you still have his...what is it you have again?"

She gritted her teeth. "I have our father's ear."

"Ah yes, his ear." Feigning cluelessness, she asked, "And what does that get you exactly?"

Her gray-blue eyes cooled as she thought but a moment before answering, "Everything."

"Except for a palace on the Mount." *For someone so wise, she has a lot to learn.* "You need to dream bigger, Athena."

"And what do you know of my dreams?"

"I know they are the same as mine."

"How so?"

Athena pretends she does not notice how alike we truly are. "All the other gods are led by their passions, desires, and emotions. Not us. We can put a certain aspect of ourselves on hold to gain what matters most."

"And what is that?"

"The wise one asks me?" She gave a suggestive smile. "You already know the answer."

As Aphrodite rose to her feet, she executed a respectful curtsy toward the headless statue and exited the ancient temple, leaving Athena deep in thought.

The answer to her question was poised at the tip of Athena's tongue.

"Power."

21

THE WING(LESS) MAN
APOLLO & HERMES

Hermes swiftly sped through the open land, a blur of motion in the fading daylight. After his prolonged absence, he was determined to reconnect with all the gods, ensuring he remained well-informed and in control of the flow of information. Surprises were not his cup of ambrosia, and his knack for staying ahead of them was a source of pride.

It was always advantageous to be the *bearer* of tidings rather than the one reliant on them. Moreover, the art of dispensing information and shaping its delivery to the uninformed held a *special* kind of power. Hermes excelled in the gossip arena, a master of his craft.

The swift-footed god slowed down once he saw Apollo sitting underneath a tree. *Oh, he looks at peace. Such a shame I have to disrupt it.* He shouted from above, "I have been searching all over for you."

"You found me." Apollo remained utterly motionless, his

gaze fixed on the work before him. "The muses are punishing me for not spending enough time with them." Taking a quick glance at Hermes, he noticed the intruder was now floating above him. "Quick, give me a word that rhymes with orange."

The clever god pondered for longer than he would have liked before shaking his head hopelessly. "That will be a problem for the ages."

Apollo pressed his lips together, wondering why he wasted time asking Hermes.

"What are you working on?"

With precision, he put ink-pen to papyrus paper and wrote a line of poetry to match the melody flowing in his mind. "I am finishing up on Hebe's Day of Understanding Theme. I am rearranging the chords to fit my alto-singing voice. My gift to her shall be a brilliantly inspiring song of awe and wonder."

"Lyrics by Apollo, music by Apollo, performed by Apollo." Hermes landed firmly on his feet, tilting his head to the side, and pinched his finger and thumb together. "A tad bit pretentious, am I right?"

He squinted, not appreciating Hermes' attempt at humor. "It is impossible for a god to be pretentious."

"And yet, somehow, you made the impossible possible." Hermes clapped wildly and let out a high-pitched whistle. "Bravo to you. Standing ovation. Encore!"

Apollo rolled his eyes, determined not to let Hermes further distract him. His concentration remained unwaveringly tethered to the sheet, absorbed in the mystical beauty of artistic creation.

Is Apollo really going to ignore me after all I did for him? Silence was never a friend to Hermes—silence was always too much to bear. "So...what happened?"

He will not leave until I tell him about my night with Athena. Sighing, the divine musician relented to Hermes' determined persistence. "Nothing happened."

"What?" *This does not make any sense.* "Everything should have gone perfectly." Not caring that Apollo preferred the pen above his companionship, Hermes crouched before him. "Did you play the lyre I made for you long ago?"

"I played."

"What of Dionysus' wine I set aside especially for you both to drink?"

"We drank."

"Did you use one finger or two?"

Wisely, Apollo decided not to dignify the question with an answer.

The birds chirping in the background were music to his ears and momentarily gave him a sense of joy until they flew away. "Athena is too much in her head. She could not let go enough to relax and be in the moment."

"That is it? You are going to give up?"

"By the Gods, no!" Realizing that Hermes had no intention of leaving him alone anytime soon, Apollo put his pen and paper down. "I will just give her some time...some space."

"No, no, no." Hermes shook his head adamantly. "I think that is the *last* thing you should do."

Despite his better judgment, he asked, "Really?"

"Yes! Give the goddess no time, no space. Be in her face every day and night."

Why should I take any suggestions from Hermes? Coming back to his gods-given senses, Apollo shook his head. "Name a goddess you have successfully wooed as proof I should take your advice."

My evidence is your twin sister, whose thirst I was able to quench earlier today. Hermes knew better than to say his thoughts aloud. "Touché. You have gotten the best of me. I do not have a goddess to show you my words are true. However, Athena does seem very conflicted."

Apollo nodded in agreement and reached for his pen. "I know what you mean. There is something Athena is after, but I just cannot put my finger on what exactly it is."

"She is a full-born." *There is no denying they are a special breed of god.* "Something is always going on with them."

"Only The Fates know."

"The Fates only know how to spin a tall tale as masterfully as they spin a golden thread."

Apollo jerked his head in Hermes' direction. "The Moirai are not ones to mock," he whispered harshly. "They choose the day of our birth, measure and plot our destiny, and determine our death."

"Gods do not die." Looking up at the clouds temporarily covering Helios, he added, "Besides, the future can be predicted, and as such, one's destiny can be undone."

The memory of the shocking vision he had at the touch of Hebe sent a chill down to his bones. His ridged fingers shivered, vibrating his pen. *If only Hermes' ramblings were true. Alas, kismet is set in stone.*

"Therein lies the difference between us. I am determined to change my lot while you prefer to wallow in it." Before Apollo could interject, Hermes spoke over him, "Case in point, while you were here sulking by your lonesome over your failed night with Athena, Ares spent the day escorting her through hills and valleys."

The pen froze in his hand as he glared pointedly at Hermes.

"I saw them leave," Hermes stretched the truth to fit his narrative, "but I do not know where they went." *And here comes jealousy to rear its ugly head.* "She came back alone."

"What are you trying to imply?"

"I do not know," he lied effortlessly. "But they were gone a very long time."

He stuck the pen over his ear. "Hermes, be careful how you gossip about our Prince and his whereabouts."

"Or what? Face Ares' wrath?"

"It is not Ares you need to be worried about." He stood up and glared at Hermes, pointing a finger an inch from the tip of his nose. "You be careful with what you are implying as far as *Athena* is concerned." He jammed his sheets of paper into his satchel and stormed off into the surrounding trees.

Hermes snorted and crossed his arms. Apollo's anger only delighted him all the more. "I hear you loud and clear!"

22

(HERMES) HAS IT
ARTEMIS & ATHENA

Let me try this again.

Artemis moved with silent grace, stalking her prey through the woods. Her footsteps were careful, ensuring no sound betrayed her presence, for startling the target would be a costly mistake. As she closed in, the clearing ahead presented the perfect opportunity for her to strike.

Taking her place among the dense undergrowth, Artemis retrieved an arrow from her quiver.

Ready...

With practiced ease, she drew back the string of her bow, narrowing one eye to aim with precision.

Aim...

Her breath slowed, her focus sharpened, and in a fluid motion, she released.

Fire!

The arrow sailed through the clearing, narrowly missing its target, and embedded itself in the sturdy trunk of a tree.

"Great Zeus!" Athena, startled by the near miss, came to an abrupt halt. Her sharp silver-blue eyes immediately locked onto the arrow lodged in the tree at her eye level, and she yanked the wooden stick from the bark. The metal tip was carved into sharp, jagged edges—enough to severely damage animals and gods alike. Suspicion arose in her gaze as she followed the trajectory back to the direction it had come from.

As Artemis stepped out from her concealed position, Athena's posture shifted into a defensive stance. She stormed over to the huntress, waving the arrow over her head. "You almost shot me!"

Tracing a finger along her bow indifferently, Artemis shrugged. "I thought you were a deer."

"Since when do deer walk on two legs?"

"You are the first, my *dear* Athena." She gave a mocking curtsey. As if on cue, laughter rang out through the forest.

Athena ignored Artemis' infamous Nymphs, who preferred to remain hidden amongst the leaves and threw the arrow on the ground. "That is *not* funny."

"Relax. If I wanted to hit you," she stepped to Athena as if to challenge her, "I would have hit you."

Yes, this is true. I should be happy Artemis did not feel like striking a god today. "Is there a reason you had this tree behind me for a target?"

Artemis beamed brightly. "I wanted your attention in the most dramatic way possible."

"Congratulations. You have it."

"Remember when I was young—a little goddess running around with the other little gods? Even back then, I could shoot an arrow better than any of them."

As a youngster, Artemis' talent was quite apparent. "You would always hit the bullseye. I have never known you to miss. Ever."

Artemis continued, "I remember the day our father said it was unbecoming of a goddess to hunt. He declared I was supposed to put down the bow and pick up anything that was not so...godlike." She smiled at Athena. "And in your wisdom, you challenged him. 'Why is it good for a god to hunt and not a goddess?' It was such a simple question, but enough for him to rethink his stance."

"And here you stand today. A force to be wrecking with." Athena could not help but be delighted. It was nice to hear that Artemis appreciated how she helped her so long ago. "The gods should be able to choose any path in life. God and *goddess* alike."

Artemis raised a fist in solidarity. "Here, here!"

The wise one surveyed the lands around them. The area was known to be settled by men rather than a suitable place for giant creatures to wander. *This forest is different from Artemis' usual stomping grounds.* "What are you doing out here anyway?"

"I was searching for you. You are incredibly easy to track."

"Why? Just to tell a story?"

A mischievous look in her eye revealed her true motive. "Rumor has it you and Apollo are in a relationship."

Rumor, huh? She clenched her fist, wishing a specific god's neck was in her grip instead of the arrow. "Since when did *Hermes* change his name to Rumor?"

"Calm down. I came all this way to say I am happy for you."

"You are?"

Why would that be so hard to believe? "My brother means everything to me. And if you make him happy, I could not be any more thrilled."

"There is nothing to be happy for." She hated to have to discuss such topics with nosey people. But it was Apollo's twin, and so Athena indulged her. "We are *not* in a relationship."

Taking a step back, she asked, "Why not?"

"It is just not the right time for me."

The lone twin put her hands on her hips, flexing her toned arms. "What, you think you are too good for Apollo?"

"Artemis, please." Already, the conversation was going to a place Athena had no intention of continuing. "This has nothing to do with you." Trying her best to avoid the impending conflict, she walked away.

"I should have known this would happen. Had I the chance to warn my brother, I would have told him to think twice before getting involved with a full-born." She knew she struck a nerve in Athena, even though Athena was working overtime to hide that fact. And so, to push her over the edge, Artemis added, "You and *Aphrodite* are the same."

Athena spun around and pointed the arrow directly at Artemis' nose. "I am *nothing* like Aphrodite."

The huntress smiled triumphantly like she had caught a deer in a trap.

It irked Athena to witness the look of satisfaction spread over Artemis' face. "And the next time you see *Rumor*, tell him I will pull out his tongue." Without uttering another word, Athena dropped the arrow, turned, and disappeared into the dense forest once more.

"Well, that went much better than I could have predicted." The lone goddess bent over to pick up her discarded arrow.

"Look out!" A chorus of feminine voices yelled, causing Artemis to quickly spin in the direction of rustling from behind.

To her dismay, she was met with two tall, well-formed figures approaching her from the thick greenery. She reached behind her and pulled another arrow from the quiver strapped to her back. Each weapon pointed at the two not too far from her.

A powerful voice rang out from one, "Are you sure you want a fight? It would be unfair since there is only one of you and two of us."

Slowly, she circled them while effortlessly spinning the rods between her nimble fingers. "Not for long."

"We mean you know harm," said the other one with his hands stretched out, showing he held no weapons.

"Prove it," she dared, pointing her arrows in their respective directions. "I am Artemis, daughter of Zeus. You are trespassing on the King of the Gods territory. Declare your reason for doing so at once!"

"We are here to represent the Gigantes Kingdom on the

behest of the King of the Gods for the celebration of Princess Hebe. I am Otus." The god had a clean scalp and a well-trimmed beard. He wore an elegant yellow robe with his family's crest, and although his body was covered, the outline of his bulging muscles was impossible to hide.

"And I am his brother, Ephialtes. We are The Aloadae." And like Otus, Ephialtes wore a yellow robe, a clean scalp, and a neatly styled beard.

"By the gods!" *They are identical in appearance.* Looking from one face to the other, she lowered her arms and, thus, her weapons. "How will I tell the two of you apart?"

"Easily." Bringing his hand over his heart, his eyes lingered on the slit of her skirt, exposing her extended, shapely thigh before settling back to her hardened expression. "I am Otus, the one who has already fallen in love with you."

The other one cracked a small smile after hearing his brother's response. Mimicking Otus with a hand on his chest, he added, "And I am Ephialtes, the one who has not."

"Well, I am flattered by your confession." And turning to the other, she quipped, "And I am offended by yours." Artemis remained distrustful but had enough confidence to re-holster her arrows. *One thing is for sure, they are dressed for a celebration.*

The two giants exchanged an amused glance until they realized the goddess had turned around, heading back into the forest.

She held a finger to the sky as she walked. "Follow me into Mount Olympus."

At once, Otus and Ephialtes hurried along behind the daughter of their King.

23

BIG BROTHER
ARES & HEPHAESTUS

The Underworld of Mount Olympus.

Ares trudged through the depths of the Great Mount, lined with sporadic torches casting ghostly shadows along the stone walls. The weight of the past hung heavily in the air, and he could not help but feel a sense of foreboding as he ventured further into the heart of the palace.

The last time I made this trip, Prometheus was a prisoner.

Yes, the dungeons were secure enough to hold even the Great Prometheus.

Ares recalled the Titan's son held in chains wrung around his hands, feet, and neck, so taught, he could not move.

I remember thinking what a harsh punishment he was dealt, not knowing that eternal isolation would only be the beginning of his torture.

He descended the circular steps deeper into the dark pit.

Prometheus is a constant reminder of what happens if one

crosses the King of the Gods. Yet, I did not need such a reminder. I already learned that lesson as a youth.

Ares' footsteps reverberated through the grim corridor as he approached the cells. The echoing sound was almost a herald of his arrival, and as he neared the final set of bars, the lone hooded prisoner turned to face him.

Ares let out a slow breath, only then realizing how long he had held it in. *At last...*

The contrast between the two brothers was stark—dressed in his battle armor, Ares exuded strength and regality, while Hephaestus remained a shell of a god, wrapped in an over-worn robe.

Even though the Prince had an imposing stance beneath the stern façade, an inkling of concern creased his brow, signaling that whatever had lured him into the pit did not bode well for Hephaestus.

I warned Hebe this would be my death.

Ares grabbed the cold bars of the cell. Only one thing was on the menacing god's mind at that moment. "Did you *touch* Princess Hebe?" his voice was deathly smooth.

Hephaestus fell to his knees where he stood. "My prince..." The question was simple, yet the answer would mean certain execution. He spoke with his eyes glued to the floor, not out of disrespect but to show humility. "I—I took her hand."

"But did you *take* anything else?" his words were slow and deliberate, giving Hephaestus enough time to craft a response carefully.

If only his words could fit as masterfully as the metals he welded together. "No, Prince Ares." He shuffled his knees toward the god and pleaded, "I took nothing else. I did nothing else. I *swear* it!"

Calmly, Ares bent down on one knee, staring straight into the darkness of the pitiful god's disfigured face. "But did you *want* to?"

Hephaestus cowered on the floor, with incoherent groveling. He clasped his hands together, begging for mercy.

"You will do well to bite your tongue. Lest the Goddess Styx hold you to your oath." Satisfied with the god's terrified reaction, Ares stood tall and commanded harshly, "Get up!"

Hephaestus darted to his feet, his posture horrible because his shoulders crunched to one side and his knee twisted to the other.

The warrior's heart ached with unresolved anger, a latent fury waiting for the right moment to unleash. *Curse the gods!* He struggled to reconcile the sight before him with the faded memory of the infant born atop Mount Olympus so many years ago.

"Earlier that day, before you were born, I was on a stroll with our uncle Poseidon. As usual, he made a great earthquake to show off his mighty strength before me. Only this time, the earth shook for much longer because I egged him on. Suddenly, we witnessed lava surge from a hole in a mountaintop, spraying ashes everywhere. It was the most magnificent sight I had ever seen as a youngling."

He rubbed his chin, the stubble reminding him that he would soon need to shave. "The night you were born, mother asked me to pick a name for my baby brother or sister. I told her I did not want a baby sister, only a brother I could play with. 'If it is a sister,' I told Mother, 'send her back.'" He smiled at the memory. "Mother again asked, 'If it is a baby brother, what will you name him?'"

Hephaestus listened intensely. Ares' story was the most he had ever heard about his mother and life in the palace. His life raised next to the unforgiving sea paled in comparison.

Ares continued, "I told Mother your name shall be like the ashes springing from a volcano. Mother smiled and said, 'his name shall be Hephaestus.'"

The weathered god felt a sense of joy after learning how his name came to be. *Who would have thought my big brother named me?* He let the question stay in his mind to avoid interrupting the tale.

"Within time, our mother was whisked away into another room, and shortly thereafter, you were born."

Hephaestus maintained his silence, his memories locked away in a mental vault, buried underneath layers of pain and sorrow. Beads of sweat formed on his forehead as he struggled to take long, deliberate breaths. It was a coping mechanism he had developed over the years to contain the panic that hid within.

On the other hand, Ares felt a growing sense of dread gnawing at him, forcing him to confront his past. Hephaestus' birth was a day etched in his mind, one he had avoided revisiting at all costs. And yet, there it was, staring back at him from behind those wretched bars, demanding acknowledgment.

"I remember when I first heard you fell from the mountain...*thrown* from the mountain..." His stomach tightened.

"Like ashes springing forth from a volcano." The most magnificent thing he had ever seen, only to be turned into something so utterly horrific not long after.

Staring his brother in the eyes, Ares whispered so low it was difficult to hear, "I thought I had cursed you by giving you *that* name." He looked up in hopelessness. "The power we gods have in our hands...in our words..." *Only The Fates know.*

Ares let the solemn atmosphere remain, and soon, a wave of peace poured over him. His voice became stronger as the worst of the story was over. "I know better now. Still, I do not think I ever got over the events of that day...*all* that transpired."

The huge knot building in Hephaestus' throat shrunk, and his breathing settled. However, Ares was far from finished.

Although I love my brother, I have not, nor will I ever forget, my love for my sister. "When Princess Hebe was born, she was as small as a dove in the palm of my hand. And like a bird, I clipped her wings to prevent her from flying too far into the ruthless world below. Alas, her feathers have returned to her, and she is now free to come and go as she pleases." Ares grabbed the prison bars so forcefully that the metal would have buckled from the intense pressure if it were possible. "Even so, I will continue to protect her with a fierceness like no other for all eternity. Ask me if I am lying."

Hephaestus had enough sense to remain quiet.

"I know *you* were the one who injured Hebe."

The accusation is true. What more can I say? What case can I plead? I am guilty.

"Hebe is the most precious thing in the world to me. If you ever lay a hand on her again, I swear to gods..." his voice softened to a whisper, "*when* your body reaches Hades, it will already be in pieces."

He tried to swallow, but his throat felt like a bolder was blocking its passage again.

Ares reached into his side, pulled out a key, and lodged it into the lock with a firm twist.

Hephaestus took two clumsy steps back as his older brother entered the cell. He may have been taller than Ares; however, one could never be sure given his hunched posture.

"You are to stay away from the princess."

He is asking me to choose life or death, but what is life without Hebe? It would have been better if I had never met her at all. She is the light in this world of darkness.

The longer he took to answer, the more Ares' right eye twitched. "Have I made myself clear?"

Reluctantly, he found his voice, "Yes, you made yourself very clear. I will stay away from her."

"Good." *Now I must try and clean up the mess Hebe made by disobeying.* "And if the King should ask who retrieved you from the Territories and put you in this cell, you tell him it was me."

"Lie to the King of the Gods?" He gasped at Ares' demand but knew a prisoner had no right to argue with a Prince. "I will do as you say. I am at your mercy."

The younger brother looked utterly defeated, collapsed on the floor with no hope in sight, yet the warrior would have it no other way. *One has first to destroy in order to rebuild.*

After a prolonged silence, Hephaestus sheepishly glanced at the muscled god towering above and saw something he never thought possible. *By the gods! He's actually...happy!*

Ares smiled so brightly that it lifted Hephaestus' spirits immediately. With a wave of his hand, the gated door opened, and Ares stepped inside, hand outstretched.

Hephaestus was shocked momentarily but decided even if he misinterpreted the gesture, he had better act before the moment would pass him by. He grabbed Ares' hand and immediately felt a force pull him onto his feet. To his complete surprise, the Prince wrapped his arms around his ribcage, locking him into the warmest embrace he had ever felt in all his life. Once his disbelief passed, Hephaestus returned the passionate embrace with equal enthusiasm.

At last...I hold my babe brother in my arms. A relief washed over him—the urning he had to rock his tiny brother so long ago never left. Ares wasted no time and kissed his smooth, unblemished cheek. "Welcome home, baby brother."

For now, it was a moment of happiness, a reunion of sorts, but both gods knew that the shadows of their past still loomed.

Even though Ares ended the visit with a warm welcome, there was still someone else they both had to answer to—a figure known the world over for his lack of forgiveness. Prometheus was the eternal reminder of the punishment that awaited all those who would dare disobey the King. And Ares silently wondered if Zeus would make Hephaestus another reminder.

24

WHEN JEALOUSY REARS...
APOLLO & ATHENA

Damn, Muses! Apollo paused momentarily and slammed a hand to his forehead.

Ever since Hermes planted a tiny seed of doubt into his fertile mind, he could no longer ignore the fruits of jealousy growing throughout his entire being.

Athena and Ares. Alone. Together?

Apollo continued his lone walk through the Ancient Land of Men. *Why would Athena be around Ares? It is no secret she thinks he is a fool! It may be that Ares requested her company. But he does not fancy her either.* The entire premise left him baffled.

Of course! His eyes widened with a new idea. *All this must be a lie conjured up by Hermes for his own entertainment.* Given more thought, Apollo shook his head profusely. *But alas, Hermes is not one to spread a bald-faced lie as truth.*

Lost in his musings, he suddenly stopped, almost stumbling over his feet. He had unknowingly wandered into the entrance of the ancient temple to find a striking figure against the backdrop of the old structure.

"What a surprise." The red-haired goddess was easy to identify even though her back was facing him. "It is good to see you in the day."

Athena turned around to see the handsome blond approaching her and smiled brightly. "Likewise."

The slight blush of her cheeks made his heart race faster. "You look wonderful, as always."

"Thank you, Apollo." She bit the inside of her cheeks to dampen her nerves. "About last night."

"No need to say anything. I got the message loud and clear." He did not want her to feel uncomfortable, not to hop away, but he was also too curious about her meeting with Ares. *How can I broach the subject?* "What have you been doing today?"

"Not much of anything," she answered indifferently, returning her focus to the cold statue mounted above them. "Did you know this temple was first built in honor of Queen Hera around the time of the 2nd generation of men?"

"I did not know." He had noticed the old building throughout his existence but had not thought much of it. "I have seen Aphrodite around this temple many times."

"Yes, she has been here a lot." *Which is what drew me back here. Seeing her praying on the altar sent my mind spinning.* "This temple is well built. Even after all these years, everything is intact. Everything...except for Hera's statute. It is missing its head. Do you not find that interesting?"

He shrugged, allowing his colorful shawl to sag from his shoulder. "Heads come, heads go." The little history lesson did not interest him at all. "May I ask you something?"

"You may."

Despite better judgment, he asked, "Is it true you were with…"

"Oh! I almost forgot." She hurriedly reached into her pouch. "I have something for you."

"What is it?"

She revealed an instrument handcrafted out of wood and polished until it glowed, resembling the color of honey. "It makes music by moving your fingers over the many holes and blowing through the opening. I was inspired last night. You have a way with your lips and the movement of your fingers…"

He examined the wooden pipe, the musician in him momentarily overshadowing his feelings for his crush. *This instrument is well made, indeed.*

"I have not blessed it with a name." Athena gave him a sheepish smile when he looked back at her. "I was hoping you would do the honors. Also, I have not even played it. I want you to have that honor as well."

"A virgin." He held it up in the air and gave her a wink. "I shall be gentle when I break her in."

Playfully, Athena rolled her eyes, which looked more blue than gray the longer he became lost in them.

It took a moment for the master of poetry to find the right words to express his joy. "This is the most thoughtful gift I have ever received."

What a relief! "I hoped you might love it."

"Of course, I love *you*...it." *I am so stupid!* "I love *it*."

Her cheeks remained flushed. "I'm happy you love...*it*." Her thoughts took another turn when she remembered she talked over him a moment before. "I am sorry I interrupted you as you were about to say something. What is it you wanted to know?"

Running the instrument between the tips of his fingers, he thought better than to allow his jealousy to get the better of him. "It was nothing. Nothing at all." Holding the wooden object high, he declared, "I will be sure to dedicate the first song I compose on this instrument to you."

Athena nodded in gratitude. "That would be lovely."

25

WATCH THE THRONE
ARES & APHRODITE

"All hail King Ares!"

The Prince reclined upon his father's imposing throne with his sword leaned against its side. The King's crown sat askew over his brow, and he balanced the royal scepter on his middle finger as a fleeting way to rid his boredom. However, it was not working.

His metal wrist and shin brace remained affixed to his frame, and with an air of nonchalance, he draped one leg casually over the arm of the throne.

Beneath the many steps before him, a modest assembly of creatures gathered in seats while a line formed outside for those seeking judgments from the King's Court. The voices in the crowd were shocked to find Ares on Zeus' seat—although none were more shocked than Ares himself.

I could be out riding my chariot. Instead, I am surrounded by four walls. Why am I torturing myself?

The massive doors of the Court opened, and the crowd came to a tempered hush when each noticed the jaw-dropping Aphrodite at the entrance.

Ah, yes. Is Aphrodite not the answer to my question? She is the reason for my torture. He laughed to himself. *For once, I am not the sadist in a relationship.* The Prince instantly sat up straight as the goddess pranced down the aisle in a figure-hugging gown—one of many.

She held his gaze hostage with no intention of releasing him and made her way to the third row and sat on an empty chair. Still reveling in his attention, Aphrodite scooped her golden waves to one side, having them fall over her right breast, leaving her left cleavage in full display. And as if she could not do anything more to entice him, she gave him a slow, deliberate wink.

Aphrodite! What I would not give to ravish her right here on my father's throne in the presence of all my subjects. Ares settled back into his throne. *This morning, I withdrew from her chambers before she woke. However, the next time we meet in secret, I will not leave in silence.*

"Your Majesty."

Ares snapped out of his haze to see two familiar faces below him. "Well, well, well." He leaned forward with a hand perched on his knee and an amused snarl on his perfectly symmetrical face. "Otus," he said, eyes moving from one to the other, "and Ephialtes."

The twins exchanged glances before the oldest, by mere seconds, spoke with a hand to his chest, "Actually, it is I, who is called Otus, and he is called Ephialtes."

Ares did not pretend to care and brushed the response away with a careless wave. "And for what reason are you two here?"

"We have come in place of our father, Porphyrion, Ruler of the Gigantes Kingdom," said Ephialtes.

"Oh, I am sorry to hear of Porphyrion's grave illness."

Otus' brows raised, unsure of where the Prince would hear such a lie. "We can assure you our father is very much in good health."

Of that, Ares was very much aware. His back stiffened, and his voice grew loud over the assembly. "If Porphyrion is *not* on his deathbed, what other reason can he have for missing the celebration of the Princess of the Gods?"

The silence from the onlookers turned to mummers as Ares again searched for the sea-blue eyes of his soon-to-be lover.

As if she could sense his search for validation, she smirked as a sign of approving his ruthless line of questioning.

"Unfortunately," Otus answered when the crowd's silence returned, "Our father is weighed down with the responsibility of running the southern Kingdom."

"A Kingdom allotted to him by Zeus, the King of the Gods." Ares deliberately moved to tighten his grip on his sword's handle, but he did not remove it from his side. "A Kingdom that can easily be allotted to another god if your father no longer pleases the God of the Sky."

"Now, now, my Prince. We do not need to turn friends into

enemies." The tall Otus stood taller, moving his hand slightly to display the weapon, he too, had at his side.

Aphrodite recaptured Ares' smoldering stare, and for once, she was unsure if it was she who was burning his heart or if it was his thirst for violence. Even though she could not pinpoint the reason for his lust, that did not stop her legs from involuntarily clenching at the sight of him above, seated at the pinnacle of power.

"Today is one of celebration. Let us not divide our interests when we can join them." Otus looked to his brother, who nodded to continue, "Earlier, we intercepted the goddess Artemis on our way here, and her beauty and strength immediately won me over."

Slowly, his gaze returned to the Giants, but his dark eyes no longer had a playful sense of brutality. His burning passion from within was quelled for the first time since Aphrodite entered the Court. "Is that so?"

The goddess of great beauty looked on with deep concern. *Why does Ares care about anyone who wishes to wed Artemis?*

"I am requesting the approval of the King to approach the goddess with the intention of marriage." He took a step forward. "A joining of the very High North to the South."

The goddess raised her hand to her bosom, hoping to steal a glance from her Prince again. However, Ares remained solely focused on the Giants. *Why does he not seek my face?*

Ares stood to his feet but left his sword leaning against the throne. "As I stand in my father's place, be sure that what I say is true. Not only did *your* father disrespect the great Zeus by not appearing before the Court, but you also have the gull to request marriage to his daughter? The audacity!"

Otus and Ephialtes mirrored the same confused expression as their brows raised and their forehead creased.

Before they had any time to react, Ares raised a finger in lieu of a sword and shouted to the Court Guards, "Seize them!"

Charging from each side of the room were two Minotaurs who grabbed them along with two Centaurs, one with a spear and the other pointing a ready arrow at the captured foes.

The Giants knew better than to resist and relented as the Minotaurs roughly pinned their arms behind their back.

Once the culprits were secured, Ares paced the dais, rubbing the stubble along his jaw. "The punishment for disrespecting the King is a thousand lashes."

The audience gasped in response, but Ares did not wait for them to hush. "However," he continued, "The Fates have favored you. For today is my sister's Day of Understanding, and as such, there will be no bloodshed in her honor." He stopped pacing and turned to the two below with weary eyes. "A pity."

Aphrodite's hand gripped her throat as she awaited with bated breath for him to cement his act of mercy.

Ares skipped down the steps and stopped just far enough in front of them that they looked to be equal height. "Leave now! And if you ever dare think to return," he warned, "your judgment *will* be carried out."

26

DISTANT LOVERS
ZEUS & HERA

MY LOVER IS NO MORE. MY WIFE IS FOREVER.

After his long journey, Zeus entered his Quarters and settled into his home. It was comforting to be back amidst the familiarity of palace life. Thoughts of Demeter were far from his mind. He *had* to push his feelings for her aside. After all, he had a wife, the Queen of the Gods, and any inclination that he spent much of his time away loving her sister would lead to certain disaster.

Demeter is right to be concerned about Hera. But why is she suddenly so worried after all this time we have been together secretly?

Upon hearing shuffling from the bedroom's closed door, Zeus buried thoughts of his mistress and prepared to reunite with his Queen.

Hera stepped into the living area and stopped short at

seeing her husband standing next to the three-legged table in the middle of the room. Her purple dress, long enough to drape the floor, hugged each curve to her frame perfectly. Her flowing brown hair was pulled loosely behind her shoulders and gathered into a sparkly clip. Her hazel eyes were hypnotizing and capable of ensnaring whoever dared to look upon them with no chance of breaking free.

Zeus was speechless, as he always was whenever he looked upon her loveliness. She was absolutely stunning, confirming all the whispers that would say she rivaled Aphrodite in beauty.

It was easy for Zeus to forget her attractiveness when they were arguing, which at certain times would be constant. But at that moment, with no words spoken, he would have given the world to ravish her again and again.

Hera cautiously looked Zeus over, wondering if he had come back to her as pure as how he had left her. *My husband, at times, in name only.* She remained skeptical whenever he returned from his adventures—an old feeling of betrayal she found hard to erase. So instead of embracing her beloved, she crossed her delicate white-arms and raised a high sculpted brow. "Why did you take so long?"

The peace and calm Zeus had experienced unwinding at home had dissipated upon the sound of her shrill voice. "The journey was a difficult one. That is why I was gone so long."

Hera could tell from his demeanor he would speak about his trek no further. However, she knew that, given enough time, she could wear him down and eventually force him to relent.

Before she could press further, Zeus picked up the elegant pitcher from the table and poured a drink. "Has Hestia recuperated enough to attend today's festivities?"

"She has not."

How much longer will you drift away from us, Hestia? Zeus took a sip of water from his cup.

Not even mentioning Hera's dear sister could temper her rapid-fire questions. *He is sadly mistaken if he thinks changing the subject will make his life more comfortable.* "Why did you agree to Aphrodite's wishes? Have you seen the spectacle she calls home on our mount? Why did you not ask my opinion on the matter?"

Aphrodite! The one I kept hidden from Hera—and the only one who would have stayed hidden if I had my way! For whatever reason, he decided to engage her. "I did not ask your opinion because you would have said no."

"That is my right." She circled him and flashed her hands as she spoke, "Here I thought after all this time, your bundle of so-called joys had finally ceased, and then, low and behold, I found you with Aphrodite."

"I had to hide Aphrodite from you the same way I hid Dionysus...albeit for different purposes," he mumbled under his breath. "Aphrodite was born fully formed around the time of Hermes and Dionysus when our marriage was on the verge of collapse."

She eyed him cautiously without saying a word. Nor did she have to. Her eyes glowed with anger.

"By the time I found out I had another daughter, we had repaired our marriage, and you were carrying Hebe." He stopped long enough to take another sip of his drink. "And so I kept Aphrodite hidden for a long time until you...found us together."

"If I did not find you, would you have kept her a secret?"

"Of course! If only to keep the peace we had finally achieved."

Nothing was stopping Hera from turning the sudden appearance of Aphrodite into another argument. However, she had long ago forgiven his infidelities from the past—plus, she had many new things to argue with him over. "I went to visit our daughter in her new home, and imagine my surprise when I saw she was not alone. Why did you put a guard by Hebe's door?"

"Protection."

"You would have a *man* protect a goddess?"

"I will have a man tell me everything I need to know about my daughter's whereabouts now that she can come and go as she pleases. Hebe will soon debut as the Princess of the Gods, able to fully perform her royal duties. I want to make sure no suitor approaches her without my knowledge."

"Speaking of suitors approaching without your knowledge, Poseidon has gifted Hebe *another* pet. As if I cannot see his true motives to curry favor with the princess."

My brother was never one to be subtle. Zeus placed his empty cup on the table and walked over to the opening of the balcony to take in the cool breeze. "It is no secret Poseidon wishes to unite his son, Hallirhothios, with Hebe. A joining of the sea to the sky, combining our kingdoms."

"Hallirhothios!" The Queen wailed with a hand to her forehead. "The bastard son of a Nymph? Hebe will not be wedded to someone of such low status."

"Hebe's station as a princess alone will elevate Hallirhothios' social positioning." *And with Hades threatening our long-standing peace, all options for solidifying allies must be weighed.* Against his better judgment, he mused out loud, "One must consider the possibility."

"I will consider nothing," she replied in a huff, nose high in the air. "Besides, it is only right for the older to marry before the younger. It is not time for Ares to find a wife?"

"Ares is far too happy instigating mortal men to settle down and help govern our Kingdom." Turning to her, he pointed an accusing finger in her direction. "Ares is the way he is because *you* have spoiled him since the day he was born."

She shrugged as simply as could be. "As is my right as his mother."

"If Nymphs are not to your standards and you insist the Prince marry, why not unite our son to Artemis."

"Artemis?" The name alone left a horrid taste in her mouth and a piercing sound in her ears. "The one who prefers to call me expletives instead of Queen?"

He nodded, stroking his dark, neatly trimmed beard.

"Over. My. Dead. Body."

"Promises, promises," he mused more so to himself while closing the balcony doors. Finally, the King waved a limp hand akin to waving a white flag. "I will argue no further."

She was ready to argue until the end of time and would have, except something much more important was weighing on her mind. Her words caught in her throat.

Grabbing his hands, she led him away from the windows to sit on the preach-colored sofa along the side of the wall.

There was never a topic too risqué for Hera to broach, except the one name that she knew was like a stab to her husband's side. *I cannot hold my tongue any longer.* Staring deep into his solid blue eyes, she asked, "How is *Hades*?"

His jaws clenched before he had a chance to control his emotions. It did not matter how much he trusted his wife's faithfulness and her undying love for him; her inquiring about his nemesis always rubbed him the wrong way.

He swallowed hard enough for Hera to see the lump move down his throat. "He is doing well."

She gave his fingers a gentle squeeze. "Tell me the truth."

Letting go of her hands, he rested his back on the couch. "He is lonely."

"What does he want? More souls to keep him company?" Hera clutched his neck desperately—any other time, her touch along his neck would have sent him with passion. "We can give Hades his heart's content."

"He is not *that* kind of lonely." His brows raised, causing subtle folds along his forehead, the signs of a King who carries a heavy load. "He wants a wife."

She slapped her lap energetically and declared, "Then he shall have one!"

Has she gone mad? "Really? Who?" The loose curls of his locks shook with his head. "Do you intend to join our

Kingdom with the Underworld by offering Hades our daughter?"

"Bite your tongue!"

"If not Hebe, which goddess would you condemn to live in the Underworld?"

Without hesitation, Hera opened her mouth to answer, "Aph..."

"No."

"Art..."

"Stop."

"Ath..."

"That is enough," he warned, cutting her off completely.

My poor Hades. She sank lower into her seat. *I can only imagine him all alone in the Underworld, away from his family. Feeling isolated and dammed along with all the souls he collects.* "And if he does not get his way?"

"We will no longer be at peace."

Hades needs me. I am the only one who can get through to him. Hera got down on her knees before her King. She clasped her hands together, pleading as never before, "You must let me speak to him."

His tone was low but forceful, "You will do *no* such thing."

"He *will* reason with me."

The jealousy Zeus felt over Hera flared beyond measure at the mere thought of Hades anywhere near her. Thankfully, as long as his brother remained trapped with responsibilities in the Underworld, Zeus knew he did not have to obsess over Hades and Hera's eternal attachment to one another.

Hades can rot in that dump he calls a world, for all I care! As if

I did not know the truth of why he had asked me for a wife. Only the Goddess of Marriage can seal a union between the gods. Hera must be present to extend her blessings to a couple. My brother cannot fool me. He only seeks an excuse for Hera to travel to the Underworld under the guise of matrimony when he has only ever wanted to marry my Queen.

"Please, Zeus. I have not seen Hades since the day he left for his kingdom. Let me see him now and right whatever wrong he has against you."

"My love." Softly, he placed a hand underneath her chin. "I know you two share a bond I will never understand." His temper was growing within him the longer he tormented his mind at the image of his wife next to his brother. "I cannot risk you going to the Underworld. I will not take the chance of you never returning." *Either by Hades' force or by her own will.* Slowly, he bent over and kissed her forehead, knowing a kiss was never just a kiss when his lips touched any part of her silky skin.

When Zeus would leave for an extended period, they would argue and then make love once he returned.

Now that our fight is over, let us finally get to the best part... making up. Reaching for Hera's shoulders, Zeus removed her shawl, exposing her sharp collarbone and a peek of her lovely breasts. "I have missed your embrace." His tongue rolled along the bottom of his lip, more than ready to put his jealousy to good use by claiming every part of her body as she screams his name in ecstasy. "We still have some more time alone before presenting ourselves in the Great Hall."

Hera smiled, drawing him in with her large swirling eyes.

"Then let us use this time wisely." She loomed over him, teasingly pulling down her straps and letting her gown drop to her ankles in one swoop.

He lit up as he took in the fullness of her nakedness. "As you wish, my Queen."

27

KISSING, COUSINS
ARES & HALLIRHOTHIOS

As the tedious procession of the Order of the Court unfolded, the Prince found his patience wearing thin with each passing moment. Not even a fleeting glance in Aphrodite's direction amidst a sea of forgettable faces could quell the restless energy.

Will this line of nobles ever cease? Watching the seemingly endless parade of dignitaries and officials file past, dressed in elaborate attire topped with their pompous demeanor, only served to deepen his sense of disillusionment.

His rulings throughout the day became increasingly erratic, his decisions swayed by the capricious whims of his ever-shifting mood. A well-timed glimpse of Aphrodite flipping her golden hair secured Aster of Imbrus a generous increase of land from the Prince's favor. However, when the goddess delicately adjusted her shawl to conceal her collarbone, a sudden wave of irritation washed over Ares, prompting him to dole out punishments with a heavy hand. Unfortunately, Tydeus of Kosone, caught in the crosshairs, found himself saddled with a new land tax that seemed tailor-made to penalize him alone.

If I remain here any longer, my judgments will create either a Utopia or lead to the start of the Apocalypse. With such a drastic difference in potential outcomes, it is far better for the King that I leave the throne than remain seated.

The ceaseless drone of decrees threatened to overwhelm him, until his newfound obsession slowly lifted the hem of her gown, revealing a tantalizing peek of bare skin as she gracefully crossed one plump, creamy leg over the other. The sight, though fleeting, was enough to keep Ares tethered to his spot.

On the other hand, I could stay a tad bit longer.

Suddenly, the grand double doors opened, revealing a figure cloaked in regal finery as he swept into the court and paraded down the aisle, stopping below the dais. With a hand on his torso, he gave a full bow. "What a wonderful surprise to see you on the throne, Your Majesty."

Ares loathed all royal names, whether Prince, Grace, or Majesty. However, the familiarity of the voice stopped the usual vomitous feeling from stirring in the pit of his stomach.

He wilfully tore his eyes away from Aphrodite and stood up once he confirmed who was indeed before him. *Hallirhothios!* Rising from his seat, Ares smoothly hung his sword at his side before descending the steps with long deliberate strides. The clanging sounds from his assortment of weaponry grew louder as he and made his way towards the waiting figure below.

Hallirhothios felt the pounding in his chest as the warmonger drew near, his imposing presence casting a shadow over the young one. The sight of Ares, with his tall, muscular frame and steely gaze, never failed to send a shiver down his spine.

The Prince reached out with powerful hands, gripping Hallirhothios' shoulders with a firmness that made the younger god flinch instinctively. But to his surprise, there was no pain, only the warmth of Ares' touch as he pulled him into a tight embrace.

"My little cousin." Ares exclaimed as he eased Hallirhothios off his feet, before setting him back down on his feet. With a smile that lit up his rugged features, Ares pressed a kiss on each cheek before drawing back to regard him with fondness. "It brings me great joy to see you once more!"

It was a rare sight to see the war god's fierce countenance softened by genuine happiness, and Hallirhothios could not help but return the smile in kind. "And it brings me even greater joy to see you, cousin."

Ares plopped his arm around the young one's neck and led to a side door away from the eyes of the court. "Come with me to the King's Study, where we can speak privately."

THE KING'S STUDY OCCUPIED A CHAMBER ADJACENT TO THE bustling Royal Court, reserved for the most confidential deliberations. The cozy space had a wall lined from floor to the ceiling with a vase array of ancient books, rarely, if ever, opened. A large window dominated the other side of the room, offering a breathtaking view of Helios' chariot pulling the sun over the clouds.

Ares disregarded Zeus' plush, comfortable chair in favor of sitting on the solid wooden desk, heedless of the scattered papers on the polished surface. He could not wait to remove the stiff crown and toss it carelessly beside him.

Meanwhile, Hallirhothios stood rigid with shallow breath before his Prince. His damp hands were clasped at his back, and he could feel tiny beads of sweat collecting on his forehead.

"Why do you look so pale? Relax! As if you have not spent countless occasions roaming every inch of this mountain with impunity." Glancing at the god's side, Ares grinned wildly at seeing a dagger enclosed in a black and red leather sheath. "I see you are carrying the gift I gave you on your Day of Understanding."

Hallirhothios patted the silver handle, fashioned in the shape of a skull. "It has never parted from my side since the day I received it." A gleam caught his eye, and he wiggled his eyebrows. "Except during my intimate moments."

He wagged his finger ruefully at the younger one as a wry smile played upon his lips. "That is when you are in most need of your weapon—that is when you are the most vulnerable."

A wink from Ares loosened him enough to let out a joyous laugh. "I must say, I am relieved at your warm greeting. I thought because I have entered my godhood, I would no longer receive the charity of being a youngling and instead be treated as a bastard."

"You have always been family, and that will *never* change." He picked up an ink pen and pointed the feather tip toward his cousin. "Besides, Poseidon would never allow anyone to disrespect his only son. Speaking of...where is my uncle?"

The longer he remained before Ares, the more it seemed like old times—as if nothing really had changed. "My father could not wait to give Princess Hebe her present, and the last I saw of him, he was on his way to deliver it to her personally. However, that was a long time ago."

He tossed the pen to the side. "Ah yes, Wolfie." Ares scratched along his jaw, wondering if Hebe had heeded his warnings to leave the pet outdoors. "Our Queen will say Poseidon spoils the princess."

"She deserves to be spoiled. Which is why I am here."

"Do tell." He folded his fingers together, allowing the sun's golden rays to highlight every ripple and bulge of his powerful physique in exquisite detail. Based on strength alone, no one could deny that he was truly a force to be reckoned with.

As if on cue, Hellirhothios' throat tightened. "As you are well aware, once the celebration begins, it will be difficult to get a moment with Princess Hebe, competing with such a large crowd of well-wishers." He wiped a trembling hand over his clammy forehead, fighting the chill coursing through his veins. "And so, I—I am seeking permission to personally give my present to Princess Hebe ahead of the festivities."

So, this is why he is nervous. He wants to spend time alone with Hebe. His eyes flickered, a spark igniting a familiar surge of heat radiating underneath his skin. Ares embraced the raw power pulsating through him. "Hallirhothios, normally, I would grant your request without hesitation. However, as of today, neither my sister nor you are a youngling. Therefore, there will be no more unsupervised *playdates.*"

"Even though you said otherwise, things have changed." Slowly, he nodded, his gaze fixating on the billowing clouds roaming the mountaintops. Amidst the tranquil beauty of the natural world, he found solace, a moment of relief for his twisted stomach. "But I understand why change must come. I shall leave my gift in the pile with all the others. I can only hope to revisit the Princess on the personal invitation of the King."

Ares maintained an unwavering focus on his cousin, his eyes piercing through the air like a sharpened blade as he waited for the younger god to meet his eyes once more. Time seemed to stretch out before them, and then, as if drawn by an invisible force, Hallirhothios' gaze returned to meet Ares', along with the returning anxiousness. "But let me be resoundingly clear," Even though his mouth felt as arid as the desert sands, he pressed forward, "I want my intentions to have Hebe as my bride known."

In an instant, Ares sprang from the desk as he closed the distance between himself and the other god. Standing toe to toe, their imposing figures loomed large in the confined space, their noses mere inches apart. With each exhale, a rush of air swept past, tousling the curls that framed his cousin's face.

Despite Hallirhothios' new ascent to godhood, he was far from naive, and Ares recognized the challenger's gambit for what it was—a play for power within the realm of Olympus. *He dares to inquire about marriage to my sister!* A primal urge stirred within him to assert his dominance over anyone, whether friend or foe. Ares itched to unleash any of the various weapons that hung from his belt. *If I cannot temper my instincts to fight my cousin, there is no hope for any of Hebe's suitors.*

As Hallirhothios took a cautious step backward, the imposing figure of Ares' seemed to undergo a subtle transformation before his eyes. He no longer saw the god of war as a formidable and menacing presence, but rather, he beheld him through the lens of youthful awe and wonderment. "Ares, since I was yay high running around the palace with a wooden stick, trying my best to imitate you, I have always wished for the impossible. For you to be my brother." Relief flooded through him as the strength returned to his arms, dispelling the lingering sensation of weakness that had plagued him moments before.

With newfound confidence, he reached out, his fingers brushing against the rough stubble of Ares' cheek. "Now that I am older, I understand nothing is impossible for a god. Hopefully, someday soon, we *will* be brothers."

Damn it all to Hades! The inferno raging within him gradually subsided, its fierce flames slowly smoldering to embers, cooled by the distant memories of babe Hallirhothios in his arms. Ares retrieved the crown, placing it securely on his head. "I will inform the King of your interest in Hebe so that arrangements will be in place for the next time you arrive on Mount Olympus."

Had the ceiling stretched infinitely higher, he would have soared with unbridled joy into the heavens above.

With the Prince bestowing a tender kiss upon his brow and a lingering embrace, they turned their steps towards the halls of the Royal Court.

As they departed, their footsteps echoed against the polished marble floors. Hallirhothios' thoughts ceased to dwell on his potential bride, his mind now consumed by his prior conversation with the gossip god.

Oh, Hermes, my fellow bastard. Who is the fool now?

28

THE WINE'D UP
ARES & HERMES

The colossal doors swung open, revealing the next visitor approaching the King's Court. This newcomer strode confidently into the chamber, instantly captivating the undivided attention of all those present.

Ares gripped the arm of the grand throne, and his features contorted as if he had just tasted something exceedingly bitter. Before him stood Hermes, the favored son of Zeus. Ares could never quite figure out what endeared the swift-footed god so profoundly to their father and, surprisingly, his mother. True, Hermes possessed undeniable charisma, a trait Ares begrudgingly acknowledged. Yet, there had to be more than a good personality that attracted the King and Queen to the always-calculating bastard.

Ares rolled his eyes, finding it challenging to endure the carefree smirk gracing Hermes' punchable face. *The bastard always looked like he was up to something...because he was always up to something.*

Hermes approached the throne with a bounce in his step and executed a deep and respectable bow. "Ares, Prince of the Gods." To the onlooking crowd, it would be easy to mistake Hermes' conformity to tradition as a show of support for the one on the throne—when, in actuality, Hermes was exceptionally good at masking his genuine emotions.

Ares is neither charming, intelligent, nor pleasant, yet Aphrodite and all the goddesses and Nymphs of the land vie for his favor. And how did he do to gain such a following? Not by merit but by the luck of birth order. He has everything while deserving nothing.

Even though Aphrodite had set her sights on the warring god, Hermes knew better than to act out his jealousy in front of the audience in the court. He knew it best to be far more strategic.

"Hermes, I see you have returned from your journeys. And where along the land has your travels taken you?" The Prince inquired casually, idly picking at his fingernails as he awaited Hermes' response.

"Here, there and everywhere."

Ares' thick brows raised when he noticed the bulging bag slung over Hermes' shoulder. Leaning forward with both hands resting on his knees, he fastened his gaze on the messenger god. "And what treasures have you brought back from the distant corners?"

"I am pleased you asked." Reaching into his pouch, he

produced a glistening bottle. "A fine libation from the wayward son of Zeus."

Ares shook his head in mild exasperation. "Has Dionysus deigned to grace Olympus with his presence at last?"

"No, it seems he prefers the earthly realms," Hermes remarked with a wink. "Much like yourself."

"But I am here now, seated upon my rightful throne," he declared, extending his hand expectantly. "Hand me the bottle."

Hermes hesitated, his grip tightening around the bag as the murmurs of the courtiers grew louder in the background. "It is a gift for the King,"

"I now sit in place of Zeus. And because you are my father's son, I will grant you the luxury of repeating my command. Have over the bottle." Ares only repeated the order because Hermes was his father's son. Anyone else would not survive disobeying a direct order.

"As you command," Hermes acquiesced, begrudgingly ascending the steps to the throne. With a deferential bow, he presented the exotic drink to the interim ruler.

His face contorted as he scrutinized the dark red liquid. *There is nothing special about this.* Twisting off the lid, he sniffed the sweet scent to confirm his thoughts. "Juice from the vine?"

"It is not what you think. A little is good. Too much is trouble," he explained, placing his satchel with the remaining bottles at the throne's base.

"The crown thanks you for your gift. You are dismissed," Ares said as he shooed Hermes away with a dismissive hand.

However, Hermes had no intention of departing the Royal Court empty-handed. "Might I add?"

Ares arched a skeptical brow, silently urging Hermes to proceed.

"The King of the Gods' crown sits upon your head as if crafted especially for you. However, such a symbol of authority should not be worn alongside armor. Rather, you should wear the finest linen and silk, flaunting royal luxury."

Ares' brows drew together in a subtle furrow.

With a final nod of deference, Hermes turned on his heel to depart, skipping smoothly down the steps and through the aisle.

In 5, 4, 3, 2, 1—

"Hermes." Ares' voice sliced through the air, halting the messenger god in his tracks.

He heard Ares dismounting the throne and drawing near from behind. Swiftly, Hermes pivoted on his heel, ready to confront the armed god.

"My father awaits in his chambers, but I have yet to welcome him home." Ares' words lacked his earlier bravado announced. "After being away for so long, the King deserves privacy with his Queen. However, when time allows," he continued, extending the satchel back to his brother, "ensure he receives what is rightfully his."

Once more, Hermes executed a respectful bow. "As you wish, my prince." As Ares brushed past him, Hermes let out a grin as he observed the audience of the court. *That was much too easy.*

However, the smirk on his lips quickly dissolved as his

eyes fell upon Aphrodite amidst the spectators. Her piercing glare bore into him, and for the first time in his existence, the allure of Aphrodite's gaze failed to ignite the usual stirrings of desire from within.

29

SISTER, SISTER
APHRODITE & HEBE

"How does she do it?" Hebe whispered, her voice barely audible over the commotion outside the palace.

From afar, the young Princess stood in awe as Aphrodite strolled by all those in her wake, unmoved by their outpouring of love. She held tightly onto her leech as Wolfie sat perfectly still at her sandals.

The gorgeous goddess lazily flapped her fan, bored with all the attention she was receiving. Having gods and creatures alike stumble over her beauty was so common that she was often oblivious to their grand overtures, which made the rare instances where she was not lusted over, all the more apparent.

Ares left the Royal Court so distraught with Hermes' mind games that he did not even glance in my direction! Out of the sea of faces, Aphrodite caught a familiar gaze beyond the crowd. *Just who I was looking for!* Without hesitation,

Aphrodite hiked up her gown and dashed toward the princess who stood by the Palace courtyard.

Before she could reach out to the young one, a bulky figure with a bruised left eye stepped out of seemingly nowhere, forcing her to stop.

"Stop at once!" Xander ordered, slamming his spear between them.

Aphrodite took a small step back before regaining her composure. The person in front of her had a stern face with unwavering eyes. He dressed as a guard, yet she knew there was something *peculiar* about him.

Is he a...man? A slight smile crawled along her lips. It did not take long to notice the increased beat of his heart and the red blood pumping through his veins and cherry colored his cheeks. Once she was sure of her assessment, her smile widened. *He is a man!* Subduing a mortal was light work for a goddess of her stature.

"W-what business do you have here?"

With batted lashes, she refused to let him break away from her haunting stare. "My business is with the Princess," she said, then gently touching his chest. "Or would you rather my business be with you?"

His heart began to flutter...or was it his stomach? Everything was a blur, and he was confident his knees would soon buckle if Aphrodite did not release him from her mental prison.

If only my touch could easily sway Ares.

Hebe could not let the scene unfolding before her continue. "That is enough, Aphrodite."

The goddess blinked once, then twice, and looked over Xander's shoulder to Hebe, finally breaking her hold over the guard. "Oh, alright! If you insist."

"Aphrodite means me no harm, Xander. You may step down."

He shook his head, removing the last bit of the trance that seemed to hoover over him. "Of course, my princess." With a bow, he stepped behind Hebe, but not too far away, and dared not make eye contact with Aphrodite again.

Grrrrrrr!

Wolfie stood on all fours, glaring at the approaching goddess, exposing all of her razor sharp teeth.

"Enough!" she commanded with a shake of the leech. "Do not mind her. She is over protective."

This must be Poseidon's gift to Hebe. Wolfie. Aphrodite forced a smile, showing two perfect rows of teeth. "No worries. I have a ton of experience dealing with all types of bitches." The alluring goddess giggled her laughter like a melody in the air and gave a proper curtsy. "My princess."

"I am so glad to see you here," Hebe gushed, a smile lighting up her face as she rose on her tippy-toes to greet Aphrodite.

"Where else would I be?" she asked, taking Hebe's arm to lead her on a cool stroll around the inner court.

She was taken aback by Aphrodite's forwardness, not at all used to non-royals touching her so freely. *Aphrodite is new to Mount Olympus and needs to learn proper conduct.* The joy with which the blonde goddess laughed with delight and caressed her hand was all it took for Hebe to relax and sink into Aphrodite's embrace.

"Now, have you picked out your ceremonial gown?"

"Yes, earlier today."

"Good. May I be so bold to offer you some suggestions?"

"You may."

"I have noticed you always wear your hair down, whether loose or in pigtails—it is an unnecessary distraction. For tonight, it would be best for you to wear your hair up in a loose bun. That way, everyone will be drawn to your face unencumbered."

Hebe nodded eagerly, her eyes sparkling with excitement. "I will do all that you say."

Aphrodite stroked Hebe's hand. "I cannot wait for you to see the gifts I brought."

"Oh, please tell me! I cannot bear to wait!"

"If you insist," Aphrodite chuckled, pulling Hebe into a tight embrace. "My gift to you is an entire new wardrobe fitted for your entry into godhood."

Her mouth opened wide, and she slapped her cheek excitedly. "I would love to dress like you! Maybe then the gods would look my way instead of averting their eyes when I walk by."

Aphrodite stopped on the marble path, facing Hebe with a serious expression. "The dress one wears may get a god's attention, but a dress alone is not what *keeps* a god's attention."

Staring into Aphrodite's eyes, she felt like she was about to fall into the abyss. "Will you teach me what I must do?"

"Of course, I will teach you. Why would I not? After all, we are sisters."

For the first time during their delightful interaction, Hebe's body instinctively jerked away from Aphrodite's hold. From her time as a babe to that very day, one thing she knew for sure was that she was a Royal, and the goddess before her was not. "No, we are not sisters."

Aphrodite remained quiet, letting the sting of rejection hang in the air. More so for Hebe's emotions than for her own. *One such as her will feel horrible at the thought of her harsh but true words hurting me.*

Taking a deep breath, Aphrodite spoke softly, "For most of my life, I thought I was the only child of my parents. And one day, the revelation that my father Zeus had other children was the happiest day of my life." She took both of Hebe's hands in hers and offered an innocent smile. "No, we are not sisters. But... we can pretend."

Her round eyes grew wider at the thought. *Artemis would rather glare at me than talk to me, and Athena is too focused on Kingdom matters to pay me any mind. In this short time we have spoken, Aphrodite has given me more attention than Artemis and Athena combined!* Hebe swayed their hands in delight, her eyes sparkling with newfound joy. "I have always wanted a big sister."

"And I have always wanted a little sister!" Aphrodite responded, matching Hebe's enthusiasm.

They squealed in unison, jumping together in a joyful embrace. As they shared a moment of sisterly affection, Xander stood nearby, patiently waiting. However, Hebe's attention was suddenly drawn elsewhere. She glanced off to the side and noticed Artemis making her way over to the courtyard. Abruptly, Hebe pulled away from Aphrodite.

"I must go and prepare for my celebration," she said hastily and walked toward Xander, leaving the great beauty behind.

Aphrodite barely had enough time to curtsy in farewell before Hebe passed Artemis on her way inside the palace.

Artemis stopped in her tracks, acknowledging the departing princess and a growling Wolfie with a slight bow, her demeanor as stoic as ever.

Soon, Hebe and Xander disappeared from view, leaving Artemis standing beside Aphrodite.

Aphrodite narrowed her eyes, sensing Artemis' standoffish interaction with the princess. "Am I missing something?"

Artemis crossed her arms and tilted her head. "A brain, perhaps."

She carelessly flipped her tresses over her shoulder. "Why have a brain when I have beauty?"

Artemis sighed audibly, shaking her head in exasperation. "You were introduced to the Kingdom so unexpectedly that the rest of us have not had the opportunity to explain Olympus politics to you."

"Us? Who is *us*?"

"Me, Apollo, Athena, and Hermes, the Low Gods, otherwise known as The King's Bastards." After a slight pause, she added, "Although Athena will always object to being labeled a bastard."

"What must I know about the Royal dynamics?"

"Hera does her best to maintain a distinct line between her younglings and those who belong solely to Zeus." Artemis paused, choosing her words carefully, "We are not to fraternize with the prince and princess unless the King and Queen permit us."

Her lips curled into a teasing smirk. "Is that so?"

"It is so." Artemis delivered her warning with a firmness that brooked no argument. "Those are the rules." And with that, she left Aphrodite in the very same spot where she found her.

Aphrodite watched her retreating figure, and a hint of amusement played on her lips. "It would seem that I know something that Artemis does not know." Unfazed by the restrictions imposed by Olympus' politics, she surveyed the courtyard, already plotting her next move. "Rules are meant to be broken."

30

LOT IN LIFE
HERMES & ZEUS

A LITTLE IS GOOD. TOO MUCH IS TROUBLE.

Hermes stood tall before the entrance to his father's quarters. He slung his satchel across his shoulder and rested his hand casually on the sling.

I hope I can talk my way out of this one. He tapped lightly on the large frame.

The door swung open, revealing Zeus in his royal attire. The only absence was his crown. Upon seeing his youngest son, his face lit up with unbridled joy. Throwing all royal etiquette aside, he opened his arms wide and shouted in triumph.

"My son!" He gave him a big hug, lifting him off of his feet. "Come in, come in."

"My King." Still in the hug, he patted Zeus on the back. "Father, it is good to see you."

After their warm greetings, Zeus moved to sit on the

grand chair while Hermes remained standing, separated from the King by only a low circular table. While custom dictated that the King should have received Hermes in the Royal Court, the informality of the moment led Zeus to forgo the usual rigid protocols.

"What have you busied yourself with on your return home from your assignment?"

Hermes sneaked a grin. "Aphrodite, of course." *I should be careful with how I speak about his daughters, and usually, I would, but Aphrodite is a special case.*

"I have already warned you about that one." The King wagged his finger. "You are cunning. Aphrodite? Even more so. She is a full-born, after all. As gorgeous as can be, but a handful."

"That is *exactly* how I like my goddesses."

He shook his head ruefully and settled back into his seat. "After you left on your journey, I followed through with my plan and appointed a mortal named Xander to stand guard at Hebe's door."

"I must repeat the same questions I asked when you first suggested it. How can a man guard a god?"

"Xander will be more than a guard. He will be my eyes. I instructed Xander to report whatever...more importantly, *whoever* may secretly seek to rendezvous with my youngest daughter now that she is of age."

Just what I need! Another obstacle to inhibit my free rein about the palace. He forced a smile. "A father always knows what is best." *I must find a way to ingratiate myself with the new guard.*

"Now tell me, how were your travels?"

Hermes took the chair across from his father. "It was good. I love exploring the world. It amazes me that the men do something new every time I visit the earth."

He rolled his eyes. "Starting fires is something new?"

"Oh! Apparently, a new myth is spreading around the lands of a phantom feminine creature who kills any man who dares to insult her."

Zeus let out a sigh. "If only the tale were true." *Enough of this talk of men!* Zeus leaned across the table and whispered, "Did you find *him*?"

Hermes cleared his throat. He was given a task by his father and was disappointed in himself for not accomplishing it. "I did not," he answered regretfully.

Zeus broke eye contact for a moment, saddened by the news.

"Dionysus will appear when he wants to appear. You know how he is. He is so dramatic! I am sure there were times I was in the same Tavern as him, and he disguised himself so I would not recognize him."

"Why do you assume that?"

It was then he reached into his bag and presented the gift. "Because he ensured I would know he created this new drink."

Zeus opened the bottle and took a whiff. "What is it?"

"Red nectar. He calls it wine."

He swirled it around. "It looks like grapes from the vine."

"Ah, it is, but it is not. Dionysus' wine is a peculiar drink. When a lot is consumed, all our defenses come crumbling down, and we can no longer hide our true self." Sitting comfortably in his seat, he continued, "The fires are spreading in the lands in part to this new concoction. The men act out more on their every desire. A little is good. Too much is trouble."

Taking the satchel from Hermes and putting it to his side, Zeus said, "I will be sure to try it soon."

Now that that matter was settled, Hermes was more interested in what Zeus had been up to while away. "And how were *your* travels?"

The King gave a knowing grin. It was as if Hermes was a lad all over again, sitting on his knee waiting to hear another adventure story.

He pressed on, "What was it like in the Underworld?"

"Even as a little god, your eyes would light up when I told you tales about Hades."

"Why would they not? The Underworld sounds amazing."

"Your brothers and sisters would hide their faces in terror if I mentioned that name. Never you."

"Father, you know I go anywhere you want me to into the world. I always do as you say." He clasped his hands together. "Please take me to Hades the next time you visit."

All the warmth on his face grew cold. *He does not know what he is asking of me.* "Hades is a place for the dead, my son, not the living. You have so much life to live." He sighed heavily. "It is a perilous time now. Yes, you are a god of age. Yet Hades is far older. It would be nothing for him to trick you into staying for good."

"But..."

"No."

He knew his father's words were final, and so he decided not to continue to badger him.

"Besides, Hades has brought to my attention that you have been wadding in the dark waters."

Great gods! He stiffened up, swelling with pride. "Hades has been watching *me*?"

I should have known Hermes would welcome being on Hades' watch. "You are to never go into those waters again. Understand?"

He nodded his head without saying a word.

"Good. Is there anything else we need to discuss?"

Yes, there is one more thing. "Earlier, I arrived at the great throne to see Ares sitting on it."

Zeus could not contain his surprise. "It is his right, though he has shown little interest."

"I heard a commotion inside as I waited to enter the court. It turns out that Ares, acting on your behalf, banished the Gigantes Clan from ever setting foot in your Kingdom."

"What were his reasons?"

"Porphyrion, Ruler of the Gigantes Kingdom, sent his twin sons in place of him for Hebe's ceremony."

"Ares has always maintained that the Giants were untrustworthy." Zeus combed his trimmed beard in contemplation. "I find Porphyrion's choice not to attend Hebe's monumental occasion aggressive."

"More like passive-aggressive," Hermes said, pressing the tips of his fingers together. "That is not all that took place in the Royal Court. I found out that the Giant Otus requested Artemis for a bride."

Zeus gripped his jaw upon hearing the news.

"No cause for you to worry. Acting on your behalf, Ares rejected Otus' proposal and banished them from your Kingdom. However, the fact that one of the Giants fancies Artemis proves we should not jump to unsubstantiated conclusions because of Porphyrion's absence. I believe Ares acted in hast and did not weigh out the political implications of his actions."

Slowly, Zeus nodded, considering everything his son had to say. "Oh, how I have longed for Ares to take an interest in Royal matters." He rubbed his forehead in a circular motion. "I will not undermine my son's decision by overturning it. The Giant clan would be mad to even *think* about rising against the High Gods. It is in their best interest for peace to prevail."

"True. As of now, the Giants are far from being a threat. But who knows what threat they may pose in the future." The timing was right for Hermes to put his newfound knowledge of history, courtesy of the wise one, into action. "Under the urging of Athena, I have been reading the history books about yesteryear and how everything came to be."

Athena...other than Hermes, is the only one I favor. "Smart lad."

"It seems the gods are in such a long-lasting peace because you, Poseidon, and Hades drew lots to share power."

Zeus glared at him intensely but kept his lips firmly shut.

"The sharing of power keeps the peace at bay." He took a deep breath and added, "Your children, *all* your children, shared in helping the High Gods maintain power after the Great War." With a shrug of the shoulders, he offered, "Maybe we should have some shared power for our help in keeping the other kingdoms at bay by *not* siding with them should they plan another rebellion."

What foolishness is this? "The Lots for each domain of the earth has already been drawn. *You*, of all people, know this."

"I do." *I was there when the Lots were drawn.* "The sky is yours, the sea is gone, and the underworld is claimed."

I know now where this conversation is going. "The earth is neutral territory."

"Maybe the earth should not be neutral anymore."

"All this to keep a peace that is already here?"

Hermes leaned back and crossed his arms. "All this to keep the peace so that it *remains* here."

Try as he might, the King prevented Prometheus' prophecy from resurfacing in his mind. The last thing he wanted to obsess over was which of his offspring would be first to rally treachery with the Giants or whoever else.

As Zeus contemplated all that Hermes had just laid out, another matter weighed heavily on his mind, something the messenger god had broached that deeply unsettled his very soul. He lowered his voice, ensuring his wife could not overhear their conversation from the other room.

"No one must ever know what *really* happened on that fateful day my brothers and I drew lots."

"I have never told a soul," the younger god responded through clenched lips. For he knew the truth coming out would not do either of them well. "The best god won on that day. That is all that matters."

Zeus stood up as his son did the same, and they had a final embrace. "Good to have you home, my beloved."

31

THRILL OF THE HUNTER
ARTEMIS & ARES

Artemis trekked along in the heart of the ancient forest, dense with towering, moss-covered trees, having finally made her kill.

Over her shoulders, she carried a freshly slain buck. On such an occasion, her mood would have been exhilarating. However, as the day neared its end, Artemis knew her hunting ritual would have to be cut short.

Blasted Hebe and her Day of Understanding! I would rather be anywhere else!

Unexpectedly, she stopped at the unfortunate sight before her. *As if my day could not get any worse.* "Ares!"

The cruel god sat against a tree with his sword driven into the grass and a large rock in his hand. He did not acknowledge her. He only watched with an intensity that was his trademark. He bore the rugged features of a brash warrior, with a chiseled jawline and a stern resolve.

Long ago, the two would faithfully scour the forest on the hunt for the next kill and dismemberment. But over time, their outings became fewer and fewer until they stopped altogether.

Artemis! On any other day, Ares would have smiled at the chance to agitate his favorite scouting partner. However, there were already too many problems to handle without adding more. "Are you hunting alone? Where are your Nymphs?"

"They are around. They are always around."

A chorus of giggles wrapped in the wind engulfed them as if on cue.

"Silence!" Artemis commanded, and at once, the laughter ceased. She placed the lifeless buck on the forest floor with her bow and quiver strapped to her back. Her eyes were as sharp as arrows in his direction. "What are *you* doing here?"

He met her gaze with a wry smile. "And where else would I be?"

She crossed her arms, already bored with their conversation. "I do not know...tending to your princely duties in the absence of the King."

He waved away her fake concern. "The King has returned, so I am relieved of *said* duties."

Clashing sounds rang through the trees from Ares swiping the heavy stone at an angle against his blade.

"The King's return does not negate your other royal responsibilities. But why should I try to impart knowledge to one as stubborn as you?" Ares was so busy sharpening his sword that Artemis wondered if he had heard a word she had said.

"I am in no mood to play with you today, Artemis."

The only time he is genuinely happy is when he plunges his weapon into blood and guts. She shook her head ruefully. "Never before has there been such a miserable prince."

"My mother always told me I was one of a kind," he mumbled, more to himself than her. As Ares' eyes fell upon her leather boots and traveled toward her upper body, he felt the allure of each piece of her garment. The supple hide of the black panther tunic, molded to her sculpted form, left very little to his imagination. *I can see why the Gigantes twin was willing to relinquish his freedom and succumb to marriage.*

"Why do you have a cut out on one side of your tunic?"

She looked down at her leg poking out in full view. "The slit provides me greater movement and flexibility when on the hunt."

Slowly, he rubbed his chin. "If one slit provides all that you say, *two* slits would make one unstoppable."

"No matter what I wear, I am unstoppable."

Obviously, she is in one of her moods. "Today, you should regard me as your hero, not your enemy."

"Why today of all days?"

"Because not too long ago, I banished the Giant Otus for requesting your hand in marriage."

With a hand planted firmly on one hip, Artemis gaped in disbelief. "Without informing me of his intentions? You do not speak for me!"

He wanted to give her a standing ovation for her performance but concluded his time was better spent perfecting his weapon. "Did I not already tell you I am in no mood to play? We are alone. There is no need for you to put on a show."

She averted her gaze, refusing to meet his triumphant stare.

"Unless I was mistaken and you have some interest in Otus. Would you like me to grant his request?"

Preferring to ignore his question, she asked one of her own. "What do you think?"

"I *know,* when it comes to marriage, I *can* speak for you."

Unfortunately, Ares knows me far too well. Artemis saw no point in arguing her point, knowing full well he was correct. Admitting he was right grated against her pride more than anything else. "Forget about all of that! If what you said is true and the King has returned, Hebe's ceremony should commence shortly, correct?"

Ares nodded. "The servants are preparing the Royal Court as we speak, and we will celebrate Princess in all her glory."

"Do you not think her celebration is premature?"

The sound of stone striking metal ceased. *I see today she intends for us to battle it out—why else would she try to rile me up by mentioning Hebe.*

"Everyone denies it to my face; however, I know I am not the only one who believes Hebe has not truly achieved godly knowledge and understanding."

The prince plunged the sword back into the dirt and stood up. "What Hebe has achieved or lacks is of no concern to you or any of Zeus' bastards."

Artemis remained undeterred. "Do you want to know

something funny? With you, a prince with little to no ambition, Hebe, a princess with no sense and even less courage, and that other one, as legend has it, born too ugly to love..."

Ares remained silent, allowing Artemis to continue.

"Proves all of us bastards have outshined all of you born of royal blood."

She is much too pleased with herself. "Remind me, Artemis. What was your gift to the King on your Day of Understanding?"

Artemis' eyes gleamed with fierce pride as she recounted the best moment of her life. "Before Helios began pulling the sun across the sky, I found the Titan's son, the great Prometheus, chained on a huge rock for eternity."

Artemis' voice was filled with pride as she recounted her daring feat, her words punctuated by the thud of Ares' footsteps drawing nearer.

"And right when I heard the eagle cry from overhead, I took out my dagger, sliced the son of the Titan, and pulled out his bloody liver without any mercy."

Ares remained silent, his intense stare fixed just inches from her face.

With a triumphant smile, she continued, "I gifted our King a piece of his immortal enemy, and since that fateful day, no one before or after is courageous enough to do anything so grand."

Finally, he responded, "My dear Artemis. Prepare to have your most prized memory shattered by the one *you* deem a coward."

But before Ares could depart, Artemis intercepted him,

her foot firmly planted on the deer. "Wait! Are you not going to skin my buck?"

"No. I have Hebe's ceremony to prepare for." He gently tugged on her furry strap, his voice carrying a bit of teasing. "And be sure to change into something more elegant for once. You would not want to disappoint the princess."

32

A GIFT AND A CURSE
THE ROYAL FAMILY

On cue, Apollo raised his hands high, his fingers gracefully moving through the air, and then brought them down in perfect harmony with a sea of instruments. The inspiring melody resonated like a divine symphony, befitting the exalted audience of gods, goddesses, and creatures alike.

The King and Queen of the Gods, Zeus and Hera, graced their thrones, dressed in garments of splendor. On a gods Day of Understanding, it was customary to venture into distant lands and return bearing gifts for the King. Hebe, having just completed her maiden trip, was poised to deliver her inaugural address in the Great Hall.

As the anticipation in the chamber swelled, the High Gods Demeter and Poseidon stood just outside the closed doors the Hall. Demeter extended her hand toward Hebe, offering her a reassuring squeeze before taking hold of Poseidon's arm.

The double doors opened, and Hebe stood to the side, away from view, and watched as the two High Gods marched in step with the music down the red carpet to their designated seats at the front of the assembly.

In the *second* row of the Hall, the Low Gods were seated: Athena, Artemis, Aphrodite, and Hermes. While some might have perceived their placement as a sign of their father's favor, Artemis understood the underlying truth. The Queen orchestrated this seating arrangement, ensuring that the bastards remained close enough to the throne to be reminded of the vast chasm separating them from it.

Artemis looked passed Aphrodite and made eye contact with Hermes. She then motioned her head directly in front of them.

Hallirhothios sat in the most prestigious row, and Hermes did not need Artemis to explain the scene before them. *Poseidon's bastard sits in front while we stare at the back of his head.* He nodded his head in silent agreement with Artemis.

Aphrodite stared at the Queen's sparkling crown and jewels. She loathed how beautiful the goddess looked on her throne and how all eyes were drawn to her. "The color of Hera's gown does nothing for her," Aphrodite whispered to Artemis. "I expect better from a queen."

"That is your first mistake." Artemis gave a cheeky smile. "I expect nothing from a cow."

The goddesses giggled to themselves, their small commotion drawing Athena's ire. She nudged Artemis with her elbow. "Behave, you two," she commanded sharply.

Artemis rolled her eyes while Aphrodite paid Athena no

mind. Instead, she whispered gleefully to Hermes, who sat on her other side. "Did you hear? Artemis just called Hera a cow."

"Tell Artemis, if Hera's a cow..." Hermes leaned as close to Aphrodite's ear as possible, staring straight ahead. "I am a thirsty calf."

Suddenly, Aphrodite no longer found the joke funny. "I will do no such thing," she huffed.

Awaiting her entry into the ceremony, Princess Hebe was extremely nervous, having second-guessed her present. Rather than returning a long-lost son to the King, she contemplated how her parents would react to receiving a wild beast from the wilderness.

Why did Apollo say my my gift is poison? And is it true what Ares said? Is Hephaestus really the pariah of Olympus?

Twisting her fingers together, she glanced down the other end of the empty hallway. *Where is my brother?*

Ares had never called her bluff before.

Does he really mean for me to go through with my presentation alone?

Her thoughts floundered when Apollo's heavenly voice sang her gifted theme, and she took her first steps through the doors into the Great Hall:

There she is
Dressed in splendor
Filled with the sun and sky above
Forgiveness and mercy
We are not worthy

Yet she will bless us anyway
And there she is
Eyes of wonder
Filled with the moon and stars above
Laughter and healing
We are receiving
So let us honor her this day

The inspiring song came to an end as the youngest goddess, Hebe stood at the foot of the steps that led to the thrones. The audience, in awe of her pure and unspoiled beauty, struggled to contain their admiration.

King Zeus radiated with pride from his throne. Hebe, his youngest daughter, held a special place in his heart and was cherished by all mankind. Unofficially, she was known as the People's Princess.

A tiara graced her head, with shining diamonds like the stars above. Her hair was elegantly gathered into a bun, with a few artfully loosened strands framing her face. Her cheeks held a delicate touch of amber, and her lips were tinted with a soft shade of pink.

The Queen had personally selected a gorgeous gown for her, a pristine white creation with jewels interwoven into the fabric. Her upper chest was exposed for the first time, drawing attention to a hint of cleavage and the seemingly out-of-place metal necklace Ares gifted her earlier in the day.

Even so, Hera looked proudly at her daughter as she stopped at the top of the aisle in full view of Demeter sitting in the front row. *My darling daughter, the spitting image of my beloved Demeter. If only Hestia were here to complete this perfect picture.* She could tell Hebe was fighting nervousness but tried her best to appear confident.

The King stared at the lone empty seat in the front row—taunting him. *Ares should have escorted Hebe down the aisle, yet he is nowhere to be seen!* A soft touch from his wife was enough for his fury to evaporate into the air. *I will deal with Ares' insubordination at another time. I will not let him ruin Hebe's special day.*

With a nod from Hera, Zeus addressed the Princess, trying in vain to suppress his fatherly pride in his gorgeous daughter. "Princess Hebe."

"Dad and mom!" *Oh no!* Hebe paused a moment as muffled laughter rang through the crowd. She always forgot to follow the protocol in the royal assembly. *May Thanatos take me now!*

It burned Hebe all the more to hear Artemis' distinct laughter among the few. Once the crowd's giggles had subsided, Hebe briefly paused to collect her thoughts and readdressed the court with a proper curtsey. "My King and Queen of the Gods."

"And how was your first trek into the world as a goddess," The Queen asked.

"It was more than I could ever dream."

Hera beamed as only a mother could at the successful trip. "I hope you remember you are to return with a gift for your King."

Shuffling her feet, she mumbled, "I did return with a gift."

"Very well, daughter." Zeus motioned for her to continue her story. "Where did you go?"

"The usual places we journey to on our first outing. I made sure I was not glanced upon in my goddess form by mankind."

"That is very well of you." *Why is she so evasive?* "But again, where did you go?"

She fiddled with her thumbs in front of her. Her heart was pounding so loud in her chest that she wondered if even the back row could hear it. "Athens, Arcadia, the Unknown Territories..."

A gasp of horror swept through the crowd.

Hera leaned forward in outrage. "Hebe!"

Zeus shot a furious glare at his wife, silencing any further interruptions.

He then turned his gaze back toward Hebe and lowered his voice. "You...did...*what*?"

She swallowed hard, unable to find a way out of the mess she created. "I went to the Unknown Territories. I just wanted to see..."

He cut her off abruptly, "No god is to ever set foot on their first journey into the Unknown Territories alone."

"I did not think..."

"You did not *think* that is correct." He tightened his fist into a ball, digging his fingernails into the palms of his hands.

"I am sorry."

'Sorry' is not good enough. "You will be punished for this direct disobedience."

Hera placed a calming hand on Zeus' arm, hoping to quell

the storm of anger that threatened to erupt in a burst of lightning.

Just then, the double doors squeaked open, and everyone turned to look at the sudden intruder.

"Ares!" Hebe said underneath her breath, unable to keep the smile from her face.

Ares burst through the towering doors, his steps echoing down the grand aisle. Clad in a white tunic, he obeyed Hebe's directive and mirrored the color of her gown. His short garment had slits strategically placed on either side, accentuating his sculpted thigh muscles with every stride he took. The contrast between the white fabric and the sun-kissed skin of his legs created a striking visual, commanding the attention of the onlookers.

The Prince's feminine admirers could not help but swoon in delight, their hearts fluttering at the mere sight of him. Their eyes eagerly settled on the outline of his prominent bulge, drinking in every movement, overcome with desire. Meanwhile, their masculine counterparts could only watch with clenched fists and simmering jealousy, unable to match the magnetism that Ares effortlessly exuded.

"What an attention whore," Hermes muttered loud enough for both Aphrodite and Artemis to hear.

Artemis shrugged, rethinking the King's earlier proposal. *Marrying Ares does have some perks.*

Zeus drummed his fingers against the armrest with vigor, watching Ares make his way to the front row. There, he enveloped his favorite uncle in a warm embrace before turning to greet his beloved aunt Demeter with reverence, pressing tender kisses upon both her hands. Zeus rolled his strained eyes. *Leave it to my son to show up late and still find ways to waste my time.*

Once Ares finished his greetings, he stood beside his sister; his towering presence cast a protective shadow over her petite form.

As Hebe turned to face him, his eyes caught sight of her necklace, and a smile graced his lips. Gently, he placed his hands on her upper arms, feeling the tremors beneath her skin. Pressing a kiss to one cheek, then the other, he leaned closer to her ear. "Remember," his voice lowered to a soft murmur meant for her ears alone, "be brave."

Hebe exhaled deeply, feeling a wave of relief flood through her. Side by side, they turned to face the two rulers of the gods.

Perched regally upon her throne, Queen Hera beamed with pride as her two darlings stood before their subjects. *Ares and Hebe!* She clutched the cream pearls that circled her long neck at her sudden moment of realization. *The Prince and Princess shall...*

Before she could finish her thought, Ares said, "King and Queen of the Gods, please excuse my interruption."

"I am surprised you decided to join us."

"Likewise, I was surprised by your invitation." The crowd erupted into laughter, and Ares followed tradition by bowing his upper body forward.

Zeus settled back onto the throne, his menacing blue eyes

still on his disobedient daughter. "Your sister took it upon herself to visit the Unknown Territories."

Ares stood firm, not intimidated by the great throne he had recently sat upon nor the King who was now on it. "This I know."

Zeus and Hera exchanged stunned glances.

"I know because I accompanied her."

"Ares," Hera's whisper was barely audible as she uttered his name in disbelief.

Undeterred, Ares pressed on, his hand resting on the hilt of his sword. "It is not a crime for the princess to go to the Territories with another god."

He is sadly mistaken if he thinks this confession will appease my anger. "You would *dare* take your sister to a place so precarious?"

Ares gestured toward Hebe. "As you can see, she is in one piece."

"How long will you be able to say that about yourself once I..."

"Zeus!" Hera cut in. Her pleading expression was enough to tame her husband temporarily.

Zeus rose from his throne with a thunderous command. "Guards! Remove the assembly from these proceedings!"

His voice echoed through the grand hall, sending shivers down the spines of those present. The guards sprang into action, swiftly ushering the attendees out of the room. Yet, instead of abating, Zeus' fury grew with each passing moment, casting a heavy atmosphere over the chamber.

"The prince and princess did not commit any crime and

are back home safe and sound." Hera nodded with encouragement. "Go on with the proper procedure as before."

Zeus still had doubts, but reluctantly, he let the issue drop for the sake of tradition. Listening to his wife, he carried on, "What did you bring back in your travels?"

The two siblings shared a fleeting glance, a silent communication passing between them. Hebe's gaze remained lowered, deferring to Ares to take the lead.

"Our gift for you is sitting in the dungeon as we speak."

What have they done? Slowly, Zeus leaned forward. "What is this gift?"

Ares looked cocky as he revealed, "Your son." And for added drama, he dared speak the unspeakable name, "Hephaestus."

Hera gasped, her hand flying to her mouth to stifle any further sound. It was as if an unseen force gripped her insides, twisting and pulling at her very core, leaving her feeling unsteady and unsettled.

Zeus dug his fingers into the craved armrest. *This Ares has always been the bane of my existence.* "You dare to bring *him* back *here*?"

Ares could not resist. "Shall I have him again thrown from the All-Seeing Room?"

What? "Father?" Tears began to stream down Hebe's face. *Hephaestus was right to be scared for his life. I should never have brought him back home.*

Zeus stormed toward Ares, barely able to subdue his rage.

Impulsively, the warrior's fingers clenched around the hilt of his sword, though Ares knew better than to unsheathe it. An act of brazen treason could not be so easily retracted.

They stared each other down, eye to eye, without saying a word.

Finally, the King glanced back toward his Queen. "I will go to the dungeons alone!"

"Zeus, Zeus!" Hera called after him as he burst through the doors. She hurriedly followed, leaving the two siblings alone in the Royal Court.

The horror etched on the King's face would have been satisfying to the Prince if it were not for the anguished cries of his Queen Mother echoing in the halls. Dread crept over him. *What have I done?*

"This is all my fault." Hebe buried her face in her hands, sobbing uncontrollably. She had believed she was guiding her long, lost brother toward a life of luxury, but instead, she had condemned him to the depths of Hades.

Ares' heart ached at the sight of her distress. Without hesitation, he held her in his arms and comforted her as she buried her head into his chest. "The worst is over now."

The irony was not lost on Hebe. On her Day of Understanding, she was reduced to a cradled babe.

"Hush." Ares stroked her hair tenderly, not caring about the tears and drool pooling on his bare skin. "Do not cry."

She could not stop her tears so simply. "You *lied* to the King of the Gods for me."

"Hebe, not only will I lie for you, I will steal for you." He cupped her chin and added, "I will *kill* for you."

"I should have listened to your warnings." *I was a fool to think I could ever be equal to my siblings.* "Why did you help me?"

"Father already hates me. I can take his scorn. You cannot." He stopped stroking her dark hair long enough to look her in the eyes. "I will always be here to help you. And even though you fight it, you will always be my little sister."

33

INDECENT PROPOSAL
ARES & HERA

After some time spent comforting Hebe in the Royal Hall, the only other person's well-being weighing on Ares' mind was the Queen.

He was a chaotic ball of force, storming through the palace halls, not caring who had to dart out of his path lest they get trampled. Each stride of his powerful legs sent a gush of air, swirling around the slits of his tunic, exposing his nakedness underneath to passersby—a particular detail Artemis failed to mention when highlighting her new style of dress.

Undoubtedly, he resembled a mad god to those who did not know why he charged forward as though the Olympus Halls were the pathway to an unsuspecting village. Whatever others might have thought, Ares did not care. His only concern was to catch his mother if she had a downward spiral from the unfolding messiness.

The warrior prince braced himself as he reached the Quarters of the King and Queen, barging his way into every room. As the firstborn son, he saw no need to knock or be discreet. What belonged to the King was also his, and the same went for the Queen's possessions. He scanned each lavish room until, at last, he spotted his mother seated in the formal living area, staring into nothingness.

For a mother to labor in pain only to have her babe ripped from her bosom and returned many years later was a torment too inconceivable for him to imagine.

All it took was for her to lift her head in his direction, and time reverted to that dreadful night on Mount Olympus. Her eldest son towered in height and broad in muscle, and yet, through her eyes, he was small enough to cradle in a blanket.

Hera did not know if she stood up or if Ares lifted her to her feet. All she knew was what she felt. Her arms wrapped securely around his neck, and his arms tightened around her back.

I will never forget the sound of my brother's cry and the crash unleashed when he hit the waters below. How much louder were his cries to the ears of his mother?

Fading memories of Ares as a youngling resurfaced, depicting Hera rocking him in her arms after he returned home covered in bruises from a rough day of adventure. Although Ares thought he was easing her pain, he could not escape the feeling that she was soothing his pain as well.

Finally, the Queen was first to pull out of the embrace only to search Ares' troubled eyes for answers to a thousand questions she had in her mind, with no words to speak them.

Taking her hand, he brought her fingers to his lips and kissed them. "Where is the King?"

Shaking her head, Hera fiddled with the material of her dress and sat back down on the sofa. She felt drained as if all her energy was zapped out of her. "I chased your father as far as I could. He wanted to go alone to see...*Hephaestus*." The cursed name could barely roll off her tongue without her wincing in anguish.

He nodded at her response. Ares did not want to think the worst, but it would not surprise him if he heard another cry followed by a loud splash below.

She ran her fingers along her neck, unsure if she really wanted the answer to her next question. "What does *he* look like now? Hephaestus."

"A monster," he answered honestly. There were many gods and monsters, and Hephaestus did not resemble any *god* he had ever seen.

"He is still ugly."

"I cannot say for sure. However, he has a hunch, and his stance is twisted. He wears a hood, so I did not see his face, but *your* hazel eyes stared back at me."

Had anyone else made the comparison, Hera would rightly consider it an insult. However, coming from her beloved son, she took no offense. "I remember his eyes."

Sitting beside her, Ares confessed, "I blocked out that time in my life. The day he fell mere feet away from where we now sit."

These were memories that Hera had hoped would remain dormant. She whispered, "Ares..."

He continued, his voice tinged with lingering pain, "I remember thinking if my father could order the death of a newborn son for not being perfect, what chance did I have?"

"Oh, Ares, no." *I did not know how much of what happened made him suffer so.* Her heart ached for her son. "Why would you think such a thing?"

Ares met her gaze, his eyes holding traces of the youth he once was. "I was a youngling, mother...with youngling thoughts. I became afraid of my father that very day—afraid of what he may do if enraged enough." He was once a babe with the fears of a young one, but now he was no longer a youth. No longer fearful. "As I got older and less afraid, I felt I had to protect you from my father."

"Your father would never hurt me."

Such a half-truth. "Not physically. I know that now." He brushed the edge of his thumb tenderly against her cheek. "He hurts you in other ways, ways I cannot protect you from. No matter how much I want to."

His hand lingered against her face for a moment longer, caught in the trap of her beauty. Although she looked put together, Ares knew the truth. Underneath all the layers of clothing, she was broken. *If a mother's love for her little one is said to be priceless, how much more is the love of a son for his mother?*

"When Hebe was born, I would not let her out of my sight for fear Zeus may grow angry one day and hurt her too. But he is good to her. I know now he would never harm her." The Prince rubbed his forehead, still in deep thought. "Remember when I was a child and said I did not want a little sister?"

"Yes, I do."

"After Hephaestus fell and you were again with child, I vowed to the River Styx that whatever you birthed, I would love and protect him...*or* her. Always."

Everything was falling into place. Ares said all the things she wanted to hear. He was never one to self-reflect, and Hera did not want to let the moment pass. "And I gave birth to Hebe. Who you love and protect. Always."

"I would do *anything* for her."

She placed a hand on his knee. "Anything?"

"Yes, anything." *What is so hard to believe?* "I would die for her."

"That is well and good, but would you *marry* her?"

"What?" His body jerked, causing her to remove her hand from his knee. "No, I would not!"

"Why? How is marriage worse than death? I am not asking for your life."

"Oh, but you are, mother. And Hebe is my little sister!"

She let him regain his composure before again digging in. "The gods marry siblings all the time." Getting up, she poured him a warm drink. "Zeus is my brother. Your grandparents are siblings. Why, your great-great-grandmother and your great-grandfather are mother and son."

Taking the drink from her, he mused, "Then shall I marry you?"

"In a perfect world," she cupped his cheek lovingly as she spoke, his stumble prickling her palm, and kissed his forehead. Again, sitting next to him, she added, "You would be an honorable husband to me, but I am already married. Your sister is *not*."

"Hebe and I compared to you and my father—it is *different* between us."

"How so?"

"When Zeus was born, you were..." his voice trailed off, knowing that being eaten by her father was not the memory he wanted to bring up to prove his point, "...you were not raised together. So when you finally met Zeus, you could develop romantic love for each other."

That part of her memory was a blur. It was better to have a hazy past than to remember being devoured alive. "This is true. I was not raised with my brother, Zeus."

"Hebe would always be with me before I headed off to war with men. I love her. But not in *that* way."

Returning from battle and having Aphrodite draw me a bath was a unique experience. Her water was not as hot as what Hebe would draw, and her scents were not as spicy as Hebe would mix, yet the desire Aphrodite stirred within me is nothing I have ever felt for my little sister.

His inability to think this through will not deter me. "Once you are united, you will no longer be siblings. You will be husband and wife. Romantic love can and *will* come in time if you marry her."

Ares squinted while observing the calculating goddess he knew all too well. "Why do you care to push us together all of a sudden?"

"I saw a vision when you and Hebe were standing before the assembly, dressed in white. I see how much you love her and how much she loves you. The Prince and princess shall marry."

Ares stood up in a flash. With his back to her, facing the balcony, he confessed, "I want to hear the snapping of broken bones. I want to smell the stench of burnt flesh. I want to witness the depravity of men when they declare another group of men, no different from themselves, enemies..."

His impassioned soliloquy only caused her to roll her eyes.

"My home is down there, watching the earth fill with blood. It will never be here in the skies sitting on some stuffy throne."

"Hades is seeking a wife, and nothing stops him from requesting your sister if she remains unwed."

He raised a scruffy brow. "Hades?"

"Yes. And he threatens war if Zeus cannot find him a spouse."

She is fearmongering. "Zeus would *never* allow it. He has no intention of mending ties with the Underworld. Zeus wants to keep Hades at arm's length and no closer."

"Is that what you think? Your father is weighing his options. If not Hades, he is considering marrying your sister to Poseidon's son."

"Ahhh, Hallirhothios." Ares stroked his jawline. *If she is playing games, I will play one of my own.* He moved his fingers in the air as if figuring out a complicated puzzle. "Joining forces with Poseidon makes the most sense if Zeus wants to defuse a potential threat of rebellion from the Underworld."

Her beautifully stoned face cracked with worry. *He is so*

driven by the game of war even his dear sister is reduced to a piece on a military board!

"Even though Hallirhothios is a bastard, he is the only child of Poseidon and, as such, heir to his father's Kingdom."

Hera's nails dug into her palms with the release of her clenched mouth, "And what of *our* kingdom?"

Our Kingdom! Calmly, the warrior prince turned to examine every inch of his mother, seeing that her devious plan was written over her entire face. "You do not want our Kingdom divided between other gods. You want *your* legacy to be intact. Herein lies the *real* reason you are pushing for my marriage to Hebe."

"My legacy is *your* legacy. Everything I fight for is to the benefit of my younglings. Did you not see all the eyes fixated on you in the Royal Hall? Did you not hear the gasps with each step of your sturdy legs? Ares, the handsome Prince who possesses the strength of a thousand men and holds the keys to the Kingdom. The gods silently envy your inheritance while all the goddesses compete for your attention."

"The gods do not scare me. And why should I worry about the goddesses?"

"Because they will do anything to gain power. The goddesses will never know how to love you truly. The pure of heart will be last, but the victorious one will be *cutthroat.*"

Cutthroat. His eyes flashed with the rush of ichor through his veins.

Hera pressed her nails into his skin, not caring that, for him, pain equaled pleasure. "My words are not to inflame your desires. Such a conniving goddess *will* be your downfall.

I wish to protect Hebe from the same fate of marrying a ruthless god that would seek her crown and take advantage of her gentle kindness. What better match for her than a god who already has his crown? A prince. Her brother. My very son."

"Well, fortunately, you are in luck." He placed his cup down on the table. "You now have another prince, another brother, another son to marry Hebe off to."

She had already forgotten Hephaestus had returned.

"Like you and Zeus, Hebe and Hephaestus did not grow up together, and so love will foster between them." It was only fitting for him to fearmonger his mother like she did to him. "The more I think about it, the more I like the idea of their marriage."

Her eyes flashed, and she jumped up from her seat. "You would offer your *sister* to a monster?"

"No different than you offering your *daughter* to one." His voice lowered an octave, and his face hardened. "Hephaestus may be a monster on the outside, but I *am* one on the inside." Stepping directly in front of Hera, he was an inch from her face. "Make *no* mistake of that, mother."

The Queen turned away from her son, her body trembling in response to his outlandish counter-proposal of Hebe and Hephaestus.

It was a silent standoff, a mother torn between her love for her son and her constant need always to have her way.

Ares firmly grasped her shoulders, his skilled thumbs kneading her tense muscles. Although she was angry, he understood that time would eventually mend the rift between them. "I will always love you." He leaned down and planted a reassuring kiss on the delicate curve of her neck. Almost magically, her taut muscles gradually relaxed under the tender caress of his lips.

Oh! Ares knows precisely how to pull at my heartstrings. The last thing Hera wanted was to reprove her son's affections. However, drastic times called for extreme measures, so she remained frozen, stubbornly refusing to return his profession of love.

Her lack of response left him feeling defeated. "Good night, Mother, my Queen."

Before his arms could fall back to his sides in surrender, Hera covered his hand with hers. With her back still facing him, she closed her eyes and felt his kiss on both sets of fingers, and then he withdrew from her.

"I charge you to make sure Hebe's presents are safely delivered to her room," she whispered.

"I will."

She listened until his steps faded entirely into silence, leaving her alone with her inner thoughts. "This conversation is not yet over, my son. The Prince and princess *shall* marry."

34

BLACKOUT
ZEUS & HEPHAESTUS

'FROM YOUR DECLARED OFFSPRING, WILL COME ONE WHO WILL DEFEAT YOU AND TAKE ALL THAT IS YOURS'

HEPHAESTUS SAT HUNCHED IN THE CORNER OF HIS DIM CELL. The insects that scuttled across the cold, stone floor were his only companions. The lone sound reverberating through the chamber was the monotonous water drip from a leaky ceiling, forming a steadily growing puddle in the far corner.

He grabbed the satchel tucked away in the corner and strapped it over his body. Although he had stuffed the old leather bag with food for his journey to the Palace, the abrosia offered to him by Hebe was enough to fill him with satisfaction.

His thoughts drifted back to his time beneath the sea when his only friends were the silent, red fishes that swam with him. They never spoke nor understood his words, but they were his sole company, providing a one-sided conversation that eased his solitude.

And yet this prison, as Hebe had called it, was more than I could have hoped for. But what happens to me when the King and Queen learn of my presence?

Hephaestus heard heavy steps coming down the pathway and quickly stood up, his jaws dropping in shock and awe.

Zeus had turned the corner, his regal crown perched atop his head. His imposing figure commanded immediate attention, and there was no mistaking who he was even before he uttered a word. His were the arms that could hurl lightning bolts with a mere thought. The same hands grasped the dungeon's cold, unforgiving metal bars.

Seeing his father's approach, Hephaestus retreated against the damp stone wall. He slumped down, his body a portrait of defeated resignation. The solemn expression on Zeus' face conveyed the verdict before any words were spoken.

Hephaestus understood all hopes of reconciliation were shattered. At this point, he could only wish for a swift end to his wretched existence.

"My god...my king," he whispered in humility.

"Stand up," Zeus ordered in a low voice. "Let me examine you."

"As you wish." Hephaestus stood up wobbly, trying to catch his balance as he left the shaded corner and entered the light.

What a sight to behold. Still separated by imposing metal bars, Zeus scrutinized his son with a pencil-sharp gaze. "Your leg...you were born with a crooked leg. Your back is hunched over...that I remember." *Never before had I seen a god so lopsided.* "Remove your hood at once."

Without question, Hephaestus did as his King commanded, revealing his horrid face.

Upon beholding the left side of his son's face, Zeus faltered. "Bu-but that scar...that was from the fall." Anyone else would have gasped at the sight of an ugly god, yet all Zeus could focus on was the beauty in the pitiful eyes staring back at him.

He attempted to straighten his posture, but his back refused to obey.

"What do *you* remember?"

His question was vague, but Hephaestus knew precisely what he was referring to. "I try *not* to remember."

Zeus persisted, "What do you remember?"

He thought for a moment as the images flooded back into his mind's eye. "Falling...falling so far and for so long. And then a splash. I remember struggling for breath and red fishes all around me. Then darkness."

The King listened intently. "That is all?"

"Yes." He lowered his head as though he failed the test. "That is all."

A lone tear trickled down the King's weathered cheek, followed by another, and yet another, each tracing a path of sorrow and regret. A lump formed in his throat that made swallowing almost impossible. "Then you do not remember that right before your fall...I was holding you in my arms."

The limp god glanced up, too shocked to respond. *I knew I*

was unwanted, but I did not realize it was my father who tossed me into the sea.

Zeus wiped away his steam of tears, forcing himself not to look away from his son. "We gods are a prideful bunch. Each youngling I had was more beautiful than the last. And then you were born with no...no...symmetry. I felt ashamed. It was the first and only time I had ever felt such an emotion. And tears fall from my eyes now because, after all this time, I am feeling the same emotion again."

Hephaestus' leg protested against the strain of supporting his weary frame, prompting him to shift his weight against the cold, unforgiving wall.

"I have many regrets in life. By far, my biggest is the night of your fall. Yes, you were thrown away, but you were never truly abandoned. I know that may be hard for you to understand." He gestured toward Hephaestus' cloak, decorated with the exact Royal Seal he had swed into his gown.

Cautiously, he nodded even though Zeus was right—he did not truly understand. "When I was still a babe, the goddess Maia held me to her breast when I needed a mother's love. She kept me clothed and fed, and...she would sing the loveliest of songs as I slept. The older I became, the less of her I saw until...I never saw her again." He shut his eyes tightly and did not open them again until he heard metal scraping against the hard floor.

As Zeus opened the cell gate and took several steps forward, Hephaestus' heart raced with dread. "I only ask one thing of you."

Will he ask me about who found me? His heart felt as though it would explode at the thought. *Will I have to keep my promise to Ares and lie to my King?*

When the King stretched forth his hand, the memories of being hurled off the mountain by his own father were still hauntingly fresh. Such a betrayal ran deep, and he cowered further into the corner.

What have I done? Zeus understood how a gesture, such as a hand from him, could seem like a threat to Hephaestus. Still, his hand remained. "Forgive me, my son."

Hephaestus' hazel eyes widened, and he took a deep breath. *Is he really asking me for forgiveness?* The longer Zeus waited for a response, the more Hephaestus realized that it was so. "Of course I forgive you! I forgive you and more."

Before he could reconsider, Zeus pulled his newfound son into a long embrace, with only Hephaestus' pouch preventing their torso from touching. *If Prometheus had his way, this would be the son poised for revenge. But no longer.* "You will always have a home on Mount Olympus from now on. This I promise you."

35

S.M.I.L.F
HERMES & HERA

A soft but distinct knock echoed through the chamber's ornate door, drawing Hera's attention.

As she approached with a flip of her wrist, the doors swung open, revealing a tall, slender god framed against the corridor's shadows.

She clapped her hands in delight, "Hermes!"

A playful smirk graced his face. The young god allowed himself a moment to savor the sight of his Queen in all her glory. She had shed her ceremonial attire, opting instead for a captivating green gown that delicately traced the curves of her feminine form, accentuating her striking hazel eyes.

If it were *possible* for a god to have a crush on his stepmother, then Hermes would have a crush on Hera. But it was not possible. He loved his life too much to dare draw his father's wrath.

"My Queen," Hermes said with a formal bow. His eyes

shifted from one end of the room to the other. "Are you alone?"

She peeked out into the hallway to make sure *he* was alone. "Yes, I am alone." She leaned against the frame and left enough room for him to enter. "Hurry up and come in."

He was not accustomed to visiting the royal Quarters so late in the evening. However, since Hebe's Day of Understanding had come to such an abrupt ending, the young god took a chance the Queen would not object to a private audience so close to bedtime.

She touched her hip and tranced her eyes all over him. "Hermes, my *little* orphan god."

He smiled in response to her playful address, a name she would often use, though there was one aspect he could not help but contest—he was certainly no longer little.

"I know my husband sent you on one of his errands. Were you able to visit your mother on your journey?"

My mother? Hermes understood that Hera acknowledging Zeus' former mistress meant she felt no threat whatsoever from her presence. *And why would she be threatened by the dead?* He mused to himself. "No, I did not visit Maia's resting place."

"Pity," she said, only for pleasantries sake. Hera gave him a once over, smiling brightly. "You look well. It is always good to see you."

Is she truly alone? He glanced behind his shoulder toward the closed bedroom door. "Where is my father?"

She huffed and brushed his words away with her hand. "He is busy handling something."

Hmmm. Father did not give me any details of his journey to the Underworld. I shall see if I can get the information from his wife instead. "What something is he handling?"

"It does not matter now." Grabbing his hands, she pulled him across the room and sat him beside her on the couch. "Come tell me all I need to know."

Their routine was always the same. Hermes played the role of Hera's eyes and ears, a job he secretly relished. It gave him the perfect pretext for private moments with the most influential god among them all. It also gave him a legitimate excuse to admire her stunning beauty without the guilt of betraying his father's honor. "There is much you need to know."

"Do tell."

"Well, earlier, Ares decided to pass the time sitting on the King's thrown doling out judgments as he saw fit."

She slapped her thighs. "Wonderful."

Quickly, he held up a finger. "Not so fast. In the Royal Court, the twin Otus from the Giant Clan professed his intention to marry Artemis."

"Good!" Hera reached over to the jar on the small table before them, but Hermes intercepted her, gently taking the jar and pouring out a cup for her. "I want nothing more than to have Artemis out of my sight and away from the palace."

"Well, I am sorry to inform you that Ares refused Otus' offer and banished the twins from your Kingdom." He handed her the cup.

"Why would he do such a thing and block the chance of her marrying? I will get to the bottom of this."

"And what of him banishing prominent members of the Giant Clan from your Kingdom? Why make an unnecessary enemy?"

Before she sipped the drink, she muttered, "Oh, to hades with them!"

He suppressed a chuckle. Hera's natural spunk amassed him to no end. "That is not all you need to know."

"Tell me more." She took a sip and returned the golden cup to the table.

"My queen." In a hushed tone, he declared, "You are in danger."

Hera did not scare easily, and it had been long since she last felt any danger. But she was by far intrigued. "How so?"

"A certain goddess is determined to become Queen by snatching your crown."

Who would dare even to speak such a thing? She curled her hands into a ball. "Treason."

"Of the highest order," he agreed with an undertone of laughter.

Her eyes darted over to him accusingly. "Then why do you make fun?"

"It is humorous that a goddess could be so...ambitious."

"Yes, hilarious," she said, clearly not amused. "Tell me, who dares to usurp my role of Queen of the Gods?"

Leaning into her, with a hush, he asked, "You tell me first, what business is Zeus handling?"

And here we go! Hermes only gives after he gets. He uses his words as currency and, with it, has become the wealthiest god this side of Olympia—figuratively speaking.

Hera rose from her seat, attempting to create some distance between them. Yet, Hermes was quick on her heels, refusing to let her slip away from his inquiries.

"Hebe and Ares were in the Unknown Territories. Somehow they found my son..." she braced herself before saying the forbidden name, "*Hephaestus.*"

How could this happen, and I missed it? I make it a point to catch up with everyone on my return from faraway lands, and this time I did not have the time to check in with Hebe. He was not used to being caught by surprise. *How much better would it be for me to have told the Queen what Hebe did instead of the other way around?* "What happened? How is Zeus involved?"

"Ares and Hebe brought Hephaestus into the dungeons. Zeus is talking to him now."

"Do you know what Zeus plans to do with Hephaestus?"

"I do not know."

Imagine having a newborn torn from its' mother and thrown into the abyss. She must be devastated by the memories. Even though her back was to him, he reached out to her with a hand hovering over her shoulders but thought it best to comfort her with words instead of touch. An invisible barrier surrounded the Queen where non-royals could not physically handle her—though she could do as she pleased.

Even if Hera would not object to his compassionate gesture, Hermes did not trust himself to maintain set boundaries.

"I know this must bring up a lot of memories for you. Yes, Zeus is my father, but I do not understand why he did what he did."

She turned to face him, her eyes as dry as the desert. "I cannot talk about this now."

He nodded. "I understand."

Forcing a smile, she demanded, "Put me back in a good mood. Tell me, who wants my crown?"

He crossed his arms and asked, "So why did Zeus visit the Underworld?"

By the gods! "That business does not concern you."

"I make it my business to be concerned," he stated matter-of-factly.

Being a Lower God, he is not privy to this information, yet he persists. "Hades is restless. He threatens an uprising if he does not get what he wants."

"Which is?"

"A wife."

He smacked his forehead. "The poor fool."

She placed her hands on his chest and, ever so slowly, curled her fingers into his clothing. It was a threat, a not-so-veiled threat. "Who dares to make me an enemy?"

Now, it is time for the setup. Her hands stirred a rush through his body, causing the traitor's name to flow effortlessly out of his mouth. "Aphrodite."

She let out a laugh so loud it made her feel joyous. "Now I see why you were so amused." *Yes, he could always put me in a good mood.* "Have you seen the horror she added to the mount? Gaudy beyond belief!"

"Subtly was never her strong suit." He crossed his arms and mused, "I am still perplexed about how she got her way."

"*Your* father."

He cracked a playful grin. "*Your* husband."

"*Our* king," she sighed helplessly. "And now Aphrodite sets her sights on my crown? She is the last of his bastards to show her face in my palace, and she already has a home on this mount. Not even you or Athena can boast about a home on Mount Olympus. I do not like the precedent she is setting. She will not be victorious in her endeavor. I will make sure of it." Hera laughed haughtily.

"Precisely! I knew you would get a good laugh out of this situation." He eyed her mischievously as he prepared his exit. *And now it is time for the kill.* "For it is *nearly* impossible for Aphrodite to become Queen."

Her giggles were stifled momentarily as Hermes reached for the door handle but stopped and turned around.

Hera got the message. "I will let you get back to your thoughts, my Queen." He bowed. "You have a good night."

Hermes' words repeated in her thoughts as Hera stood alone in the living area.

...Nearly impossible for Aphrodite to become Queen.

Nearly.

36

DAUGHTER DEAREST
ATHENA & ZEUS

"The sky is falling," Zeus declared with urgency as he stomped into the old sanctuary, a place filled from top to bottom with the dusty books of the gods. Neglected and rarely visited, it was a wonder that the ancient structure still stood a ways from Mount Olympus.

The hallowed space was filled with the scent of old parchment, and the dim light filtering through the cracked windows cast an eerie glow over the forgotten tomes.

"Father," Athena greeted him calmly. She was seated at a table with an open, tattered book, her finger tracing the weathered pages. Come here beside me." She extended her hand in welcome as Zeus took a seat beside her. It is good to see you back."

His eyes were glossy but brightened at the sight of his daughter. It was such a joy for him to see all of his children, save for Dionysus, gathered to celebrate Hebe's Day of Understanding, even though the festivities did not end on a high note.

"There are an abundance of rumors spreading because of today's commotion. What possessed Hebe to enter the Unknown Territories, a forbidden place?"

"She searched for a gift unlike any I had received." Zeus did not wait for her to beg for an answer. "The Princess brought me my second son, born from the Queen, Hephaestus."

Athena's eyes opened as wide as her mouth. "I cannot believe it!"

"It is true."

"How are you feeling?"

"A mix of everything." His face lit up through the shadows of the room. "Oh, how I longed to see him..." he let his voice trail off, not wanting to confess more than he should. "But never mind all of that. What was the outcome of your little outing today?"

She hesitated before nodding in understanding. "Oh, yes." So much had already occurred that she almost forgot what he was referring to. "I spent the day with Ares so he could teach me his ways of war."

"And what did you learn?"

"I learned that Ares is dumber than I could have imagined." She touched his hand and whispered, "He is an absolute idiot."

"A useful idiot." He patted her hand. "Ares may not see things the way you and I do, but he does see. Did he not teach you the first rule of battle? Do not underestimate your opponent."

Athena sighed, wanting to argue her point but deciding to let the topic rest. She started her journey with Ares to understand his thoughts and ended up intrigued by his life of combat. "I must admit, I do find his warring fascinating. But I wonder. Should such an endeavor be trusted to one such as him?"

"If not him, who? Not everyone can enact the atrocities required of him with—"

"...a smile?"

"*Without* a heavy heart."

She nodded, a loose strain for her red hair falling over her eyes. "I was worried Ares had higher ambitions and could be a threat towards your throne, but you were right all along."

Zeus took note of her.

"Ares is happy exactly where he is."

Do you hear that Prometheus? Even Athena sees my children are no threat to me. He reached into the satchel he had strapped around his shoulder. "Never mind all of that. I have something for you." He dipped inside his bag, pulled out a sparkling green jewel, and dropped it into her cupped hands.

"A necklace?" *It is breathtaking, but he knows I do not wear jewelry.*

"Not just any necklace." He nudged her on. "Look closer.

The chain is old, ancient. Her mouth opened wide in disbelief. "Is this..."

She knows. "It belonged to your great-great-grandmother."

"Gaia."

"I was raised by my grandmother Gaia. She always wore this necklace and told me it was the first precious stone she made when she created the earth. And I give this to you, my precious goddess."

"I am honored you would gift this to me."

"If not you, who?"

She shrugged, wrapping the necklace around her finger in anxiousness. "I did not know I could be given something so special. I am neither a High Goddess nor royalty."

"You are royalty. You are my daughter."

He knows that being his daughter alone does not make me royalty. "Is that why Aphrodite is now living on Mount Olympus? Because she is your child? Shall all of your bastards and I now move there?"

He took off his satchel, threw it on the table, and rubbed his forehead. *I cannot even explain how that happened.* "Your sister is extremely persistent. She wore me down. I was so delirious I do not even remember what I agreed to."

Aphrodite did tell me that a closed mouth does not get fed. Yes, a mouth has to be open to eat, but will it relate to this matter? Shall I examine for myself?

The Sky God ran his fingers through his thick hair. "I cannot sleep. This is where I would always come when I could not stop my mind from racing."

"What is causing you so much trouble?"

"Hades."

It is so unlike Hades to start problems unnecessarily. "Why would your brother be causing you any trouble?"

He rubbed his forehead, trying in vain to stop the

thoughts in his head. "He is not at peace, so the rest of us cannot be at peace."

She shook her head. "I do not like the sound of that."

"Hades is threatening war if I do not meet his demands." Sometimes, it was too easy for Zeus to tell his daughter more than she needed to know.

"And what are these demands?"

It is wrong for me even to tell her what I did. "I should not discuss this with you. It is matters that should only be discussed with the council."

"And yet here you are." *I know him all too well.* "You knew you would find me here. You were searching for me for this very reason, not just to give me Gaia's necklace."

He relented to her assumptions. *She is right.* "You are my wisdom. I always felt a little bit of me disappeared when you leaped from my head fully grown."

Athena laughed, never tired of hearing him tell her birth story. "You say that all the time."

He closed the book in front of her, taking a serious tone, "I am here because I received the message you sent me."

"What message did I send?"

"The one you sent through Hermes, indirectly."

Good. The speedy god spread the message just like I intended. "His mouth is big and wide."

"You know he cannot keep his mouth shut but do not underestimate him. Hermes knows when to open his mouth and when to close it. More power lies in the secrets he keeps than the secrets he tells."

That is something for me to remember. Hermes is a crafty one.

"But as soon as you told Hermes your theory of my sons rising against me, he was sure to let me know."

"Sons...*and* daughters," she corrected, "rebellion of the gods is not confined to the masculine." *The gods underestimate the ambition of the goddesses. This is the one time being a goddess can result in our favor. The gods would never notice us coming, too concerned with the threat of each other while the goddesses lay in wait.*

"And what would you have me do?" he asked rhetorically.

"I can tell you what to do. I can give you ideas."

She knows I was flippant. "You *cannot* give me ideas because you are not a High God."

"I am not a High God. This is true." *I am done with holding my tongue and sending messages through third parties.* Before she could stop herself, she demanded, "So make me a High God."

The King was taken aback by her bold request. "You know I do not have that kind of power."

"Change the rules." She was a rock rolling down a hill, gaining momentum. She could not even stop herself.

"I cannot just change the existing rules."

"Make new ones," she slammed her fist on the table. *He is the King of the Gods!* "You can do that."

"Everything I do regarding council has to be voted on, and I have only one vote of four."

"You should have a bigger council." *I have thought about this for a long time but was too timid to act. Since sending Hermes did not achieve my desired result, I need to make it as plain as possible to the King.*

"As I am sure Hermes also explained to you. Your children

need more power. If not, we *will* rebel." *When in doubt, throw out a threat. After all, it worked for Hades.* "And the fact is, there are more of *us* than there are of you."

Zeus did not immediately respond to Athena's avalanche of words. The life of a king was relentless. Between his ongoing feud with Hades, the unexpected reunion with Hephaestus, and the discussions of potential rebellion with Athena, there had been no respite for the god who bore the weight of it all—a ceaseless cycle of danger and governance demanding his unwavering attention.

Getting up from the desk, he kissed his favorite daughter on the back of her head. "Good night, my child."

"Good night, Father," she squeezed his hand before letting him go out the door. "What is this?"

Zeus looked back to see Athena with paper in her hand. *It must have fallen out from my satchel onto the desk.*

With the paper in hand, she read:

Now minus 1

Will soon be undone

An addition to 5

Can subtract and divide

When it comes to 3

The end will it be

Lastly, multiply by 2

But the result, you cannot undo

Woe, woe, woe is you!

She glanced up from the page. "Father. What is this?"

"A supposed telling of my future." Walking back to her, he said, "You are wise. Can you explain this riddle?"

Her eyes traced over the words again. "When did you receive this prophecy?"

"In the wee hours of the morning."

"Well, it is a clever play of words and numbers."

"I do not believe in prophesies."

"Neither do I. However, coincidently, the first part of this riddle has come to pass."

He flapped his fingers, urging her to continue.

"*Now* minus 1..." Looking back at him, she explained, "You had three younglings with Hera, but for so long you were missing one, minus 1...until today—'will soon be undone' the missing one, Hephaestus has returned, and finally, you are made whole."

Zeus did not speak a word. Instead, he took the paper from his daughter and repeated, "I do not believe in prophecies." Turning away, he left the room, closing the door behind him.

Finally, I told my father exactly what I wanted. Athena leaned on the edge of his desk and sighed. She felt like Atlas lifted the universe off her shoulders and back onto his own.

Aphrodite is right. A closed mouth does not get fed. From now on, my mouth will be wide open.

A slow smile crawled along her face.

...and I will devour everything in sight.

37

OFF WITH HER HEAD
HERA & APHRODITE

*F*LOWING HAIR, ROSY CHEEKS, AND LINGERIE SO SHEER, *I* MAY AS *well be naked.*

Aphrodite's heart skipped a beat as she heard the creak of her front door being pushed open. "You are here so soon, my love." The loving smile on Aphrodite's face turned sour. Out of all the gods she expected to visit, Hera was last on her list.

Hera stepped into the home uninvited, not thinking she needed an invitation to march through any part of Mount Olympus. Nosily, she took her time to walk around the new addition to the palace.

Aphrodite suppressed a sigh as her unwanted guest wandered around, inspecting the intricacies of her abode.

Why did she say, 'My love?' "Were you expecting someone else?"

Aphrodite hesitated before answering, "I was not."

"You lie." Hera did not even look at her to accuse her,

preferring to rummage through the various decorations around the room.

"I am expecting someone else *later*."

The queen glanced down at the goddess's bosom, noting that her nipples were visible through her gown. "You seem to be missing your covering."

"This is how I dress for bed."

"Have you ever heard of leaving something to the imagination?"

Aphrodite smirked. "I can assure you, there are still some things you cannot see."

The royal curled her lip and continued her march around the area.

Aphrodite trailed behind Hera, her blood boiling with each thing she picked up. *How dare she riffle through my possessions like she is at the market?* "Why are you here?"

Hera spun around with a wicked grin. That was no way for Aphrodite to speak to her.

I know that look far too well. "My Queen," she corrected herself with a curtsey that took minimal effort.

How dare Zeus mock the royal order by giving his bastard a place on this Mount? "I have come to survey what you had Zeus build for you."

Running her hand lightly across her white couch, she stated, "What a generous father I have."

"Indeed." Picking up a small bust of a woman as a centerpiece on a round table, Hera added, "What a wasteful husband *I* have."

"Indeed."

Putting down the ornament, Hera turned to the other woman. "Is it not interesting how we can see the same thing in a different light based on our own experiences?"

"I view my new home as a suitable compromise. I am not allowed on the high mountain, so my home is just underneath it...for now."

Hera's expression became solemn as she closed the distance between them. The flames from the torches flickered in the background. "You do not belong on this mount at all."

"And yet here I am." She opened her arms wide to prove she was, in fact, there. "Hera, no need to be angry with me. It is not my fault your husband cannot stop his dalliances with whoever he fancies."

She pointed her finger. "You watch what you say."

"I will not." Aphrodite stepped closer to her so Hera's finger was right between her breasts. "I *will* speak my mind, oh Queen of the Gods. And, I will claim what is rightfully mine. Starting with my home on Mount Olympus."

Look how high and mighty she acts with just a bit of royal treatment. Besides Hephaestus, it looks as though Zeus created another monster. "By any chance, were you expecting Ares tonight?"

"Why would you ask that?"

She peeked directly past Aphrodite's shoulder to the warrior's helmet sitting in the corner of the room.

Aphrodite noticed the armor Ares left behind still out in the open for Hera to see. There was no denying who had been in her home and who would be returning.

The poor goddess is tongue-tied. "I take that as a yes. Know this, Aphrodite. You will never take my son away from me. As if it were possible."

"If it were not possible," she cracked a smile, "why, pray tell, are you here?"

Her eyes may have twitched, but they did not falter. "Be forewarned. My son loves no one but the sword. He can have his little tryst with you and put you away until he needs you again." Looking at her with pity, she added, "Just do not wait for anything more. That would be sad, sad indeed."

Aphrodite was fuming, but her expression remained frozen, not to reveal her genuine emotions.

Hera stopped just short of the exit. "Nice décor." And with that, she left her subject alone to stew in her hatred.

In a fury, Aphrodite stormed over to a small secret room tucked away in the corner of her home. With a swift motion, she flung open the door, revealing the dimly lit space within. There, on the floor, lay the head of a statue, its stone features illuminated by a shaft of moonlight filtering through the window.

Aphrodite's hands trembled as she reached down and lifted the figure, holding it up to her face. The cold stone eyes stared back at her. She studied the chiseled features, feeling a surge of rage rising within her.

The silent statue seemed to mock her with its impassive stare. With a frustrated growl, Aphrodite clenched her fists on the verge of shattering the stone into pieces.

Hera, Hera, Hera. I beheaded you once...and I shall behead you again.

38

DRESSED DOWN
ARES & HEBE

In the late hours, Ares stood in his ceremonial clothing and waited inches from his neatly made bed. Although his Quarters were private, they were close to those of the King and Queen, a privilege befitting his status as the next in line to the throne.

In the calm stillness, Ares' senses were suddenly stirred by the frantic energy of Hebe bouncing around the room. Dressed in his cream ensemble, he observed her in silence.

She threw her arms in the air, almost spilling the scented oils in her hands. "My party was a total disaster!"

"Because you made it so."

Her movements stopped long enough for her to pout, still looking every bit of a youngling.

"Do not cry now."

"I will cry if I want to."

Even though everything is her fault, I can not stand to see her sulk. He let out a soft smile. "You looked more beautiful than ever today in your glittery gown and your hair up high."

Her face instantly lit up. "I only styled my hair differently because I followed Aphrodite's advice."

His ears perked at the mention of his soon-to-be lover.

"Out of Father's bastard daughters, she is so warm and loving to me!"

There was no way for him to stop the bigger smile forming on his face. "I am happy *she* makes you happy." His hand found its way to the sharp grey object nestled between her breasts. "This necklace I gave you was the only thing you wore at the ceremony that did not sparkle. Why did you decide to put it on?"

"In case you followed through on your earlier threat *not* to be by my side, I wanted to make sure I had a part of you with me."

Taking hold of the small dagger, he pressed his lips against its cool surface. "I will always be by your side."

After a short embrace, she pulled out of his arms long enough to ask, "How long will you be away from Olympus?"

"I will be gone for the night. Why?" His brow furrowed slightly.

Her fingers toyed nervously with the fabric of her gown as she hesitated. "I was hoping to sleep here."

"You can have my bed while I am away."

She bit her bottom lip. "I was hoping to sleep here...with you."

He let out a long, slow breath. *Tonight will be her first night alone in her new home away from the Royal Quarters, and she is* scared to be so far away. Part of this is my fault because of the creepy stories I told her as a youngling. "Hebe, there is nothing left in this world for you to fear. You now know the truth. There are no such things as monsters."

She nodded lightly before swiftly redirecting her focus across the room and back to meticulously preparing the Prince's clothing. However, unlike his usual battle armor, she instead laid out garments of finer fabric on his orders. *Ares rarely if ever dresses formally.* "You gave me little warning to bathe you tonight."

"Only because I do not need a bath, only a change of clothes and some lavish oils."

Hmmm? Gathering bottles of fragrant oils on a side table, their scents lighter and more delicate than the usual musk associated with the battlefield, Hebe turned to find Ares standing before her.

"You are now of age when gods will approach you for marriage. Was there any available god that caught your eye before your night came to such an abrupt end?"

"Everything was such a blur." Gently rocking a vile between her fingers, she gave a sheepish smile. "Which available goddess caught your eye?"

"Only you," he teased, kissing the tip of her nose as she scrunched her face.

"Of course, you did not find a goddess to settle down with. Why pick one when you can have many." She narrowed her dark eyes. "Like father."

"Make no mistake, Hebe. Even though our father had many, he only picked one." His powerful arms were outstretched, waiting patiently as she unwrapped the linen along his upper body and around his waist.

"For so long, after hearing many whispers and half-truths, I thought our mysterious brother was banished from Mount Olympus." Once she finished unraveling his tunic, she folded the thick cloth into two halves. "But that is not what happened. I heard what you said today while arguing with our father."

He clenched his jaws, but his eyes did not waver from her intense stare.

"Did father throw Hephaestus into the sea? Is that the reason why he is scarred and crippled?" She watched as the pounding of his heart matched the rise and fall of his chest.

"I did not summon you here to interrogate me." He snapped his fingers. "Now go and fetch my fragrance. Prepare a blend of oils to tease the senses to ignite a burning flame from the one who I allow close enough to take a whiff."

Hebe nodded, and she turned on her heel and made her way to the collection of fragrances. She wasted no time selecting the finest oils and essences, her fingers moving with practiced precision as she measured out the perfect blend.

She called out to him, "You have never before asked me to service you in such a way."

Ares did his best to remain silent.

"Are you going to meet someone special tonight? Is that why you will be gone for so long?"

Instead of answering, he asked a question of his own. "If you spent more time mixing instead of talking, my fragrance would be ready."

Hebe rolled her eyes as she continued her work. Once the concoction was complete, she took a moment to inhale its heady aroma, a smile of satisfaction gracing her lips. With the vial securely in hand, Hebe returned to Ares, ready to unleash the potent smell upon its unsuspecting recipient.

"Dose my usual spots. Neck, chest, and between my thighs."

Using a slender stick, she delicately dipped it into the fragrant bottle before rising onto her tiptoes to apply the scent to both sides of his neck. "I, too, would like to meet someone special," she murmured.

Her voice held a trace of longing that he could not ignore.

She trailed the scented stick down the center of his chest and emitted a playful sigh while tracing circles around his belly button. "If only you would tell me how to keep him once I find him."

If she only knew how much her body masks her innocence and how easily it would be for a god to take advantage of her. "You are much too naive. If I had my way, you would be confined to this mountain."

"And if I were locked away, where would you be?"

"You ask too many questions."

She outlined his abs with the perfume. "Because you never answer any."

Ares' patience wore thin, and he seized her wrist firmly. "Hebe, be quiet and do what you are told."

"Whatever you say...my *prince*."

He snatched the vial from her hand and finished applying

the fragrance himself. "Must you torment my very being by calling me *that* name?"

"Must *you* continue to keep secrets when I have officially entered godhood?"

He closed the bottle and casually tossed it onto his bed. Then, he reached out, gently tilting her chin upward with his hand. "Do what you are told."

She brushed him away and crossed her arms defiantly.

"Go and fetch my clothing."

She huffed and went over to his garments. "Apollo warned me that we would be fighting more now that I reached my Age of Understanding," she muttered under her breath.

Blasted, Apollo! "What nonsense is he filling you with?"

"It is not nonsense. Apollo knows. He *sees* things."

"Then surely he will see my fist connecting with his temple the next time I see him."

"Do not dare punch him for speaking the truth."

"He speaks lies." Again he stretched out his arms so that Hebe could better wrap the long black fabric into a tunic around his body. "I only fight my enemies. Never will I fight my family."

"Did I not see your hand rest on your sword when you argued with our father today?"

"Zeus and I were merely play fighting." He winked.

The Princess stomped her foot. "Why are you allowed to go wherever and do as you please while I have a guard at my door who follows my every move." She gestured with her hand, confirming that Xander was standing outside Ares' Quarters.

He took hold of her arms, gently massaging her shoulders to ease out her crankiness. If she were still a babe, he would have already rocked her to sleep, and tucked her into bed. "I know you are now grown. But you still have a lot to learn."

"How will I learn if you do not teach me?" She pouted, her eyes pleading.

Not wanting to drag their conversation out any longer, he reached for his belt, instead of waiting for her to do it for him, and buckled it around his waist. "Some things are not meant for me to teach you."

He waited for her to respond, but since she did not, he continued, "Stay the night in my bed, and I will send my most trusted soldiers to deliver your presents to your chamber."

Once he had gathered all his belongings, he left Hebe alone, gently closing the door behind him.

As the latch clicked shut, Hebe was left in the dim light of the room, the faint scent of his fragrance lingering in the air, a reminder of his presence—that would soon vanish as well.

"If *you* cannot teach me, brother. I will find someone who will."

39

STRANGER DANGER!
PERSEPHONE & DEMETER

Demeter strolled along the familiar pathways leading to her home, using it as an opportunity to scrutinize her crops. As the Goddess of the Harvest, timeliness was crucial in her line of work. She had to keep a precise understanding of the growth rates, blooming patterns, and harvest schedules of every crop. Any distraction had the potential to disrupt the delicate balance of nature she maintained.

By the gods!

Running her fingers through the cornfields, she felt the hardness of the kernels under her touch. "Because of my rendezvous with Zeus, I missed my window to tend to my crops, and now everything is thrown off schedule!"

Frustration welled within her, and in a fit of rage, she yanked out the cornstalks in that row, tearing them from the earth and crushing them underfoot.

Eventually, she succumbed to despair, collapsing onto the

ground, her face pressed into the soil. Here, among the critters of the night, she found solace in the earth, her most faithful companion.

In the silence of the field, she heard a familiar melody:

The sky was made
The ground was laid
The winds flow through the night
The rain will fall
The seeds grow tall
And the sun will give us light.

Demeter's heart raced as she sprang to her feet, her senses electrified by the hauntingly beautiful voice that resonated through the air. Panic gripped her, and she cast her eyes about, desperately scanning the surroundings for the source of this ethereal melody.

In the distance, a solitary figure stood with her back turned, oblivious to the approaching goddess. With a sense of urgency, Demeter dashed towards the mysterious singer.

"Persephone!"

She did not move a muscle. *By the goddesses!* The brown-haired goddess spun around to see her mother running full speed in her direction.

Demeter grabbed hold of her daughter by the shoulders and shook her. The young goddess went limp, not doing anything to fight back.

"I am sorry, Mother." She knew there was no excuse for

her actions, but she gave one anyway. "I know I should not be here. I thought you would be gone for a little while longer."

She brushed the twisted hair out of Persephone's face so she could look into her daughter's bright hazel eyes. So young and innocent, yet Persephone was no longer a babe. "You should not be out of the boundaries I set for you."

"I wanted to explore more of the land. I am fine. No harm has come to me."

"That is because I found you first." Her words were hushed as if she were afraid someone was eavesdropping. "You do not know how dangerous it is for a young one such as yourself to wander alone."

But I am also dangerous. She tightened her lips. "I am no longer young, Mother. I am like you now. I have grown up. I have reached the age of understanding."

Demeter wanted to laugh at her daughter's naivety, but the unknown danger prevented her from doing so. "Persephone. Yes, you are like me—a beautiful goddess. Yet, there is so much you do not know. So much I have shielded you from."

"But why must you shield me? Why can I not be free to come and go as I please...as you do?"

"I cannot explain everything to you now." *Even if I had the chance, I would not know where to begin.* "You *must* trust me."

The young one wrapped her arms around her waist but refused to make eye contact. Instead, she gave her full attention to the dandelions in the grass. "I do trust you, Mother. I have to trust you. You are all that I know."

"Then promise me you will never leave the boundaries I set again."

Persephone looked back at her mother, examining her overall demeanor. *I know she will only accept one answer, so I will give it to her.* "I promise."

Demeter gradually calmed down, her daughter's promise acting as a soothing balm to her wounded spirit. As she gazed upon Persephone, it struck her with renewed clarity that she had indeed made the right choice in severing her relationship with Zeus.

Demeter's finger grazed her daughter's cheek. Now that Persephone was fully grown, she bore an uncanny resemblance to Hera.

Hera! Oh, how tickled she would be to see how much they resemble. Such a shame Hebe and Persephone could not be raised together, sharing a bond as sisters—the same bond I share with Hera.

Demeter took the younger one's hand and walked along the pathway to their hidden home.

But Persephone's father is Zeus. I will never tell her who her father is, and I will never tell Zeus he has another daughter. This betrayal of my sister will cost one of us our life. And I cannot—I will not risk that life being my daughter.

40

TOUCH ME, TEASE ME
HEBE & HERMES

"I should not be sitting on your bed."

Xander, Hebe's guard, sat nervously beside her. His posture was rigid, and beads of sweat glistened on his forehead. "I cannot *believe* I am here."

The bedroom was bathed in soft torchlight, aided by Selene's moon, filtering through delicate curtains that billowed gently in the night's breeze.

She was as surprised as Xander at how easy it had been to entice him onto her bed. All it took was for her to go onto her balcony and beckon him with a finger to find his way into her room. And if it was not her sole finger that enticed the guard, it could have also been the long white night dress she wore with straps low enough to reveal the roundness of her firm breasts.

The princess had plans to spend the night in her brother's room but after tossing and turning for the better part of an hour, she decided to return to her new palace. She did not want to spend the night alone and with Ares gone, there was no point for her to stay in his drab room. Once she went back to the other side of the mountain, she enticed Xander to follow her up the winding staircase into her inner chambers.

Just like Ares had promised her, he had instructed his soldiers to transfer her gifts from the Great Hall into her bedroom. When they walked inside, the wall along her spacious bedroom was stacked with gifts of varying sizes from her loyal subjects. At any other time, Hebe would have dived into opening her presents. However, for tonight, she was far more excited to unwrap Xander.

Besides their whispers, the room was quiet, saved for the periodical scratching sounds coming from one of the many closed room doors.

Scratch, scratch...

"Why did you lure me into your chamber?"

The Princess was too busy admiring Xander's bare upper body to respond. He was a mortal of average stature, with broad shoulders that previewed his strength. His rugged face bore the lines of experience fused with the smooth, hairless skin of youth.

Finally remembering his question, she answered, "I need your help."

"How can a man help a goddess?" His brown eyes darted anxiously around the room, fearing he would be caught away from his designated post.

"By letting me do all that I have ever imagined to you."

With the softest hands he had ever felt, she massaged his naked chest.

"All?" He swallowed so hard, for the first time in his life, he made an audible gulp.

A naughty grin floated along her pink lips as her fingers found their way down his bulky muscles. "You men are shaped like gods. Except, you are very weak. I am sure even *I* could subdue you," she teased.

His warrior's spirit briefly returned at the mere mention of a challenge. "I would not make it easy for you...my Princess."

A midsize bruise on the side of his ribcage caught her attention. "Who gave this to you?"

He forced a strained smile. "Your brother, along with this bruise to my left eye, when he stormed into your Quarters earlier today."

Oh, Ares! "I will make sure you feel no pain tonight. Only pleasure."

Her hands found his powerful thighs and began to caress them in a circular motion. The sensations rushing throughout his body were too much for him to bear.

Scratch, scratch...

The only thing stopping him from proving his strength was the knowledge that a man had no business touching a goddess. Only he could be used for *her* pleasure, and in doing so, he could only *hope* she would return the favor.

Painfully slowly, she used two fingers to crawl from his thigh toward his mounting erection and finally rested her palm on the throbbing force hiding under his tunic.

"Ohhh!" His eyes rolled to the back of his head as he clenched the bedsheets for some semblance of relief.

"Xander?" she whispered, her voice summoning him to refocus on her. She leaned into him with her eyes closed.

He heard her silent plea. *My princess is waiting for a kiss, and I must obey.*

Xander knew he had no time to waste and lowered his head toward her waiting lips...

Suddenly, the door swung open, and Hermes swiftly entered the room.

I knew it! His eyes, normally twinkling with mischief, now blazed with anger as he found the mortal man who dared to intrude upon the princess's private quarters.

"Hermes!" Hebe was too stunned to move—her hand remained stuck on the one body part she could not excuse away as innocent.

Scratch, scratch...

Already on the verge of a heart attack, Xander shot up with his hands covering the stiff bulge between his legs.

Hermes towered over him, incensed at the growing evidence of the guard's passion. "The audacity of you to present yourself in the princess's room!"

"I—I..."

"I should kill you...but then Ares would kill *me* for not letting *him* kill you."

Hebe clasped her hands together in prayer. "Hermes, please do not do such a thing!"

The god did not hear her cries. And even if he did, he

would not let mere tears stop him from having his way. In a commanding voice, he barked, "You! Get out!"

"I-I... can ex-explain..."

Hermes' gaze was unyielding. "I said, get out!" he thundered once more.

Without another word, Xander quickly exited, leaving the room completely silent for far too long to Hebe's liking.

What am I to do with this little one? Hermes paced the chamber's confines, pulling at the root of his tussled hair. "When your father hears of this..."

She darted behind him with a few hurried steps, her cries imploring him, "Do not tell my father."

Either he did not hear her, or he *would* not hear her, Hebe was not sure which one it was, and so she did the one thing she was never to do. The young royal hitched up her white slip and knelt before him in the middle of the plush round carpet.

The orphan god stopped pacing at the sight of her humbled below him. *A princess has no business pleading to a peasant! Her actions are absurd, and she knows it.*

Hebe held her hands out as a sign of offering. "Please, do not tell the King. I, Hebe, Princess of the Gods, beg of you."

"It is not your place to beg me anything."

Every inch of her body refused to budge, not wanting to release him from his discomfort. "Xander is my only friend!"

His piercing eyes locked onto hers as she knelt, imitating an obedient pet. He leaned in closer, his voice firm, "Do you value your friend's life?"

"More than anything."

"Then leave him be. It would be best if you had never tempted that poor youth. He did not stand a chance against the allure of a goddess."

"But he wanted to come to my bed."

"You may think so, but what you say is not true. Only the gods have freedom. Mortals do not."

Hebe wanted to understand the wisdom that Hermes' was imparting, but she truly did not comprehend the gravity of his words.

"Never invite Xander into your room again." Hermes softened his stance. "Promise?"

With her eyes brimming, she nodded in agreement. "I promise."

"Now *I* beg of you...get up!"

Happily, she bounced back on her feet and retreated a few steps, her back now against the opulent bed.

Scratch, scratch...

Hermes looked around the otherwise empty room. "What is that noise?"

Hebe shrugged, barely paying him any mind. "What noise?"

"Never mind." Hermes walked toward the nearby window, his body language returning to its usual relaxing state. "I heard you did the impossible and brought Hephaestus back to Mount Olympus."

Hebe remained by the bed, her eyes dropping to the floor briefly before she met his eyes. "I did."

"What is wrong? You should be proud of such a feat."

"I did not know my poor brother was thrown from the peak. I always thought it was an accident of some sort."

Obviously, the King and Queen were protecting her from the truth.

His silence was telling. "So it is true? Father did do it."

I will not confirm what she knows to be true.

"I cannot fathom how he could do such a thing. The most father would ever do to me was puff out his chest. Today, in the Royal Court, was the very first time he has ever yelled at me."

"Not even as a curious youngling, Zeus never disciplined you?"

"Never. Ares would yell at me if I was naughty." She giggled. "And then he would give me a treat to stop me from crying."

He nodded in understanding. *Ares oversaw Hebe's punishments because he never trusted Zeus' temper with her or his mother.*

Scratch, scratch...

"Tell me." His curiosity got the best of him, and he again approached her with an intense stare. "Is it true the Prince is a monster?"

Hebe turned away, her fingers clenching the edge of a nearby table as she spoke. "The only monster I know is my father for what he did to Hephaestus when he was a babe. Earlier, he called out to me from below my balcony, but I refused to speak a word to him."

Oh, to be a born princess and face no repercussions for defying the King of the Gods. He moved closer to Hebe.

"I do not care to speak of it anymore." She turned back to face Hermes, suddenly drained by the day's events. "Can we talk about anything else?"

That is all I needed to hear. Ever the inquisitive god, he continued to close the distance between them, earnestly probing further. "Why *did* you tempt the young lad into your chambers?"

Her cheeks flushed with embarrassment. "I cannot believe I was so bold."

She giggled, took a step, and unexpectedly caught a glimpse of her reflection in the hanging mirror. Without question, the goddess reflecting back at her, was one to admire.

I was too busy relishing Xander's changing physique I overlooked my own.

The outline of her petite figure was barely hidden under the sheer cloth of her nightgown.

My breasts are round and swollen. She cupped them from below and watched them jiggle the more she fondled them.

My nipples are poking out. Hebe pulled and twisted them. *Begging to be seen by all who look and licked by all who dare to taste.*

The titillating emotions she felt running her hands all over Xander returned as she slid her hands further down her slight frame against her taut stomach and beyond.

My hips have spread wider for a god to draw me near like what father does to mother.

She then settled on her buttocks and squeezed her plump, creamy checks in delight.

And my butt...

"Huh!" Her fingers brushed against a silky wet spot. *What is this?*

The moisture between her legs seeped through her gown and darkened a circular patch under the curve of her buttocks.

"I am wet." Suddenly remembering she was not alone, she looked back at Hermes while rubbing three slippery fingers in the air. "Why am I so wet? Is there something wrong with me?"

His teeth were clenched as tight as possible. He had purposely refrained from interjecting, not wanting to explain more to her than what was his place. The quiver of her voice was the only reason he relented, "No, there is nothing wrong with you. You are perfect. What you are doing is good. It is far better for you to relish every inch of your body and find pleasure in touching yourself...alone."

"But..." She shifted her weight from one foot to another. "I wanted to... feel the touch of another."

"And you will."

His words were gentle and stirred within her, a glimmer of hope in her eyes.

"On the night of your wedding, as I am sure your father has already made you aware," he quipped.

Great Zeus! Hebe sighed. "It is not fair."

"It may not be fair, but it is what it is. The rules are in place for your protection. Yes, Xander is no god, but he *can* make you a mother."

"A mother? Oh, if only! Having a babe would be grand!"

"Not for a princess. A babe born without a marriage is no life for a god." He adopted a more sober tone, "*I should know.*"

His words fell on deaf ears. Her body was filled to the brim with desire with no form of relief, and so her frustrations grew. "Why must I be so careful while Ares does as he pleases with goddesses, nymphs, and the like?"

"You do not know what Ares does and does not do."

She hummed a melody only she knew as her eyes danced sheepishly around the room.

"Or you *do* know?"

Without any more prompting, she spilled everything. "Tonight, I dressed Ares, but he was *not* dressed for war. And the fragrance he splashed all over his body was *not* meant to entice soldiers."

He clutched his fingers together. *Aphrodite!*

Hebe did not notice his reaction because she was having one of her own. Crossing her arms in a huff, she pouted. "It is not fair that Ares is going out to do what I cannot."

"Draw no conclusion from whatever you witnessed. As Prince of us all, Ares knows better than to spill his seed recklessly."

Seed? She looked up at him wide-eyed, as clueless as could be.

I know she is officially at an age of understanding, but she is still far too naive. "Disregard what I said." *It is not my place to tell her about these things.*

Scratch, scratch...

"That incessant noise is driving me mad!" he said,

following the sound before stopping at a closed door. "The noise is coming from this room."

"No, do not—"

Her warnings came too late, and Hermes opened the door as Wolfie ran out the other room, her teeth snapping at the sight of him.

"Wolfie, stop!" she yelled, chasing behind her until she could finally scoop her into her arms.

Lucky for Hermes, his legs were as fast as his tongue, and he darted around the room long enough to avoid her bite.

"Please do not tell my father I am keeping her inside my room for the night." She snuggled, Wolfie against her cheek. "I want someone beside me in bed while I sleep."

"Do whatever you want. I am just glad I still have all my fingers intact." He made his way over to the door he had entered. "Go to sleep, my little princess."

I love to hear him call me little princess! Giggling, she obeyed and happily pulled down the covers and hopped into bed. Why could Hermes get away with calling her little and not Ares? For now, the question had no place in her mind. She lay Wolfie next to her pillow and curled up around her.

"And one more thing." He stood in the door frame. "If by chance you *forget* the promise you made to me this very night and just so happen to have Xander on your bed again, remember only this: For a man, you spit, but for a god, you swallow."

Before she could respond, a fierce wind blew from his mouth, blowing out all the torch flames in the room with one swoop.

As Hermes exited Hebe's chamber, he made his way to the entrance of her quarters, where Xander stood, anxiously awaiting his return.

He uncomfortably shifted his feet as Hermes approached. The recent exchange had left him nervous and uncertain of how fast or slow he would be tortured for his disobedience... or much worse.

Hermes and Xander regarded each other silently.

"What I saw here tonight will go no further."

Xander took an involuntary step back, his hand clutching the hilt of his sword. "My god, Hermes. I—I can never repay your mercy."

"No, you cannot." Hermes remained reserved before adding a sinister smile. "However, you *can* spend the rest of your days trying."

Xander's fingers trembled as he swallowed hard and asked, "What must I do to show my gr—gratitude?"

And now it is time for the execution. "You will report to *me* of Hebe's dealings before you report to the King. Do you understand?"

The distant sound of a trickling fountain provided a faint, calming backdrop to the scene.

Xander nodded resolutely. "Without question."

As Hermes departed, his steps echoing down the corridor, Xander lifted his gaze and met the eyes of Hebe, who had observed their secretive exchange from her balcony.

How long has she been watching us?

Unfortunately for him, her expression did not give away

her emotions. Hebe instinctively tightened the folds of her silk gown and retreated into her room, closing shut her balcony doors shut behind her.

41

BETWEEN THE SHEETS
APHRODITE & ARES

Aphrodite collapsed against the pillows on her luxurious bed, and her limbs splayed out in utter abandon. Every curve of her body seemed to pulse with a fiery intensity, her senses alight with a pleasure so intense it rivaled the crackling flames of the fireplace.

"Uhhh!" she let out a desperate gasp as Ares slowly removed his heated fingers from within her deepest parts.

He remained focused on how her long legs trembled, and her bosom jiggled intensely before diminishing into smaller spurts. Her delicious breasts were taunting him, daring for him to feast until his heart's content. He longed to entirely give into his desires and take them between his teeth and suck on her hardened nipples for all eternity, but he knew the very mountain in which they laid would crumble under her unrelenting cries of passion.

Aphrodite opened her eyes just in time to see his tongue

lash out and lick her sticky substance from his glowing hand, and his eyes beamed red as if he had just drank the juices of ambrosia.

He stared her dead in the eye and growled, "I want more."

The visual of his glistening pecs, mixed with his husky voice, sent her body into another uncontrollable tailspin. Within time, her body relented, overcome with exhaustion. *How long has it been since I last had someone satisfy me with only a hand?*

Before she could think of an answer, the Prince brushed a thumb against her cheek and lightly kissed along her neck onto her lips, slowly working his tongue into her mouth before completely devouring her.

She could hardly catch her breath, and she did not want to. Ares was full of surprises. *What a god!*

She expected him to dominate and take charge of her body, but it was his constant burst of roughness followed by moments of unexpected tenderness that sent her climaxing into the highest of heights. *Could it be? Have I met a god who can match my stamina?*

The weight of his bare chest crushed against her breasts, and her legs were spread just wide enough to feel his hardened tip graze her slippery entrance.

Breaking out of their embrace, he hovered over her, drinking in every inch of her curvaceous figure. "Your breasts, your waist, your hips..." Ares whispered in a rugged voice as he traced his fingers down Aphrodite's naked body. "There is nothing more beautiful than you in Selene's moonlight."

The breathtaking goddess giggled as they lay between the

bedsheets, twirling her hands through his thick, yellow hair. "Ares, the fierce god whose rage boils over at a moment's notice, sounds, dare I say, poetic?"

He stared at the curl of her lips and reveled in the musical sound of her laughter. She lay nestled within the shelter of his arms, and it took everything in him not to wrap her in them tighter. "You bring it out of me." Upon further reflection, he added, "You bring out what I did not know was there."

And it scared him. As soon as the words escaped his lips, the only thing that had frightened him in a long time. The warm fuzzy feeling in the pit of his stomach was foreign to him, yet it felt so good—too good. It was addictive.

"There are other things I would like to bring out of you," Aphrodite whispered with a seductive grin. Her hand traveled from his smooth chest down his hard stomach toward the stiffest part of his body, and she wasted no time in grabbing hold of as much as possible. His staff was standing at full attention. It had yet to go down since their dalliance began.

"Again?" he asked, feigning annoyance. He quickly found her hand and guided the rhythm of her strokes. "Are you sure you want to get me started again?" he nipped at her ear, a deep growl creeped out.

"You did not stop. You only paused. In fact, I do not think you will ever stop."

Yes, it was nighttime, but her vibrant blue eyes could still lock in his stare. He pounced on her, his lips hungrily finding hers as he pushed his hips between her legs. He engulfed her body with everything in him, his mind wholly consumed with her essence.

Throughout their encounter, Aphrodite purposely heightened all his senses. His touch, smell, taste, the sound of her voice moaning in ecstasy, the look of her voluptuous body. However, subtly lowering her divine energy was enough to cool down his burning desires.

Slowly, she broke away from his kiss and eased him off of her, and he suddenly did not feel the need to fight her resistance. She smiled to herself as he lay facing her on his side. *Good!*

The timing was right for her to express the more critical things on her mind when he was receptive enough to hear them.

"After you suddenly left the Royal Court today, I walked along the grounds and saw your sister."

His face lit up. "Hebe mentioned how wonderful you were to her."

"The princess is an absolute doll! I so enjoyed her company."

"I am glad you treat her well."

"How could I not?" Aphrodite made sure to snuggle closer into his arms. "And if not me, I am sure the others do the same," she lied.

"You would be wrong. Athena is always by my father's side, so she has no time for Hebe, and Artemis is...well, Artemis is Artemis. She has never liked my sister."

It did not take me long to figure out that befriending Hebe is a surefire way into his good graces.

"Sometimes I am too rough on her." He rested his hand on her golden cheek. "She needs a feminine touch."

That is just what I wanted to hear. "I will do what you cannot." Her delicate fingers traced the patterns on one of her many pillows as she spoke. "Is what they are saying all over the Mount true? Has the unwanted second son of the King returned to Olympus?"

Hephaestus. "What they say is true."

Her hand fluttered to her lips. "Have you seen him?"

"I have," he admitted, his gaze drifting momentarily to the dancing flames of the fireplace.

"Is it also true he is...deformed?"

"Yes. He is deformed." A shadow crossed his features, and Ares hesitated before meeting her eyes once more. "But it does not matter what he looks like. He is still my baby brother and is home where he belongs." He clenched his fist, the muscles in his arm tensing with the force of his memories. "Had I been older, stronger... Zeus would not have gotten away with banishing Hephaestus to the Unknown Territories. That horrid land is no place for a god—a Prince."

Her eyes softened as she listened to him speak. "You *love* him?"

"How could I not?"

"You do not even know him."

"I do not need to know him. I have loved him from before he was born. I always wanted a baby brother."

Aphrodite's heart swelled with warmth at the depth of his steadfast love. "He is blessed by The Fates to have you."

"Blessed to have me? No," Ares replied, shaking his head with a faint smile. "He would be blessed by The Fates to have you." He leaned into her, hungrily taking in all of her with his gaze. "Unfortunately for him, I have you now. And I want to enjoy my blessings for as long as I can."

He was ready to pounce on her again, and she firmly placed her hands on his chest, gently pushing him away to ensure she still had his full attention. "I had an unexpected visitor earlier."

Ares held back a moment, not liking that someone else was in her home. *But who?* "Who other than me would visit you so late at night? Someone with not-so-pure intentions."

"You would be right." She raised a brow. "Your mother."

He groaned over her exaggeration. "I am sure she only wanted to see your new home. It is the talk of the Mount."

"Is that so?" *He is already making excuses for her.* "She only wanted to rile me up. Hera hates me."

"*Hate* is such a strong word. She does not hate you." *How can my mother completely suppress her outage for the bastard children of my father?* "My mother had finally made peace with all of Zeus' infidelities, and then you arrived after being hidden away by your mother for so long. It is all very complicated."

"Complicated? Why? It is so crystal clear to me. The Queen of the Gods is jealous, horrible, manipulative...shall I go on?"

"I have never felt this way about another ever in my life the way I feel about you." Shaking his finger at the tip of her nose, he warned, "Still, you be careful with the words you choose to say about my mother."

"Listen to me and listen well." She was so close to his face that he could feel her minty breath against his skin. "Your mother is a spiteful old *hag!*"

Before she could react, he lunged at her, pinning her arms against the bed's headboard. His expression was no longer gentle but fierce as if on the attack. "You purposefully try to make me angry. Anyone else, I would tear them limb from limb."

"But you *do* tear me limb from limb." She opened her legs wider, guiding his body in between them. "And I love it!"

Again, he pounced on her, and she wrapped her legs tighter around him, inviting him inside without a word spoken.

"I have only had a part of you." She clamped her legs tighter, desperately seeking his elusive member. "I want *all* of you."

She was driving him crazy with passion, so much so he was losing control—the *one* thing he could not afford to lose.

No one has had all of me.

The seed of a future King had a value beyond measure and should not be planted indiscriminately. Ares had long ago mastered command over every inch of his body...only to find out he had nine inches looking to start a rebellion.

"Stay here another night with me," she purred into his ear.

Every fiber of his being yearned to remain entwined with her, yet an insistent pulse began to stir within him. Before he could change his mind, he pulled away from her toward his true calling.

He sat up, purposely looking away from her naked body sprawled across the decorative pillows. "I cannot stay. I have somewhere else to be."

She held a pillow against her bare breasts. "What is more important than where you are now?"

The god gazed out toward the window, the late-night breeze cooling his fevered body. The stars in the sky served as a constant reminder of how tiny everything else appeared in this vast world. "A little village across the lands. I started a confrontation there; I must finish."

Would he dare leave my bed for more bloodshed? "And your throne? What of it?"

"My throne is occupied." Getting up from her bed, he reached over to his helmet on the nightstand. It did not take him long to find the rest of his armor. He dressed silently, wondering what thoughts were running through her mind—he did not have to wait long.

"For now, it is occupied. But not forever."

He paused a moment before fastening his belt.

"When you were sitting on the King's seat, I saw your power, courage, and brawn." She sat up straighter, her eyes as wild as the flames dancing in the fireplace. "You threatened Otus and Ephialtes, and you did not waver. They felt your words were true and made no attempt to challenge your authority. You stood before us all, every bit a King." Soon, she sank back into the many pillows behind her, defeated. "Then Hermes came along, and in an instant, all your posturing was for not."

"Zeus will rule the gods for as long as Helios' Sun sails across the sky each day."

"Did not Cronus say the same about his reign?"

"I would not know what Cronus said, and neither would you. His days as ruler were far before we were born."

The naked goddess had no intentions of backing down. "The Fates know, although we are immortal, our days in this world are not promised. *Zeus'* days in this world are not promised. Many gods are trapped in chains in the Underworld. Do I not speak the truth?"

"What you say is true."

"You deserve to one day be King."

With all his might, he refrained from raising his voice along with his suspicions. "Why do you care more for my birthright than I do?"

"Because as you deserve to be King...I deserve to be by your side...as Queen."

Of course! Along with my father and mother, Aphrodite plans my future as though they were The Moira. "If a time comes when my father crosses over to Hades and I become King, even with you as my wife, my mother will still be our Queen."

Damned Hera! She crossed her arms, along with her brows, making no attempt to conceal her contempt.

Ares remained silent as he sat down on the edge of her bed. With his back blocking the light, his features darkened, and his anger rekindled. "Or is my mother also dead in your little fantasy?"

She glared at him like an opposing warrior, but without a weapon—without a hint of fear.

Had a Nymph dared to utter such nonsense—a Nymph would not have dared. He pressed his thumb against her lips with enough pressure that she could not open them even if she wanted to. "Far better for you to stay silent."

Ares reached over her head to retrieve his dagger from the side table, and she watched as he attached it to his belt.

His mistake was again looking into her eyes, deep enough for him to become lost in them. He stood up before he could sink any further into her blue abyss.

"Aphrodite. I know you see so many things for me in my future, yet there is *one* thing you do not see."

"What do I not see?" She watched as he turned from the doorway.

"That this...is all there is." Without another word, he put on his helmet and marched through the door.

She blew out the candle closest to her and sat alone in the darkness. The emptiness of the room mirrored the hollow ache within her heart. Her lover had abandoned her, disappearing into the night, lured by a battle yet to begin.

Hera did say he would never settle down. She lay in the bed, her body aching to be caressed by his hands again. *This little setback will not deter me. I want the crown.*

And I always get what I want.

42

HERBS AND SPICE
MINTHE & HADES

"Stop! It is me!"

Hades opened his eyes in a flash to find Minthe struggling underneath the total weight of his naked body as he strangled her in the privacy of his master bedroom.

I am surprised she is able to speak.

He knew all too well the paradox of his slumber—a time when his disciplined limbs could be swayed by instinct alone. It would be a lie to say it was the first time he woke up to Minthe gasping for air.

The scene was, unfortunately, a familiar one. His touch, though strong, would have never been so brutal upon a fragile nymph if he were fully aware of his surroundings.

My habit of choking others in my sleep is a reflex that stemmed from my youth. At least, that is what Minthe told me the first time I found myself in this predicament.

Finally, Hades released her and rolled onto his back. His

eyes fixed blankly upon the ceiling. Minthe coughed and rubbed her bruised throat.

If the Water Nymph had been like most of the other souls in the Kingdom, there would have been no breath for her to salvage. However, she was among the few who still possessed the breath of life.

Hades listened to her struggle, offering her no words of sympathy or arms of comfort. "I have warned you numerous times to never sneak into my bed without prior notice. I cannot control what harm may come your way."

"And I have warned you..." She wagged a pointed finger, allowing her natural aroma to linger in the air. "I like being choked."

The King of the Dead found her natural minty scent utterly delectable. Unfortunately, his mistake was revealing long ago how deeply her fragrance aroused him, and ever since, she would intentionally wave her hand when they were in public, deliberately inflaming his passions.

Pretending to pout, she added, "Unfortunately, sneaking into your room unannounced is the *only* way I can get you to fulfil my fantasy." She flashed a broad smile accompanied by fluttering lashes.

Her playfulness was all he needed to return his attention to her. A Nymph's essence could not be compared to a goddess, yet they had a style of beauty all their own.

Her skin was as smooth as polished marble, its pale hue contrasting perfectly with her vibrant green hair. Her eyes were like two pools of deep forest green, and her delicate nose had a sprinkle of freckles. Not to mention, her lips were a luscious shade of rose, always curved into a seductive smile that could ensnare the heart of even the most stoic god.

She is a sight to be seen. His eyes dipped lower. *And I want to see more.*

Hades delicately traced his fingers along the woven fabric that enveloped her breasts, snaked around her stomach, and ventured between her legs.

She was wrapped up tight.

He clenched his jaws—far too much fabric for his taste. "I see you prepared a puzzle for me."

Her eyes danced around as if she had somehow peered into his thoughts and found amusement in his frustrations. "Only because you are so smart."

If she was not coming up with something new to do in bed, she was thinking about coming up with something new to do in bed.

The Nymph sat up in the large bed and rested her elbow on a decorative pillow. "Besides, I would hate for you to be tired of my body already."

While Hades had not anticipated any visitors for the night, Minthe would have been the first to argue that she was not a mere visitor of his bedroom but rather a resident.

My nights were always spent alone for what seemed like an eternity until Minthe invited herself into my room. That marked the beginning of what she referred to as an 'open invitation'.

She exposed herself to me in ways I had never experienced before. Fortunately, being a god, I am a fast learner.

And Nymphs are renowned for their insatiable appetite, so why should I not indulge in her desires as she has in mine?

"I have for you a challenge."

Is she still talking?

"I wrapped a long piece of fabric like a maze around my body. First, you must find the loose end of my garment and try to unwrap..."

Before she could finish her sentence, the Lord of the Underworld straddled her hips and swiftly tore her garment from top to bottom. As a prize for his efforts, he watched delightfully as her breasts bounced in excitement of their newfound freedom.

While he silently debated which way to take her, the green haired one held onto his bare thighs. "You lost, my King."

"Did I?" With the palm of one hand, Hades stroked both her nipples until they were as hard and stiff as his erection.

At last, he made up his mind.

He flipped her onto her stomach and wasted no time, spreading her legs wide enough to enter her from behind.

"Ohhh," she moaned in anticipation, biting the dark silk sheets. Her inner thighs were glistening in the soft torchlight.

Hades was not the least bit surprised Minthe was already soaked—being choked to an inch of her life was the only foreplay she needed. He held onto the base of her neck to restrict her movements and painfully teased his rounded tip up and down her slick slit, denying himself instant gratification.

Easy does it...

She kicked her feet up in response to the slow torture. "You are killing me!" she grunted, an aching mixed with pleasure.

"Death is my domain." He eased up from of her opening, tilting his shaft along the crack of her butt and pushed his fingers into her mouth. Leaning his chest against her back, his voice was almost too deep to hear against her ear, "Tonight, I will make sure you think twice about crawling into my bed."

Before she could react, he pulled out his saliva covered hand and slipped two fingers between her thighs. He mercilessly rubbed her sensitive spot and her voice caught in her throat as the weight of his dome tickled her dark hole.

"My gods." Her hips eagerly rode the rhythm of his hand while he flicked her peak again and again until she screamed, "Please, please, my King!" Her toes curled while kicking the air, and she stifled a scream into the pillow.

"There you go, my pet," he whispered, speeding up his movement to vibrate against her most sensitive spot. "I want you to drip all over my hand...so I can taste you."

"Ohhh!"

A wave of release rushed throughout her body, followed by bursts of mini-shockwaves. Soon they grew further apart until her limps went limp in peaceful satisfaction and he crashed on top of her.

Gently, he removed his wet hand from between her legs and hungrily sucked her flavored juices off each finger. The taste of her minty cream only further enflamed his lust. *My gods, she is so delicious.*

The room went quiet, with only her heavy breathing lowering into light spurts. Hades shaft remained throbbing between her cheeks, aching to be surrounded in her sticky warmth.

She lay crushed beneath him, fully content with just his fingers, completely and utterly exhausted.

I am sure she will drift to sleep if I do not move an inch.

However, he had no intention of letting her rest. He was far from finished using her tight flesh. No, he was only getting started.

The Ruler did not give the sleeping beauty another moment of rest and instead sat back on his knees and pulled her by the hair against his chiseled front.

"Huh?" she was almost delirious.

"If I cannot have a peaceful, uninterrupted sleep, neither can you," Hades grunted, then nipped at her earlobe.

With his free hand, he pulled and pinched her nipples, and her back arched at his ravishing touch.

"Are you punishing me, my King?" she taunted, massaging her buttocks against his twitching shaft. "Because I *love* being punished."

"Famous last words." He released her from his clutches. "Get on your hands."

Without question, she did as he commanded and glanced behind her shoulder in time to see him step off of the bed and grab her hips to position her level with his waist. "Now, I will *take* what I want."

The King thrust deeply into her inviting wetness. Her knees would have buckled if not for his hands firmly holding her in place for his relentless pounding. "Every time I find you in my bed," he raised his hand. "I will take—what—I—want!" He accentuated each word with a slap on her butt, the slight jiggle making him unbelievably harder than before.

She was near tears from the uncontrollable pleasure. "I am all yours for the taking!" Her arms gave way, and she fell head-first into the bed, but Hades still held her legs in place and continued his onslaught of passion.

The arch of her back was now at a higher angle, providing Hades greater access to her rare and allowing him to plunge more of his length deeper into her tight depths. When she was able to take all of his hardness as far as possible, his steady strokes became faster as she squirmed under his clutches.

"Take every inch," he groaned, reaching around to again rub her peak as he slammed continuously inside her.

"Yes! Give it all to me!"

In the throes of passion, Hades turned his head only to catch a glimpse of himself in the mirror.

His normally croft light-blonde hair, was tussled in every direction. His deathly white skin, burning with golden cheeks. His usual even keel demeanor, overwrought with unruly behavior.

The God he saw was not his reflection.

What have I become?

In the past, Hades had dedicated himself entirely to the responsibilities of ruling the Underworld. He had patiently waited, preoccupied with the monotonous routine of his duties, all in an attempt to keep his mind from wandering back to the distant memory of the love of his eternal life.

I have become the one who I most hate. Zeus!

"Please, please do not stop," her voice was muffled due to the god pressing her face deeper into the plush pillow.

The way his fingers dug into her scalp caused a shift in his mind. Minthe was no longer beneath him...without a face, she easily became someone else in his mind.

Is this what my loathsome brother does to my beautiful Queen every night? Does he take her from behind so that he can pretend she is someone else too?

"Faster!"

No. I am sure most nights, the great Zeus is preoccupied with his numerous harlots...spreading his seed into whatever hole he can find.

"Oh! My gods!"

Leaving the Queen alone, craving to be filled by another god. Dreaming of someone who can work her body into submission.

"I am almost there!" she yelled, and he pinned her hands behind her back, pumping harder.

Has Hera succumbed to her longings and taken a secret lover? Has she found someone else to take her again and again until she begs for release?

"Yes, yes!"

He felt Minthe's slick hold pulsating and contracting all around him, but he could not stop.

Does Hera wait for me as I wait for her? Longing for me to spill my seed into her—so full, it is dripping out...Great Gods!

Before Hades could be tempted to finish inside the Nymph, he quickly pulled out, holding his twitching base for dear life, and laid on his back. Immediately, Minthe was over him, taking his length into her mouth and sucking out everything he had to offer.

"Urrrh!" The Keeper of Souls tried to stifle his relief by

sinking his teeth into one of the many pillows on the bed. *There is no need to have the guards rush in with their swords drawn.*

She continued to drain him, her head bobbing up and down his thick length while his hips jerked erratically.

"There you go," he coached as if she were his number one pupil, "drink it all up, my pet."

Looking him in the eyes, she made sure to swallow every last drop.

It was known that *one* of the ways for a god's seed to remain a seed was for it to be digested.

Grabbing her jaw, he pulled her closer. "Now, open your mouth."

Minthe did as commanded and opened as widely as possible. "Ahhhh!" She understood Hades had no intention of making her a mother, so she did not let a drop spill.

Once the inspection was finished, he let her go, and she climbed happily underneath the covers to cuddle next to him. If there were infinite hours in a day, she would spend every hour staring at him.

His firm, square jawline provided a foundation for his perfectly trimmed beard. His nose, straight and proud, would hit all the right spots if his face were planted between her legs. Not to mention his haunting gray eyes...

Her entire body quivered in the afterglow of his love. His muscular arm encircled her lower back, and she relished being the only one he ever let inside his personal space.

She traced his nipple with the tip of her middle finger. "I cannot get enough of you."

It would have been pleasant for him to say something of the sort in return to her. However, his mind was not entirely in the moment. Instead, his thoughts floated elsewhere for an undetermined amount of time.

"Hades?"

...

"Hades!"

Is she still talking? "Huh?"

Every line etched on her face was filled with concern.

I must have drifted off again. "My mind was elsewhere."

With tenderness, she gently brushed her fingers along his cheek, daring him to break eye contact. "I thought I lost you."

His entire body shuddered at her choice of words.

Embarrassing. He swallowed hard, trying to regain control of his limps. *Like sudden strangulation, Minthe has found another trigger of mine.*

He pressed on. "I am not lost. You found me."

She nodded faintly.

Although his words were true, she knew they were fleeting and that she would soon lose him again. After all, it was their never-ending cycle.

And for some unknown reason, Hades felt an insatiable need to know. He had to understand why she would not do what he could not—end their shared misery.

"Minthe. Why do you persist in sneaking into my bed night after night?"

"The truth?"

"Always."

She stretched her arms and legs wide, bursting into laughter. "Your bed is far more comfortable than mine," she confessed playfully.

He pulled her close to his form, his body's heat contrasting with her coolness. As she nestled into the curve of his neck, he became acutely aware of the steady pattern of breath against his skin, a sensation that was oddly soothing in its rarity in the Land of Death.

And...he smiled.

"Hades?"

"Yes?"

"Why do you *let* me creep into your bed every night?"

He pondered her question momentarily, only to ask one of his own. "The truth?"

"Always."

The room was too dark for her to notice the smile had long since vanished from his face.

"I would rather not be alone."

43

UNDERCOVERS
ZEUS & HERA

Hera lay cocooned in the plush covers of the grand marital bed. As she nestled further beneath the blankets, her senses were heightened, alert to every creak of the palace, every gust of wind that whispered through the chamber.

It had been an eternity since she had last witnessed Zeus' commanding presence when he stormed toward the dark dungeons. A persistent unease gnawed at the edges of her thoughts, a relentless reminder that her heart would remain heavy until Hephaestus' fate was decided.

The sound of a door opening and closing pierced the stillness. Hera's heart skipped a beat, and she could not deny the tremor of anticipation that coursed through her. Even though she faced away from the door, her intuition told her it was Zeus who had entered the room.

"I am awake," she whispered, still with her back facing him.

"I know."

Zeus began to disrobe, shedding the symbols of his sovereignty one by one. His majestic crown was carefully placed upon the ornate side table. The golden robe slid from his shoulders to the floor, leaving him completely bare.

Silent as the night itself, he slid into the grand bed, his back nestling against the plump pillows." In the morning, I will compose a letter and have it delivered to 4 gods and 4 goddesses."

Turning her body towards him, Hera shifted to look up at her husband. The dark tuft of hair that covered his torso allowed her to follow his chest's rhythmic rise and fall. "What for?"

"I want to delegate more of our responsibilities on the earth by recruiting more gods into the council." He added, "Bearing the High Gods' approval, of course. Once the candidates are gathered, we shall elect one god and one goddess to join our ranks."

This is very beneficial for me. "That is a good idea. We do need help governing mankind."

Zeus was pleasantly surprised at how receptive his wife was to the idea. "I am glad you agree. Therefore, it will be easier to convince Poseidon and...Demeter."

"I will write our siblings to inform them of your plans. We can meet with the full council after all the Low Gods are called." She paused a moment, realizing she assumed they would agree on who would be gathered. "Who will be selected?"

I must choose my words carefully. "I will choose worthy people, even though very few will be picked."

"I am sure *our* children will be among the selected?"

"I went to talk to Hebe about today's events and she spoke not a word to me." He could hold his tongue no longer. "Hebe will not be among the selected. She has not shown herself worthy."

Hera sat up, pushing the blanket towards her feet. "Hebe has *every* right to be represented amongst the gods."

"I do not believe for one moment Ares would dare take her to the Unknown Territories. Hebe obviously went on her own, and Ares is covering her lies. She disobeyed the laws of the land."

"You cannot prove it." She crossed her arms. "So you are not going to pick Hebe? You would rather have only one of our children represented on the council. Only Ares?"

"We have more than *two* children."

The goddess simmered down, remembering Hephaestus for the first time since the topic started. Again, she felt the pain in her lower body. "Where is *he* now?"

"I gave Hephaestus a room down the hallway, to the left."

He is so close, yet so far. Hera examined the patterns woven into the blanket. "How does he look?"

"He looks the same as when he was born. Except now he also has a scar on his face courtesy of the rocks he landed on after the fall."

"Oh, the gods!" Shaking her head, she covered her face in hopelessness.

"He is broken, but his resolve is steady. He may not look like a god, but has all the attributes."

She glared at him bitterly. "Looking like a god is the *only* attribute that matters." Bringing the covers back around her body, she settled again into the bed and turned around.

Zeus wrapped an arm around her and cuddled her from behind. He rubbed her stomach, unknowingly helping to soothe her tension.

"Does he remember?" Her eyes were wide open, staring out toward the starry night.

"Yes...he remembers the fall."

That day, that infamous day, has never been discussed between us after the incident. What more could there be to say? Though the emptiness was always there between us, words unspoken...until now. "Did he remember...*how* it happened?"

"No, he did not." Before she could let out a sigh of relief, he continued, "So, I told him."

Her body tensed in response to his words.

"I told him...I threw him through the All-Seeing Room."

Instantly, upon hearing his confession, she relaxed underneath the weight of his muscular arms. She rolled to face him, looking him square in the eyes, yet remained silent.

The King gently cradled his Queen's chin with three fingers, and in that moment, she was the only person in the world who mattered to him.

"You have my word," he whispered as light as the air, "Hephaestus will never know, it was really *you* who threw him from Mount Olympus."

44

THE MONSTER
XANDER

Xander stood facing the horizon in the chill of the mountain night. The daytime creatures slumbered, while the nocturnal hunters prowled in silence. With his spear held firmly before him, Hebe's guard struggled to maintain his vigil, his efforts to balance sleep and wakefulness becoming increasingly difficult.

"Stay awake, stay awake, stay awa..." Xander's eyelids drooped, only to snap open again with a start.

"...Awake, stay awake, stay awake..." His whispered mantra looped in the quiet darkness.

Meanwhile, on the second floor of the palace, Hebe lay on her back, nestled under a woolen blanket. The sudden cool mountain breeze wafted in through her open balcony doors, stirring her from her slumber just enough to feel a pressured weight on her chest.

Hsssss!

Her eyes snapped open wide, startled by the hissing sound in the darkness. Before her, a long split tongue, slick with green mucus, vibrated menacingly inches from her nose.

Hsssss!

Hebe opened her mouth to scream, but the sticky tongue jammed into her mouth, blocking any cries for help from escaping. The weight of the creature pressed down on her, rendering her immobile. She gagged as the tongue forced its way further down into her mouth, feeling the darkness creeping in at the edges of her consciousness.

Just as she felt herself slipping away, what seemed like an audible voice, shouted into the void, *Be brave!*

In an instant, fuelled by a surge of adrenaline, her eyes flew open again. Without hesitation, she snatched the chain from around her neck, and plunged the dagger into the body of the creature looming over her. With a twist, she felt resistance give way, and the creature let out a guttural cry, releasing her from its grip.

From outside below, Xander's eyes snapped awake as he looked up to Hebe's open balcony door. His heart pounding in his chest as he bolted into the palace. Ignoring the warnings from Hermes to stay away, he raced up the stairs to the forbidden room. There, in the dim light, he spotted the monstrous creature lying on the floor, its grotesque form a disturbing sight, twitching on its back unable to turn itself over.

Hebe was nowhere to be seen.

Without hesitation, Xander gripped his spear tightly, his muscles tense as he approached the creature. The size of the hybrid beast was daunting, but fear did not paralyze him. With swift, decisive movements, he thrust his spear into the creature's writhing form, again and again, until it lay still at last.

Breathing heavily, Xander scanned the room once more, his eyes searching desperately for any sign of the princess.

"Princess?" Xander's voice echoed as he moved through the room in search of her. "Princess?"

"I am in here," came a faint reply.

Without a moment's hesitation, Xander dashed to the nearest closet door and flung it open. Relief flooded over him as he beheld Hebe, curled up in a corner with Wolfie nestled in her arms, licking her face happily.

He sank to his knees, his heart still racing from the rush of fear and relief. With trembling hands, he reached up to the heavens. "Thank the gods!"

"Is it...dead?"

He nodded his head before answering, "Yes. It is dead."

Hebe raised her arm, in lacklustre triumph. "Yay," she whispered with a smile too faint to be considered a smile. Her body sank against the wall, too spent and covered in thick goo to move.

Yet even in the aftermath of their pitiful victory over the creature, one thing remained evident Xander.

This monster did not come alone.

EPILOGUE: A GIGANTIC PROBLEM
PORPHYRION

THE RULER OF THE SOUTH KINGDOM REMAINED SEATED ON HIS throne in an empty court. Once bustling with courtiers and advisers, the grand chamber now echoed with solitude. Hours had passed since his sons Ephialtes and Otus stood before his throne, recounting the disrespect they had faced in Zeus' Kingdom.

Despite the gravity of their grievances, the King's anger smoldered beneath a calm facade. Porphyrion's absence from the King's festivities was a calculated insult, one intended to stoke the flames of conflict. Yet, the King found himself unable to retaliate as swiftly as he desired. His hands, typically so free to wield power, were unexpectedly bound by the one he held dear.

Oh, how he longed to unleash the full might of his Kingdom's forces upon Mount Olympus, to answer disrespect with righteous fury. But for now, he could do nothing but bide his time, waiting for the moment when retaliation would be both swift and devastating.

He groaned, feeling the tension coiling in his muscles as he opened and closed his fist, seeking some release from the weight of his thoughts.

"Well?" she prompted, with a raise brow.

With a conscious effort, he pushed aside his internal deliberations to focus on the seductive goddess before him. Her curves, accentuated by the delicate drapery of her silk gown, held his attention captive.

"I have given you ample time to consider my proposal," she said, tilting her head provocatively. Her luscious curls swooped around her shoulders in a mesmerizing dance.

"You are attempting to delay the inevitable conflict," he countered.

"Can you not see?" she replied with a graceful sweep of her hand. "The battle has already commenced. But instead of swords clashing, it is hearts that collide. Both leave behind scars, but only one remains undefeated."

Reluctantly, he nodded in acquiescence to the one who patiently awaited his response. "As you wish, my dearest one. I shall withhold my assault on Mount Olympus... for now. Use the time I grant you to work your enchantments."

"Very well," she replied, her smile radiant as she rose from her seat, smoothing the fabric of her elegant gown. "I must depart. The palace awaits my return before the break of dawn."

Porphyrion nodded once more as she kissed his cheek, as she had done a thousand times before. He watched as she moved towards the door. Unable to contain his thoughts any longer, he tightened his lips, but the words spilled forth nonetheless. "Aphrodite?"

The goddess paused, turning back to him in the room's subdued glow. "Yes, brother?"

"I will do as I said and give you time to infiltrate Mount Olympus," Porphyrion declared. Leaning forward in his chair, he locked eyes with Aphrodite. "But if you fail to get the Prince to marry you, for the honor of my sons, when I overrun Zeus' Kingdom, Ares' severed head will be forever preserved on a spike."

Aphrodite met his intense stare with one of fearlessness. "My King," she responded calmly. "I will not fail."

To Be Continued...

DESIRES OF OLYMPUS
PASSIONS OF THE GODS #2

It is not enemies that Gods fear; it is family.

As the Royal Family struggles in the aftermath of Princess Hebe's attack, Hermes heads an investigation to unveil the truth and instead learns a secret that threatens to shake the very foundations of Olympus—if he so chooses to reveal his discovery.

To the displeasure of the Queen, a planned celebration in honor of Prince Hephaestus leads to a disastrous outcome—sparks of attraction between him and Princess Hebe.

Meanwhile, King Zeus seeks to solidify his kingdom's strength by arranging strategic marriages for his sons. When given an ultimatum by his father to choose a bride, Prince Ares finds himself torn between duty and desire.

Lust, jealousy, power, and revenge: The Passions of the Gods.

WHERE TO FIND LEAH NIGHTINGALE

Subscribe for updates and more:

Passions of the Gods

Tumblr

Tiktok

YouTube

Pinterest

Instagram

Printed in Great Britain
by Amazon

04ed041f-fa0c-4c9a-8df7-45c7d7411152R01